Named after a goddess who turns her lovers to stone, an insular New England coastal town holds more secrets than it can keep…

Torn from her hometown and her father as a child, Paige Waters' last memory of both is fraught with mystery and confusion. Now, sixteen years later, with both her parents gone, Paige returns to Alcina Cove, certain there is more to the painful story than she's been led to believe. The answers must lie within the community, buffered from the larger world by the sea; but when she finds the townspeople more reticent than ever, her only hope is the intriguing man who lives in her childhood home—if she can break down his reserve…

A fisherman turned writer, Liam Gray is haunted by secrets of his own, some of which are deeply entangled with the closure Paige seeks. But as he and Paige grow intimate, their attraction building, Liam finds himself torn between truth and betrayal. Whichever he chooses will risk his future with Paige and cause someone pain—until an even greater danger leaves him no choice…

Books by Celia Ashley

Dark Tides Series
Dark Tides
Storm Surge

Published by Kensington Publishing Corporation

Storm Surge

A Dark Tides Romance

Celia Ashley

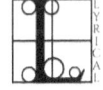

LYRICAL PRESS
Kensington Publishing Corp.
www.kensingtonbooks.com

Lyrical Press books are published by
Kensington Publishing Corp. 119 West 40th Street New York, NY 10018

All Kensington titles, imprints, and distributed lines are available at special quantity discounts for bulk purchases for sales promotion, premiums, fundraising, and educational or institutional use.

Special book excerpts or customized printings can also be created to fit specific needs. For details, write or phone the office of the Kensington Special Sales Manager:
Kensington Publishing Corp.
119 West 40th Street
New York, NY 10018
Attn. Special Sales Department. Phone: 1-800-221-2647.

Kensington and the K logo Reg. U.S. Pat. & TM Off.
Lyrical Press and the L logo are trademarks of Kensington Publishing Corp.

First Electronic Edition: May 2016
eISBN-13: 978-1-60183-758-5
eISBN-10: -60183-758-5

First Print Edition: May 2016
ISBN-13: 978-1-60183-760-8
ISBN-10: 1-60183-760-7

Printed in the United States of America

To the marks against the silence

Acknowledgements

I would like to give thanks here to Janet Hetherington, who—with much exuberance—unearthed the mythology of the goddess Alcina and suggested hers as a name for the town in which this series is set. After learning of the goddess's propensity for turning discarded lovers into stone, I added to Book II of the Dark Tides Series the stone circle named after the goddess and from which the fictional town derives its name.

I wish also to thank my wonderful editor, Corinne DeMaagd. Her enthusiasm and her expertise have been invaluable. When initially approached about turning the first book, Dark Tides, into a series, I bemoaned the task of creating synopses for the next two books in record time, but with Corinne's assistance, the task became more pleasure than pain. Corinne remains a joy to work with throughout every editorial process, and I can only hope I have not been too much of a nuisance in return.

Thank you to all the wonderful women in my writers group for their friendship, the brainstorming sessions, the spontaneous bouts of cathartic release.

I would like to acknowledge my familiarity with the paranormal. Although I have experienced nothing near to what I put my characters through in my books, I have had encounters that have changed my life view. If you would like to read more about them, I do make the occasional entry in my blog about things that go bump in the night.

Last but far, far from least, I wish to thank my readers—for their loyalty and the enlightening comments they offer about my work and life in general.

Chapter 1

"Full fathom five thy father lies;
Of his bones are coral made:
Those are pearls that were his eyes:
Nothing of him doth fade,
But doth suffer a sea-change
Into something rich and strange."
William Shakespeare – *The Tempest*

She'd forgotten how callous and greedy gulls' cries could be, and yet how evocative of place. Sixteen years of exile vanished in the sound.

Mom, what is that?

Sweetheart, don't. It's nothing.

Paige considered her friends' warnings about coming home, how they had cautioned her regarding sounds and smells splitting open the aged cask of memory. In the past, fragments had occasionally risen from the murky recesses, but they always slipped back into the dark without being fully realized. She didn't know what she feared more—the memory itself or the darkness holding it at bay.

Keeping her distance from the shoreline, Paige studied the seabirds' flashing ghostly wings through the gloom, unable to see what incited their frenzy. Beyond, waves crested in thunderous approach. Paige shoved her hands into her pockets. Out on the water, a ship appeared to barely move, the lights lining its hull burning like pinprick holes. Sunrise was not yet a glimmer where sea met sky. She turned away.

To the west, the sky possessed a dull radiance. Traffic lights and street lights burned through the wee hours in Alcina Cove, a pervasive smoky glow in comparison to the bright lighthouse signal rotating in the distance, warning sailors of the rocky coast, guiding them home. Alcina Cove had grown in the years since Paige had been gone. She'd barely recognized the meandering road that led to her old home, bordered now by the sprawl from the town's center.

The night she and her mother fled with nothing but a suitcase between them, the sky had been black except for the lighthouse beacon, the stars above blocked by heavy clouds. She remembered how the sedan's headlights had created a stark, white tunnel, remembered her mother hunched forward over the steering wheel, peering ahead through the eye not swollen shut. Rust discolored her blouse, more blood dripping from her mouth. Paige had attempted to staunch the flow with a cloth, but had given up. At thirteen, she'd understood only one thing with clarity. They were never coming back.

Mom, who did this to you? Was it Dad?

Hush, darling, it doesn't matter now.

Paige heard a noise and turned to scan the dark beach. She found nothing and started walking again away from the raucous, opportunistic gulls and their meal. The breeze wrenched at her curly hair, tumbling sections free from her ponytail. She attempted to tuck the trailing strands behind her ears, only to discover them tangled and damp from the sea air.

Her eyes burned, but back at the rental cottage, an uncomfortable bed awaited her. High threadcount sheets covering a lumpy mattress didn't make the bed any more restful. And the freshly laundered pillow case was tainted by the tang of seaborne dampness. She'd tossed and turned, disturbed by the combination of clamminess and lavender scent. It reminded her of the sheets on her childhood bed.

Eventually a desire to flee the cottage had prevailed, forcing her from bed and into the night wearing sneakers and a sweatshirt jacket over her nightclothes—a T-shirt and ratty cut-off sweatpants. Sand sliding beneath the shoes' smooth soles had, until then, been all but forgotten. It had only taken five minutes wandering the beach to get her rhythm back.

Paige turned toward the structural silhouette on the rise above the beach. A narrow chimney rose above the angled roof against the backdrop of the town's lights. For some reason she'd always pictured the chimney succumbing to gravity, broken brick and mortar scattered on the ground, as if representative of what had happened to her family. But there it stood, maintaining its crazy tilt against Newton's laws. So much for symbolism.

With her father's passing, she wondered if the house might be empty, abandoned. She saw no lights in any of the windows, some of which lacked reflection, possibly missing panes. The cedar shakes on the walls had weathered to a color like tarnished silver in the darkness, and beneath the porch overhang a shutter on a lower casement hung canted by a broken hinge.

Paige's stomach twisted in a spasm beneath her diaphragm. She pressed the heel of her palm against her belly.

"Are you aware there's a penalty for trespass?"

Paige jumped, a solitary expletive flying from her lips. Heart in her throat, she hastened several steps away before turning to face the speaker. "Sorry," she said, breathing hard. She squinted in an effort to make out a visible face in the shadows, but was unable to determine anything but gender.

"For what? The fact you're trespassing? Or using a word that would have gotten my mouth washed out with soap as a kid?"

Paige couldn't believe this guy was chastising her for swearing after he'd practically jumped out at her in the dark. What the hell? "You startled me."

"You're not from around here, are you?" the man said. Not like a question. More like an accusation. Paige bristled despite standing in the dark five feet from an unseen stranger on an empty stretch of beach before dawn. Even the ravenous gulls had abandoned their midnight repast. The waterfront was deserted.

"And what makes you so sure I'm not?"

"First, you're trespassing. Second? The accent."

Paige clamped her lips together. More than half a lifetime in Tennessee had altered her speech's cadence but hadn't fully erased the characteristics of an early New England dialect, which made for a strange accent indeed. If the man hadn't been so antagonistic, she would have admitted as much.

"Nothing to say to that?" he nudged.

"What would you like me to say?"

"'Goodnight' would work."

Her mouth dropped. "You're right. With that attitude, I probably should say goodnight."

"The next time you decide to take a stroll on this beach, seek permission, day or night."

"Understood." Paige started to turn away, but irritation got the better of her. She spun back. "I didn't realize I needed an invitation." Who did this guy think he was? There was only one man who could claim proprietary rights to this stretch of beach, and he was dead. Yanking her fist from her pocket, she jerked a thumb at her former home over her shoulder. "Do you live there?"

"I own 'there,'" he said. "Bought the place from Edwin Waters just before he died."

"Oh." One of the things she was planning to check was the allocation of the house and land before her father's death. The knowledge her father had sold her old home outright to someone hit her harder than if he'd walked away from it. Not that she would have expected him to leave it to her, but by selling it, he'd made it pretty clear he hadn't even considered that option. Tears stung her tired eyes, nausea sweeping through her stomach. "Well, doesn't look like you have much pride of ownership, I'll tell you that."

As soon as she spoke, she realized she should have taken a moment to gather her emotions under a tighter rein.

"You can tell that in the pitch black, can you?" His voice traveled like rumbling thunder.

Paige loosened unconsciously curled fists. "Look, I'm sorry. Again. That was out of line."

Paige attempted to tame her annoyance. If this man had bought her old home, he might be in possession of information she could use. The predawn gloom had lightened, revealing a hulking shadow well over six feet tall. Paige slid her left foot behind her and shifted her weight over it, hoping he wouldn't notice the movement away. She didn't want anything in her actions to indicate fear. She had learned the tactic in a self-defense course she'd taken several years past. The course had been fairly useless except the one stratagem. Never. Act. Afraid.

"What are you doing out here?" he asked after she'd taken another step back.

She paused, not quite balanced. "I needed some air."

"You don't smell like you've been drinking."

"I haven't been."

"How far did you walk?"

Paige's nails dug into her palms, fingers curled tightly once more. "Why are you asking me these questions?"

"Just trying to determine where the hell you've come from and what you're doing here," he said. "My major issue is with the patrons of Cappy's. They like to wander down to the beach to walk it off before heading home. Is that where you've come from?"

"What on earth is Cappy's?"

"Answers that question. You really aren't from around here." His tone was dismissive.

Paige's brow wrinkled. Could this guy be any ruder? "At the moment, I am from around here. I'm renting the cottage next door."

He made an abrupt movement in her direction and Paige stumbled backward.

"How long?" he demanded.

"Am I staying? Not that it's any of your business, but—"

"No. How long have you been in the cottage?"

Good Lord, was that any of his concern, either? "What does it matter?" Paige continued backing away, keeping the man in her line of sight. What had been a shadow had begun to fill in with muted color: faded blue jeans, the indistinct hue of his T-shirt, disheveled coal black hair. He possessed a handsome arrangement to his features, though the particulars remained veiled by darkness. Not what she wanted to find—the guy pissing her off in the middle of the night was good-looking. She'd rather he resemble the discarded leftovers from the vanished gulls.

"Sorry to have disturbed you," she said with mock sweetness. "As we're to be temporary neighbors, I'm sure we'll run into each other again at a more reasonable time of day."

A soft red glow appeared on the man's face, highlighting a scar running down his jaw. Paige glanced toward the ocean. The horizon had lit up like a thin line of embers.

"Red sky at morning," she whispered.

"Sailors take warning," he finished.

She snapped her attention back to him. "So the saying goes."

"That it does."

"Are you a sailor?"

His jaw worked, dark eyes narrowing beneath lowered brows. Surely he wasn't that much older than she, but something in his life had aged him, weathered him a bit—and not unattractively—by exposure to the elements. The sun lifted higher, sunlight dancing across the waves that washed over the rocky beach. His shadow lengthened along the sand, conjoining with hers. "I was. Why?"

"No longer spending your days on the sea?"

"I'm not out here for small talk. I have work to do."

"At this hour? What are you, a smuggler?"

He said nothing, but something in him stilled. Crap. Maybe she had struck on the truth. Paige renewed her retreat, surprised when the man offered an abrupt, if not quite willing, introduction.

"My name's Liam Gray. I apologize for giving you a hard time."

Celia Ashley

"No apology necessary." Paige spun on her heel and strode up the slope toward the rental.

"And who are you?" Gray called after her.

She stopped short, sneakers sliding in the sand. "I used to live in your house," she said, pointing toward what was little more than a two-storey cottage, tall, limited in width, and looking not quite so decrepit in the daylight. "And my name is Paige. Paige Waters. Edwin's daughter. I've come back for answers, and I plan to get them."

Chapter 2

Edwin Waters' daughter didn't even reach his collarbone, yet her stride on the slope would put a person twice her height to shame. Liam watched her disappear over the hill. The ponytail flying behind her looked as if she'd whipped it with an eggbeater. And her clothes, well, they resembled something pulled from a trash bin. He refused to be intrigued.

Liam crossed the porch and yanked open the door, stomping sand from his shoes before stepping into the shadowed kitchen. A kitchen once inhabited by Paige and her family. And, after all these years, she'd parked herself next door. Seemed to him she had more of an agenda than she was letting on. Seemed to him trouble had come in the form of a five-foot-tall whirlwind. The balance in his life was already fantastically out of whack. He had no desire to wage another battle.

Not bothering with light switches, Liam climbed the stairs, heading for his office. He paused in the hallway, listening to the boards creaking across the attic floor overhead. He had given up checking. Whatever lurked up there didn't want to be seen. There'd been a time when he thought he knew what resided in this house with him, but lately he hadn't been so sure. Ironic, a man who wrote ghost stories for a living unable to uncover any history about the one in his own home. Paige Waters might know a thing or two about that, but he wasn't about to ask her.

The groaning timbers silent, Liam continued past the attic door into his office. Instead of turning the laptop back on, he went to the window, staring through a scraggly pine at the cottage roof eighty feet away. The timing of her return couldn't be worse.

"What are you really up to, Paige Waters?" he whispered. After a moment, he picked up the cell phone from the desk and dialed. He suspected she planned to storm the town with questions. Certain people needed a heads up.

* * * *

Paige parked her car in a space on the blacktop circle that surrounded the stone cross bearing the names of all the sailors Alcina Cove had lost at sea. She climbed from the vehicle, swung the door shut, and approached the etched names. Reading them, the sheer number of men and women who had died in pursuit of a living on the vast ocean in the past one hundred years dismayed her. The death notification she'd received regarding her father had only informed her that his ship had gone down, and his fate was not marked here.

Around the cross, flowers bobbed in the manicured beds, planted lovingly by a local society, according to the small plaque set on a post in the middle of them. Red, white, and blue blossoms of geraniums, petunias, and some tiny flower Paige didn't recognize reminded her that the Fourth of July was around the corner. Tiny flags on wooden dowel posts spray-painted gold lined the edge of the garden.

Paige tarried a few minutes longer to study the most recent names. Some sparked a vague memory, the surnames familiar to her. Had she known a Donald Sweetwater as a kid? Or an Albert Dunwiddy? Probably. Despite its growth, the town wasn't all that large. Many families remained in Alcina Cove generation after generation. Or so she'd been informed by both her mother, when alive, and web articles Paige had studied prior to heading north.

The ocean pounded the jetty rocks behind her. The processing plant she had passed in her car yesterday filled the air with a distant thrum. Beyond the memorial, Alcina Cove's main thoroughfare lay straight as an arrow pointing inland, the residential side streets angled out irregularly from the business center. Paige decided to leave her car parked by the cross and head into town on foot. Most addresses on the small spiral pad in her purse should be located on the narrow side roads.

She stopped first at Cora Showalter's home, a woman whose name she had found in her mother's battered address book with Cora's birthday noted. Even though Paige had never heard her mother talk about the woman, the fact that Debra Waters knew the woman's birthday held some significance. Paige had sent Cora a note informing her of Debra's passing and that she'd be coming north—she couldn't quite bring herself to use the word "home"—in a few months and would like to stop and see her. Paige had never heard back, but that didn't mean anything. For all Paige knew, there'd been little or no contact between this woman and her mother since that night long ago. Cora should still be able to provide her with information.

Striding up a slate and crushed stone walkway, Paige practiced the few lines she'd prepared for introduction. She pressed the bell at the front door. Receiving no response, Paige opened the screen door and knocked on the wooden one for good measure.

"Who are you looking for?"

Paige glanced over her shoulder. A woman with unnatural crimson hair glared at her from the sidewalk. "Cora Showalter?" Paige said. "This is the last address I have for her. Does she still live here?"

The woman wrinkled her nose. "Nope."

"Do you know where I can find her?"

"Try the Episcopalian cemetery."

Paige's fingers tightened around the notepad, spiraled wire digging into her palm. "When did she die?"

"A few months back. Her daughter lives here now, but you won't find her at home at this hour of the day. She works. And she won't like an out-of-towner lurking on her sidewalk," the woman added.

Paige sighed. "The accent, of course."

"And the fact you didn't know about Cora. Any long-time resident knew about Cora the moment she passed."

"Was she that well-loved?"

The woman's mouth twitched. "No."

Paige strode down the walkway but halted a short distance away from Cora's erstwhile neighbor. "So, are you a long-time resident, Miss—?"

"Of course."

No offer of a name. Paige bit the inside of her lip. "Then maybe you knew Edwin Waters or Debra Waters?"

"Nope, can't say I ever did."

Paige didn't quite believe her. She didn't expect her parents to be known to everyone in the town, naturally, but the way the woman looked away when she answered made her suspect. Paige recognized there'd be no point in accusations, though. She thanked the woman and turned away, crossing the name *Cora Showalter* from the lined paper with a vigorous scoring.

"What have you got there?"

Paige glanced back. "Nothing. Thank you for your information." Paige started walking back in the direction of Main Street. Behind her, she heard the woman's heels clicking sharply in scurrying pursuit.

"Wait! Wait just one second."

"Yes?" Paige paused in anticipation of last minute information. The woman clattered up beside her and snatched the pad and pencil from Paige's hands.

"Let me see what you've got here."

Shocked, Paige reached to take the notebook back, but the woman turned a shoulder to her. Paige realized she wouldn't get the notebook back without a struggle. Not until the woman finished scanning the list, making little noises through her teeth as she ticked off each name. She went back and crossed through some of them before returning pad and pencil.

"There," she said.

"Why did you do that?"

"Those people," the woman explained, wagging her pointer finger over the page, "useless to try and hunt them up. They won't be helping you. They're gone, one way or another. As for the rest? You pound on the wrong doors, you're going to find trouble. People around here, they don't like strangers."

"Yes," said Paige, "I'm getting that impression."

Holding Paige's gaze while she gave a short, sharp nod, the woman backed away and spun on her heel. Paige scanned the lined page again. Her information pool had been reduced by more than half.

* * * *

Sweat stinging the sunburn on her nape and shoulder, Paige returned to the cottage discouraged. Not one of the residents on the remaining list had been home. Paige parked her car in the graveled spot that served as a driveway and climbed out to hammering coming from next door. If she hadn't totally alienated the man, Liam Gray might be of some help. After sweating all day, she lifted an arm for a quick sniff to make certain she didn't smell like a cow's backside before heading over to the house where she had spent her earliest years.

The first thing she saw as she rounded the beach-facing porch was sawhorses laden with packs of cedar shakes. On top of the nearest pack, a faded blue shirt fluttered in the breeze. Paige's gaze shot to the top of a ladder to the porch roof where Liam, shirtless, muscular, and lightly browned, straddled a pile of cedar with his back to her, hammering replacement shakes into place. Paige bit her lip.

"I'll be right down," he said without turning.

Paige pivoted away, heat flaming her cheeks with more ferocity than the sunburn at her neck. Naturally, he would be able to see the whole beach reflected in the second floor windows, including her upturned face gawking at him.

The ladder rattled with his descent. She waited until he had slipped back into his shirt before looking at him. He hadn't buttoned the garment. The soft fabric hung over his torso, negligently revealing more than it covered. "What can I do for you today, Ms. Waters? Was there something you needed?"

Annoyed with herself for her distraction and him for his sarcasm, Paige shifted her gaze away from Liam's naked chest. "For starters, you can call me Paige."

"Paige," he said. "Better? Did you need something from me?" His tone had become guarded. As it should be, she supposed. She hadn't been very friendly when they'd met before. If nothing else, the hour hadn't been conducive to the usual niceties. As for needing something from him, well, she didn't want to think about the way he looked in his open shirt. Because there was *that* need. Her mind had gone there straightaway, to that simple, dangerous, heated need. One foisted on her by solitude and loneliness and a desire to be held, to melt away until, for a while, nothing of herself remained. He stared down at her, waiting.

"I thought I might ask you about my father."

He appeared mystified. "Your father?"

"Yes. Did you not hear me this morning when I said I was Edwin Waters' daughter?"

"I heard you."

Something in his manner snapped her drifting focus back to his face again. His black lashes had lowered, partially concealing his eyes.

"Did you know him?" she asked. "My father?"

"Why would you think I knew him?"

"But you knew of him," she persisted. "You made mention about him dying shortly after you bought the house."

"Yes, I did. But it doesn't mean I knew him or anything about him."

Paige sighed. "Somebody has to."

Liam's lashes lifted. The thought process behind his dark eyes remained unreadable.

"I don't even know exactly how he died except the rather useless 'his ship went down.'" Embarrassed by her voice's beseeching tenor, she inhaled to steady herself. "Can you at least tell me that?"

He started moving toward the ladder, impatient, no doubt, to be back at his work. "I'm sure there are other people in this town better able to answer your questions."

"Maybe there are, but none of them were available today." Perhaps she was paranoid, but it was as if they'd gotten wind of her intentions and vanished, decided to take a holiday rather than talk to a stranger. Paige took a step after Liam and stopped, her head jerking up to view the second floor window. "Oh, I'm sorry. I didn't realize you had someone helping you. I shouldn't have interrupted."

Pausing, Liam followed her gaze. "What are you talking about?"

"Up there," she said, "in the window."

He took a few steps back from the ladder in order to gain a better view of the upper storey. "I don't have anyone helping me, Paige. And there's no one up there."

"But—"

Coming to stand beside her, he crouched until his head was level with hers. She could smell his body's musk, the evidence of salt air and labor in the sun. She held her breath.

"It's just a reflection of the clouds. See?" He straightened. His warm, hard forearm grazed her shoulder. "I've got to get back to work. Tomorrow you ask around again, and if you get nowhere, I'll see what I can do. Not everyone in this town is willing to open up to an outsider."

"At one time, I wasn't an outsider," she wanted to say. Instead, she strode away from him, heading for the beach. She remembered to call over her shoulder as she stepped down into the sand, "Permission to walk?"

"Permission granted," he said without a touch of humor.

Chapter 3

The light cast by the single bulb in the bedside lamp was insufficient for the task at hand. Apparently, people who rented the tiny cottage did not read. They slept, or engaged in activities that did not require illumination. Paige possessed no chance of either.

Sleeping from sunrise until noon probably didn't help her insomnia, nor did her frustrating afternoon. The recollection of Liam Gray shirtless in the late-day sun was the biggest obstacle to slumber.

Now there would be a complication she did not want. A man like him would already have a woman in his life anyway—a gorgeous woman without baggage and who didn't require a stepstool to kiss his mouth. Paige considered the many other ways of reaching that part of his body but dismissed them, tossing the paperback onto the nightstand. Overthrown, the novel skittered off the wooden surface to the floor with a loud slap. Something slammed against the bed's undercarriage and then darted out, dark and low, across the room.

Scrambling onto her knees on the narrow mattress, Paige bit back a shriek. *Was that a freaking rat?* Grabbing the lamp, she angled it down to illuminate the painted floor. Various hiding places existed: under the dresser, behind the small stove and refrigerator in the kitchenette, back under the bed, the bathroom. Paige chewed her lower lip as she considered the animal's likely route. She had no choice but to go looking for it.

And when she found the darned thing? Paige leapt off the mattress in the door's direction. Landing at a run, she flew toward the handle and yanked the door open. With any luck, she could chase the animal out.

Paige pawed through her purse for the small LED flashlight she kept. Once found, she clicked on a focused beam and began a cautious search in all the places she'd envisioned a rat hiding. Finding no success in the main room, she walked with soft, guarded steps to the bathroom and flicked on the overhead, filling the room with light. "Last place," she announced in an attempt at bravado, "unless you ducked out when I didn't see you— Oh, hello."

On older cat was curled behind the pedestal sink, yellow eyes wide and pupils dilated, flecks of gray around its muzzle and tufted in ears that laid flat against its head. Paige dropped slowly to her knees, clicking off the flashlight.

"Hey, how'd you get in here?"

The cat blinked once, ears flicking forward from the defensive. It issued a small chirp as it began to unfold from a tight ball.

"You haven't been in here since I arrived, have you?" Paige tried to figure out when the cat might have slipped inside. Surely, she would have heard if the animal had shared the room with her since her arrival late the night before. Where had it come from? "Are you wild, buddy, or someone's pet?"

A brief knock sounded on the open door. "Paige, is everything all right?"

Paige leaned back to view Liam filling the doorway, the night sky black behind him. His wet hair was skimmed back along his head, the white T-shirt he wore splotched with damp. Not rain. He must have showered.

"If you were planning to be my white knight, you're a little late." *God, Paige, stop flirting.*

"Why? Did you require rescuing?"

Hell, was he flirting back? She studied his face as he stepped inside. No, probably not. "I have a visitor."

"What?" He appeared truly shocked, eyes flying wide before his brows lowered into a frown.

"A kitty," she said.

"If you have a cat in there with you, it's probably mine."

Paige frowned. "What does your cat look like?"

"Black."

"Oh." Paige stood. "Come have a look then."

She stepped back to allow him into the bathroom. He smelled like soap, shampoo, toothpaste, and a hint of sawdust. She supposed that came from his jeans. Attempting to ignore the flipping of her stomach, she watched to see how the cat reacted to him.

Liam dropped to one knee on the white tile floor. "Shadow, what are you doing?" After a languorous stretch, the cat ambled over to him and climbed into his arms. Liam rose again, his head inches from the low bathroom ceiling, his shining black hair backlit by the bulbs in the glassless fixture.

"Shadow? You named a black cat Shadow?"

He shrugged. "Not very original, I know. I found him and took him in, and the name fit. He hasn't complained."

Paige reached out and scratched the animal behind the ears. The cat responded with a throaty purr. "How long has he been gone?"

"Yesterday. He wanders but always comes back at night. I was out looking for him when I…when I saw you on the beach last night. Well, I guess it was technically this morning." His gruff tone had softened. Paige wondered if that was the cat's doing. She pictured this broad-shouldered individual searching the night for his foundling pet and felt a sharp, visceral pull low in her abdomen.

"I'm glad you two have been reunited." She restored the flashlight to her purse. "Did you come over here only looking for him?" Paige fastened her purse, fingers hovering over the zipper tab, wondering if there'd be any chance he'd say no.

"Yes, and I saw your door was open."

She sighed. His rumbling voice reverberated through the room. Paige faced him, crossing her arms over her breasts. The cat cuddled in his sturdy arms in no way detracted from his rugged good looks. Light from the kitchen lamp glinted off his scar. Paige tapped her jaw line. "What happened?"

His expression changed. "You really don't have any boundaries, do you?"

Paige jerked a shoulder in dismissal. "I didn't mean anything. Sorry."

Liam shook his head. "It's fine. I have to get going."

"Want something to drink? I have…well, bottled water is all I have right now. I need to get to the grocery store." She laughed, trying her best to make it not sound as though she'd invited him for something more.

"It's late," he said. But he didn't move.

She met his gaze dead on, trying to figure him out. She'd never met a man she couldn't sum up in about two seconds. No, that wasn't true. She'd never bothered with a man she couldn't sum up in two seconds. There was a vast difference. That practice said a lot about herself she didn't like. The fact she was still contemplating Liam said even more about him.

Her breath rushed out. "You're right. It is. I won't keep you."

He nodded, the cat in his arms purring loudly. "How long do you plan on sticking around?"

"I cashed out my savings and took a leave of absence. I need answers to many things in my life."

He nodded. "Then I'll see you tomorrow."

"You'll see me tomorrow."

Her skin warmed. She followed him in silence to close the door behind him. Standing a moment on the threshold, she allowed the breeze off the water to dry the tiny perspiration drops from her brow as he walked away. Down by the water's edge, a soft glow caught her eye. She turned. A light bobbed at the height of a man's hand at his side, as if someone carried a lantern.

Paige stepped out for a better look, pulling the door shut to block the light from inside. Yes, someone was there, moving at the surf's edge. The lantern cast a golden glow over a man's left side as he strode in a straight line toward the far side of the beach. Nearer, she could hear Liam as he made his way homeward, his thunderous voice subdued in one-sided conversation with Shadow. Didn't he see the man? But he continued speaking to the cat, unperturbed. A neighbor, she supposed. Not an outsider, like her.

* * * *

Paige headed back to town in the morning armed with her list of residents. Maybe, with the earlier hour, she would find some of them at home. And if these didn't pan out, she'd go to where people hung out and ask general questions there. Somewhere she'd find a lead. If not, she would speak to Liam.

First, though, she needed a blasted cup of coffee.

Yesterday she'd spotted a place called the Caffeine Café and headed there. Standing in line at the coffee shop, Paige eavesdropped on the conversations around her in blatant curiosity. For thirteen years, this town had been her home. She might very well have been acquainted with certain patrons, but doubted she would recognize them now. People changed in time's passage, teenage boys even more than girls. Still, something in the dialogue around her could strike a chord of memory.

At the register, she ordered a large coffee and paid, taking a welcome swig as soon as the kid behind the counter handed the cup to her. She held the spiral tablet in her other hand and flipped it open while turning around. Someone jostled her elbow. The notebook fluttered to the floor.

"Here, let me get that."

Paige caught a glimpse of a police uniform and close-cropped sandy hair as the man who had spoken stooped to pick up the notebook. It had fallen open to the list, and she could see him browsing over the names as he stood. She held out her hand, palm up to hasten the notebook's return. "Thank you."

The man—badge pinned to a shirt strained by the bulletproof vest beneath—hesitated before dropping the pad across her fingers. Despite her annoyance at the officer's inquisitiveness, she realized an opportunity had fallen into her lap.

"Are you on duty?" she asked. "I need some information and I—Dan? Dan...Stauffer?"

He frowned. "Yes. Do I know you?"

Probably not, she thought, but plunged on. "I'm Paige Waters. You were a couple of years ahead of me in school. I was a freshman when you were a senior."

Her last year spent at Alcina Cove High, she hadn't finished the semester out, ending up in a place midyear where she knew no one. If she remembered correctly, Dan had always considered himself a charmer. She'd been too young and unexceptional to catch his eye, but with recognition she also recalled the stories of his reputation as a ladies' man.

"Paige Waters? Oh, right, you and your mother left town rather abruptly. Don't remember the reason why, though. Something personal, I heard."

Stunned he had recalled her that quickly, Paige eased past the congestion at the counter. With a gesture that Dan should join her, she headed for a table and took a seat. Stauffer followed. He sat across from her and leaned his forearms on the tabletop.

"You said you needed some information. What's up?"

Now that she'd come to it, Paige wasn't sure where to begin. She could sense him sizing her up and she wondered if his womanizing behavior had persisted all these years later. Paige spun the coffee cup between her palms in a slow circle on the table, feeling the liquid's heat through the thick paper.

"My mom passed away almost three years ago. And then I received a letter from an attorney in January of this year notifying me my dad had passed away, too. I think it took a while for the attorney to locate me. My dad had no property, nothing to pass on. He'd had a house—our house—but I found out he'd sold it. The notification just said he died at sea. I don't know the exact circumstances. I tried researching online but, oddly enough, couldn't find anything. I came back to find out what I can about his life, and my mom's, too. Perhaps you might be able to give me some assistance?"

Dan shifted in his seat, his vest creaking, handcuffs on his belt clanking against the metal tubing of the chair. "I don't get it. What do you hope to accomplish, digging around like this?"

"I beg your pardon?"

"Don't get me wrong. I'm not trying to dissuade you. I'm just trying to understand what you want me to look into. Do you think they were involved in something the police would know about?"

The paper cup jerked in Paige's grip.

Keep your mouth shut, Paige.

But Mom...

"Of course not. I thought you might have some way to uncover more details about my father's death. I don't even know where his ship went down."

Considering her a moment, Dan finally nodded. "Makes sense. What was his name again?"

"Waters, same as mine. First name Edwin."

"Okay. I'll see what I can do." Wheels turned visibly in his expression. She guessed he'd already begun formulating ideas as to why she wanted to know. During her final days, Debra Waters, in her delirium, had hinted all had not been as she'd let on since their flight from Alcina Cove. There had to be a reason Paige's father had written her from his life. Maybe he plain hadn't cared enough to do otherwise once he'd driven his wife away. Or possibly some of Debra Waters' ramblings hadn't solely been the result of opioids and cancer.

"Where are you staying while you're here?"

She hedged, hesitant to share the information. Wouldn't he think it suspicious she'd rented a place next door to her old home? "Do you have a card?" she asked. "I'll write my cell number down."

He pulled a business card and a pen from his pocket. Paige scrawled the number across the back. She asked him for another card and tucked it into her purse. Clutching her coffee, she pushed back her chair and stood. Stauffer followed suit.

"Thank you," she said.

"Not a problem. What about that list of names? What's that for?"

"People I think might be able to answer some questions."

"Be careful. People in this town don't like being approached by—"

"Outsiders," she said. "I know. I've been told. Thing is, I'm not. An outsider, I mean. I've been away. That's all."

"A long time away."

Right. She needed no reminders.

* * * *

He watched her exit the coffee shop, a damned cop on her heels. They were cordial in parting. Not like total strangers. Not like some chance meeting. What the fuck did that mean?

Stepping behind a tree, he kept an eye on her as she crossed the street to her car. She had a nice step, long and sort of uneven. Yup, the Plain Jane daughter had turned into a fine-looking woman after all. Just like Deb.

But first, before he placed any wagers on whether she had the personality, too, he'd better figure out why the hell she'd come back.

Chapter 4

"Oh, goodness, yes, come in, come in!" The face of the elderly woman who opened the door folded into a thousand smiles. Her snow-white head bobbed in greeting. Paige was taken aback by the exuberant welcome and wavered on the threshold in uncertainty.

"Do you really know who I am?"

"You're the image of your mother, dear. I know that much. Come in and sit down. Tell me how your mother's doing."

Chest tightening, Paige followed Beatrice Hunt—the only person on her list who'd been willing to talk to her—into the living room. Taking the seat the woman indicated, she perched at the edge of the cushion, folding her hands between her knees, purse dangling from her wrist. "Mrs. Hunt—"

"Bea. Call me Bea."

"Bea—"

"Would you like some tea, Paige?"

Paige settled her bag on the couch arm. "No, thank you. I have sad news. Mom passed away nearly three years back after a long battle with cancer."

"Oh," the woman said in a hushed voice. "I didn't know."

"I'm so sorry. I thought I had notified everyone."

"Is your father aware?"

Paige hesitated. The woman was speaking in the present tense. Apparently, Bea Hunt didn't know he had died, either.

Paige hadn't told him about her mother. Flowers had appeared at the funeral home in his name nevertheless, leading her to assume someone she'd notified had let him know, or he had seen the small notice she had placed in the local paper. She'd spent several days agonizing over whether she should write to her father, but in the end figured her mother would rather she didn't. The day of the service she'd considered removing the small bouquet from the room, but ultimately took the flowers home with her, together with the other arrangements that hadn't ended up at the gravesite. The bouquet had withered, and for some reason that defied her understanding, she'd scooped up the fallen petals and put them in an envelope. The yellowed envelope still sat on the kitchen counter at home.

"He knew," she said. "He sent flowers."

"Surprising, all things considered."

Paige remained mum.

"I guess I don't have to tell you," Bea added. "And it's all right. We won't talk about that."

"Thank you," said Paige. "You do know Dad's gone now, too, don't you?"

"Oh, well, yes, I'd heard that. I forgot for a moment. I never saw him. Your mother and I fell out of touch years back. She was always very independent, your mother. Ideas about everything. I found I couldn't keep up."

Paige twisted her fingers together in her lap. "What kind of ideas?"

"The wild kind. She once told me she wanted to be a famous singer. Now, she could sing, as you well know, but she had no control over the famous part. I told her that, but she didn't want to hear it."

Shifting on the cushion, Paige shook her head. An ambition to be a singer didn't strike her as all that wild. However, she hadn't known about her mother's desires, despite Bea's assumptions. Although she'd heard her mother sing in church and recognized the beauty of her voice, Paige had never been aware of any aspirations in that regard. Perhaps her mother had chosen Nashville to run to for that reason. "How long ago did she want to be a singer?"

Bea considered a minute. "Oh, I'm guessing it was before you were born."

"Did she change her mind because I came along?"

Bea thought a little longer, distress creeping into the set of her mouth. She looked at Paige and then away. "She had a lot of dreams. I guess the next one took precedence."

"She'd always been steadfast and level-headed."

Bea shrugged. Paige plunged on. "Do you know exactly what happened between Mom and Dad?"

"Not happy with her lot in life, I guess."

Paige reeled back. "Would you be happy with a husband who blackened your eye and split your lip and nearly broke your arm?"

Bea blinked, her expression suddenly bland. "I don't know anything about that, Paige."

No force existed behind Bea Hunt's statement, and no truth either. Hadn't the woman commented two minutes ago about how surprising she found it that Edwin Waters sent flowers for his wife's funeral? Paige had seen her father's handiwork for herself the night her mother woke her out of a sound sleep by shoving an open suitcase at her and telling her to fit only what she needed in the little space left inside. She didn't need confirmation from Bea Hunt and began to wonder if she'd misinterpreted the tiny star next to Bea's name. "What was your relationship to Mom?"

Clearing her throat, Bea appeared grateful for the change of subject. "I was her teacher in grade school. Later, when she was grown, we became friends. We were on the church committee together."

"I didn't know any of this," Paige said. "Mom never told me."

"She is—was—your parent, Paige. We often don't know enough about our parents' lives, nor do they know enough about their children's lives. It's natural. Is this why you're back in Alcina Cove? To find out?"

"There are a lot of holes in my life. Things I'd like to learn about my parents' relationship, about our lives together as a family, when we were one. About my dad, what he made of his life…after. I guess to start, I'd like to know how he died. The circumstances. Do you know?"

Bea's lips thinned, nearly disappearing. "Edwin was a tough one. Tough to know. Tough to love, too, I think."

Paige swallowed, giving a ring on her finger a nervous spin.

"He found himself in business with some objectionable people."

"Like who? What kind of business?" She wasn't surprised by Bea's statement, but oh, how she wanted to be.

"I don't know, really. One hears rumors. And he wasn't inclined to listen. To anybody. Incautious, too. Determined to pick the wrong path, stick with decisions out of pride, even if they were plainly foolish. And this last time? Well, I could have told him he'd come to a tragic end. You have to respect the demands of the sea. He never did."

"The demands of the sea?" Paige's fingers stilled. "What are they, exactly?"

"He had another business in recent years. Did you know that? A legitimate one. At least that's how he made it out. Taking sports fishermen out in that sailboat of his."

What did Bea mean, a legitimate business? What had her father been up to prior to that?

"Sometimes he took them places where they shouldn't have been," Bea continued.

"Like where?"

"There's danger out on the sea. That's what they paid him for, to show it to them, those places no one else would take them in pursuit of big fish. But that ship of his? It was destined for destruction."

"How? Was there something faulty in the way it was made? If so, someone should look into the manufacturer." Someone? As his daughter, that someone should be her.

Bea shook her head with emphatic jerks, setting her well-sprayed hair to jiggling. "There wasn't a blessed thing wrong with that ship. It was Edwin's disregard for the will of the sea."

Bea's turn of conversation began to worry Paige. The woman had acted lucid enough, but now…

"Every man who sets foot on a boat knows better. But your father was determined to flaunt his disregard. He started out dressing himself and whatever crew member he roped into helping him in red shirts with the company's name on them."

"What's wrong with that? I'd say that's a savvy business move, having your logo on a shirt."

"Red. They were red. No sailor with any conscious respect for the power of—"

"How do you know this?' Paige interrupted. "You said you hadn't any contact with him before he died."

"One hears things. And it wasn't just that. His last, his deadly mistake, was an improper rechristening of that ship of his. Bad luck to change the name of a ship without proper observance. He was warned but took none of it seriously."

Paige rose, uncertain how to respond to such tripe. This woman was seriously going to blame a man's demise on the fact he wore a red shirt onboard a seagoing vessel? And what did he rename his sailboat that was so very ominous? *Titanic*?

"I'm sorry, Mrs. Hunt, but—"

"Don't dismiss what I say, Paige. The gods of the sea are demanding. My own husband made a fatal error on his last run fifty years ago and never came home to me."

After gathering her purse from the sofa arm, Paige paused to address the woman. "That's very sad, Mrs. Hunt, and I can understand why you would want to place the blame on something in a realm other than our own, but the sea is a dangerous place, as you said. Ships go down all the time. But it's nature or mechanics or pilot error or—"

"No, Paige—"

"Can you at least tell me where the ship went down? Was it a storm? What?"

Bea Hunt's eyes glittered. Paige couldn't tell if the gleam came from unshed tears or anger. Choosing the former, Paige touched the woman's shoulder in sympathy. She spoke in a gentler tone. "Do you know where the ship went down? Can you tell me?"

Bea made a negative gesture with her hand. "A storm, yes. North. North of here somewhere is all I know. Are you leaving?"

Paige took a step in the direction of the foyer and then stopped. "I have other folks I need to speak with, but I'll come back. We'll have tea then, all right?"

Bea didn't believe her. A stab of guilt shot through Paige's chest. For her mother's sake, she would come back. There'd be no talk about the sea, only about the flowers growing in Bea Hunt's garden out front and maybe her mother's days in school.

"I will. I'll be back." Paige moved to the door, waving Bea back in her seat when she made to rise. "Do you want me to lock up on my way out?"

"There's no need. Who's going to bother with an old lady?"

Paige's gut churned with seven kinds of shame despite her aggravation at Bea Hunt's nonsense. She headed straight for her car and climbed behind the wheel, where she glanced through her list again. Other than Bea, the folks who'd answered their doors today did so in wary friendliness and had avoided inviting Paige in by stepping outside to speak with her. None of them had offered any information worth a damn.

Spotting Bea peering through the parted lace curtains at her, Paige waved and pulled away from the curb. At the stop sign, she leaned the notepad against the steering wheel, studying the names the woman with the outrageous hair had crossed off, supposedly in the interest of keeping her from trouble with the townsfolk. What was it the woman had said? One way or another, these people were gone. Why on earth had Paige taken the word of someone who hadn't been inclined to help her?

She'd start with Alva Mabry. After the brief and unfortunate interview with Bea, Paige knew she'd probably regret seeking Alva out, but she turned right at the stop sign. Although Paige never heard her mother say anything about an Alva, the woman's name and address had been in the shabby address book with an asterisk beside the entry in bold, purple ink. Paige was determined to find out the significance.

* * * *

Liam grabbed a beer from the refrigerator and pressed the cold bottle to the blister on his thumb. On the counter, the grilled burger sat on a plate beside cooked beets. Behind him, a floorboard creaked. He lifted the bottle. "Want one?"

He received no answer. Of course he didn't. What the hell was he thinking?

Snatching up the plate, he turned and headed outside. On the porch, he shoved a box out of his way and lowered himself onto a badly painted Adirondack chair. Knees bent, he planted his bare feet on a wooden baluster on the railing. A chill swirl of air danced across his forearm, raising a rill of hair. He ignored it. Cold air dancing on an otherwise hot evening meant nothing. Not every odd occurrence was something to sweat about. Some were just nature.

Liam bit off and chewed a meaty mouthful, then chased it down his throat with a deep swig of beer. He'd worked up quite the thirst working in the sun. Pretty soon, though, he'd have to lay off and let some of the repairs go for a while. He had other deadlines to meet. The kind that paid the bills.

Movement caught his eye out on the purple-shadowed beach. He leaned to the side for a better look through the porch railing. He took another bite off the burger, chewing slowly. "Paige Waters," he said around the mouthful. "What are you up to?"

He watched her pace, a few steps one way and then back. She wore jeans rolled up to mid-calf and the water, foaming in evening shadow, purled around her ankles at the tide line. Pulled into a high ponytail, her curly brown hair bobbed and bounced with her head's movement. She appeared to be talking animatedly. To herself.

Liam continued to observe her as he finished his meal, his thoughts growing less clinical with every passing minute. Each time they interacted, his necessary detachment became harder to maintain—especially at this moment, with the double whammy of both curiosity and attraction. He set aside his plate and headed out onto the beach, beer in hand. He thought about stopping first to get her one, but decided against it. He didn't want to appear too friendly. Besides, in her present mood, she'd probably kick sand at him.

He managed to get within two yards without her noticing. He stopped, crossing his arms. Over the growling waves, her voice carried to him, rising and falling in indistinct agitation.

"Wouldn't it be more helpful to bounce all that energy off someone else?"

She jerked about and lost her balance, the canvas shoes in her right hand sailing from her grip. Liam lurched toward her, snagging her by the arm before she tumbled into the waves. She fell against his chest. The bottle flew to the sand.

After he set her back on her feet, Paige bent and picked up the bottle, brushing off the sand. She held the container in the air. A glint of evening sun shone on the contents through the clear glass.

"You were going to offer me used beer?"

"Used beer?"

"That bottle didn't spill, and it's only half full. You've been drinking it."

"I have been. But I wasn't offering it to you."

She narrowed her eyes at him—eyes, he noticed, the color of honey—then pushed past him, starting up the sand toward the house. She glanced back. "I'll take one, thanks." And off she went at a staggered trot, heading for the stairs leading to the porch.

Liam hurried past her and leapt up the steps two at a time. At the top, he planted his feet apart to the width of the tread, blocking her way. "What's wrong, Ms. Waters?"

"Don't flirt with me," she said.

"Don't flirt?" Good God, was he? She needed watching and he, of course, was the best candidate for the task. Flirting was both stupid and dangerous. "I'm wondering what's wrong, that's all. People don't stand by the ocean in boisterous conversation with themselves if everything is fine. You haven't been drinking already?"

Rolling her eyes, she pushed his leg out of her way and threw herself down into his abandoned chair. "I wish," she stated in an emphatic manner.

With a mental shrug, Liam snatched up his empty plate from the porch floor and went inside to grab two more beers. He set the sandy, half-full bottle in the sink. He wasn't a fanatic who bemoaned a waste of "good beer." He only drank a few times a month, when he felt a change in the cycle of his life or had worked up a really rip-roaring thirst. Tonight, it was both. He could blame Paige Waters for that.

Pausing before exiting the kitchen, he tipped his head back to listen. "Are you still here?" he queried softly.

Nothing. Just as well. He didn't need to be making those kinds of explanations to Paige. Back outside, he handed Paige one bottle and took the other over to the railing. He hopped up, balancing himself on top, one foot hooked around a baluster and the other leg stretched out along the length of the rail, his spine pressed against the upright post. A month and a half ago, this stunt would have left him on the ground. Little by little he was making the necessary repairs.

"Would you like the chair?"

He shook his head. Paige tipped the bottle and her head back with a fluid motion and swallowed a third of the contents in a few gulps. Then she set the bottle on the chair arm, her face twisting in indecision.

"I don't think I like beer," she said.

Laughing so hard he nearly upended himself over the railing, Liam managed to gasp out a question. "Then why did you demand one?"

"I don't know."

She didn't know? He doubted that. "I can get you something else. Water or a glass of apple juice?"

"I'll just sip this. It'll make me drunk, right?"

"It might. You're a small person."

She nodded, taking a mouthful gingerly.

"But why do you want it to?"

"Something somebody told me."

Liam slid down from the railing. He kicked the upended crate closer to the chair and sat on it. She kept her gaze on the bottle in her hand as she picked at the label with the edge of her thumbnail. Condensation dripped down her wrist. "Why did you come back to Alcina Cove?"

Pick. Pick. "I told you."

"To find out what happened to your dad. But if that was all you wanted, wouldn't you have gone straight to the police? They'd be the best source of answers for you. There must be something else. Do you have no family here?"

She shook her head. Tendrils of hair flicked around her brow and into her eyes. She blinked them out. "Not anymore."

He waited in silence.

"I was told today that we never really know our parents and they never know us. I get that. I understand." Swig, swallow, face. Pick. Pick. Pick.

"And?"

"I guess I need to know them. I need to know what made them tick, why they got together, how things went so horribly awry. Of course, it's too late. Even if I get answers, they're hearsay, really. Someone else's opinion of why they acted as they did."

The burger and beets he'd eaten began a revolution in his gut. He wriggled the crate closer, tipping his head to look into her downturned face. "Why do you need to know?"

"What kind of question is that?"

"It's just a question. It's rather late in the game to be seeking those kinds of answers, and I was wondering why you were putting yourself through it."

She began to pull at the label in earnest. Liam took the bottle away. She bowed her head again and stared at her hand, at the thumbnail she had chipped with her actions. After a moment, she put it in her mouth and bit off the sharp edge. He gave her back the beer, sensing she'd drawn into herself, as if to become as small a target as possible. He wondered why. In the past day and a half he'd found her to be feisty and fearless. She had faced him, a rather large stranger, in the darkness without backing down, and he had to admit he admired her for it, although he'd been trying not to.

She lifted her head. "Because I…I feel I'm tainted by the past. I can't get beyond it. It has affected so many of my decisions." Tears glistened on her lashes in the growing twilight. Soon it would be dark. Her distress disturbed him. He resolved not to get up from that box until she was back in fighting mode.

"Paige."

She waved her fingers, took another gulp of beer, and wiped her mouth with the back of her hand. "I'm fine. Really. Oh, and you'll get a kick out of this. You probably know her or heard of her. I went to see someone whose name Mom had marked in her address book. Alva Mabry?"

He sat up. "The—"

"Psychic? Yeah. That would be the one." Leaning her head against the chair back, Paige stared up at the shadowed ceiling. "You know what she told me? That there's a darkness around me. She implied that I'm haunted."

Liam's muscles lost heat and elasticity as he went still as stone. The susurration of the ocean sounded far away, and the click of a firefly against the rhododendron growing beside the house beat like a stick against concrete. "She said that?"

"Yep. What do you think?"

"I couldn't say. Depends on what you believe."

"What I believe was she made a lucky guess. People like her, they learn to read other people. Of course I'm haunted. It probably showed in my face, my body language, as soon as I walked in the door. Aren't people always haunted by the deaths of others— Are you okay?"

Blowing out a breath, he rose. "I'm fine. I know you don't want another, but I'm going to grab a cold one. This one's a little warm."

In the kitchen, Liam leaned his hips against the counter, his back to the window facing out to the porch. A mouthful at a time, he drank half the contents of the bottle in his hand, his gaze glued to the far wall. Then he turned and dumped the remainder into the sink. He didn't bother to turn on the light. He didn't want Paige seeing him through the glass because surely his face would reveal more than he could allow.

Liam listened closely to the sounds of the house around him, for the creaks and snaps of normal settling and the movement beyond the mere cooling of timbers.

There's a darkness around me... I am haunted.

As much as he had no faith in Alva's brand of quackery, this time the old woman might be right.

Chapter 5

Paige gripped the beer she'd been babying. She wasn't going to finish it. She knew that. Yet she derived some comfort from the feel of the bottle, solid and heavy in her hand.

Liam had taken a long time getting himself another beer. Paige glanced at the darkened window over her shoulder before returning her gaze to the ocean. In the setting sun, the waves battering the rocky shoreline had gone blue-black, each rolling crest tipped in a wash of gold and red. Gulls soared on the sea breeze in the darkening sky with wings outspread. And there, way out on the water, another freighter winked its tiny lights. The scene tugged at her insides, pulling at old memories, causing conflicting and harrowing emotions to rise to the surface. Teeth in her lip, Paige blinked back tears.

"Enough." She struggled up from the deep, angled seat. When she stood, she caught sight of the man she had seen the night before down by the water's edge, his bobbing lantern bright against the dark sea beyond. She rushed to the porch railing, leaning forward to study the man's locomotion, spotting something not quite right in the way he moved. The screen door rasped open behind her.

"Do you know that man?" she asked Liam. He didn't answer. She turned. No one was there.

"Liam?"

Paige twisted back toward the ocean and hastened out onto the weathered steps. The man had vanished, lantern and all. Perhaps he had already clambered over the jetty of rock, but he had been moving with profound sluggishness, as if age or infirmity weighed him down.

The screen door opened and closed again. Liam appeared at her side on the step. "Were you calling me?"

She frowned at him. "Did you forget something?"

"I thought you didn't want another beer?"

"No, no, I don't. Thank you. I mean, you started to come out a second ago. I heard the door. But you weren't there when I turned around."

Liam's left eyebrow shot up. "That happens sometimes."

"Absentmindedness?"

"No, the door opening and closing with no one there."

She frowned at him before breaking into laughter. "Ooh, creepy. Got it. But you forget, I used to live here. The door doesn't open and shut on its own."

"Maybe it didn't, but it does now."

"Tighten the screws on the hinges or something. I was calling you because there was a man on the beach. I wanted to know if you knew him. He's gone now."

Liam gave the beach the onceover. "No one there."

"He vanished."

"Like smoke?"

"No," Paige said in sharp impatience, "not like smoke. I didn't see what happened to him. One second he was there, and the next he wasn't. And believe me, he was moving none too quickly. But he wasn't a ghost. Oh!" She skipped down two steps. "Do you think he might have slipped into the water?"

Unconcerned, Liam went back up onto the porch. "There's nothing splashing about down there. Probably a mirage."

Paige followed. "A mirage? Like you see in the desert?"

"It happens. If the conditions are right, objects miles out to sea will appear as if they're right in front of you. That man might have been walking on the deck of a ship that's no more than a speck on the water." He resumed his seat on the crate. Paige noticed his hands were empty. He folded them together between his knees. Instead of taking the chair, Paige remained standing.

"That would mean the conditions were right two days in a row. I saw him last night, too."

"What did he look like?"

"I don't know. It was hard to see. Curly hair and beard. He wore a hat and coat, now that you mention it. Odd time of year for that."

"Hmm. Perhaps a ghost, then?" His eyes cut in her direction as if to gauge her reaction.

Paige didn't hold back. She snorted. "A ghost? Come on. This isn't some television show."

"No," he agreed, "it isn't. It's a very real town with three hundred years of history behind it. Before I moved here, I'd heard the town referred to as Haunted Alcina Cove."

"Haunted?" Paige tried not to laugh again and was not entirely successful. "Although its residents might not always be the friendliest, and some might be downright peculiar, it's a quaint, picturesque location. Certainly not the stuff of nightmares."

"Neither are ghosts. Not usually, anyway."

"You sound like you believe—"

"I don't know what I believe." He stood. "But this is what I do. I write travelogues, and I gather and research local stories about ghosts and other mysterious happenings and compile them into books. Sometimes I combine the two, writing travelogues featuring ghost stories of the area along with the scenic spots. I can't explain everything I've found out or everything people believe they've seen."

He paused in his pacing in front of her. The heat off his body was palpable in the evening's dropping temperature. She lifted her head to look him in the eye. "Okay. I didn't mean to upset you."

"You didn't upset me. The subject just makes me a little nuts at times." He laughed. "What about you? What do you do when you're not here?"

Paige sidled away from him. His proximity made her twitchy. She reclaimed the Adirondack chair since he obviously wasn't using it. He returned to his earlier roost on the railing.

"I teach eighth grade English," she said.

"A bunch of hormonal thirteen- and fourteen-year-old boys? They must adore you."

"What?"

"You have to be aware you're a good-looking woman, Paige."

Paige waved a hand, heat flaring in her cheeks. "I don't have to be aware of any such thing. And we've gotten off topic. I want to go back to you. How long have you been making a living at writing?"

Liam folded his arms across his chest. Evening's last light flashed off the water behind him. "Making a living? Not long. And not hand-over-fist, either. But I like it. I've been writing most of my life. But a sedentary occupation was never the destiny of a Gray. Nope. I was out on the sea at sixteen and owned and operated my own trawler by nineteen. Fished the ocean for more than fourteen years."

Performing some quick math even after only half a beer proved difficult, but Paige figured she had an approximate idea of his age. Curiosity satisfied, Paige smiled. "So you gave that up? Commercial fishing?"

"About eight months ago," he said with a small affirmative motion of his head. "Sold the boat and equipment shortly after I bought this place."

"To pursue your writing? Bold move."

"Yeah, something like that."

Paige leaned forward, elbows on her knees in an awkward position on the sloped seat. "Not satisfied writing about ghosts?"

"That's not what I meant. But I don't plan to talk about it, if you don't mind."

He held her gaze as though daring her to question him. She shook her head. Another thing he didn't want to talk about, like his scar. And he didn't have to. Who was she to him, after all? A stranger who'd shown up practically on his doorstep in the wee hours, claiming an association to the house he owned. No reason for confidences exchanged. No cause for anything beyond a neighborly chat. "It's your business, not mine, Liam. We both have our secrets, I guess."

"Yes," he said quietly, "I think we do."

* * * *

Soon after the exchange, Paige thanked Liam for the beer she hadn't finished and left. Instead of returning to the cottage, she went to her car and removed a small flashlight from the glove compartment. Slipping it into her pocket, she headed down to the waterline. Despite her dismissal of Liam's ghost story, she found herself motivated to prove a flesh and blood man had been walking on the beach and not some specter of seafaring lore. Though she appreciated Liam's pursuit of a writing career, she wondered if he couldn't have chosen a more worthy topic than tales of phantoms and things that went bump in the night.

Stopping above the surf, Paige flicked on the light, casting its blue-white glow over the sand. Apparently high tide had come in while she'd been talking with Liam. A narrow scrim of tumbled shell and stone showed where the water had begun its slow withdrawal. Any footprints lay beneath the water, scrubbed away. Nevertheless, Paige continued toward the jetty, flicking the light on and off to make sporadic checks of the ground. Once there, she scuttled up onto the rocks to sit a few moments. She figured it was safe to do so. She might have been in a dangerous position if the tide were still coming in.

Paige shoved the flashlight back into her pocket and drew her knees up, wrapping her arms around her legs. She could see the lights of town against a lowering cloud cover. Sitting on a porch that had once been her own hadn't felt as much like home as this did. Jammed between the huge boulders beneath the night sky, staring toward town while the ocean rushed in and out at her back was far more nostalgic. She'd often come here to sit alone long after her parents had thought her asleep. Why? She hadn't been meeting anyone. The number of friends she'd had was fairly limited. For one thing, she'd been uncomfortable inviting anyone over. Looking back, though, she couldn't place her finger on a particular reason for that avoidance. Not her parents' fighting. She'd witnessed spats between other kids' parents and none of them cared. They all brushed it off as a normal course of events. She supposed it was, indeed, daily life, relationships. But as far as she knew, none of their mothers had been the victim of a brutal attack by her spouse.

Secrets. Her early life had been full of secrets.

Paige bit her lip and lowered her forehead onto her knees. The pounding surf reverberated from her heels on stone up through the hard mass of knee and skull. She squeezed her eyes shut against the discomfort, refusing to move.

A male voice spoke nearby in a series of unintelligible words. Sucking in a breath, Paige lifted her head, scanning the shadowed beach. Seeing nothing, she considered using the flashlight, but decided not to draw attention to herself. Not Liam, so whoever it was, she'd rather they passed on by.

A light flared. Paige narrowed her eyes, peering between her lashes. A man stood with a lantern in his hands at a distance of about twenty yards. She could see him clearly, bearded and wearing an ill-fitting coat despite a comfortable night. If he saw her, he gave no indication, but began walking away with the same slow, ambling stride she'd seen earlier.

Watching him move back along the beach, she tried to decide if she should speak to him, get his name, so she could tell Liam she had met his mirage, his ghost, in the flesh. In the lamp's golden glow, she could distinguish his coat's dusty folds, the coarse knit of his cap, his curly beard and hair, but below the coat's hem his legs were invisible, hidden in shadow. She stood up. "Hello?"

Paige scrambled down from the rocks, eyes on her descent to avoid breaking her neck. When her feet touched sand, she looked up again. The man was gone. "Hello?" She whipped the flashlight from her pocket and passed the beam in a huge sweep across the rocky beach. Still finding nothing, she hurried to the place she'd seen him last.

Suddenly dizzy, she stopped, her gaze glued to an indistinct mound on the sand in front of her. It looked like a body. Oh, God, had the old man fallen? She staggered over. Before she reached him, recall slammed like ice into her skull, a silver flash, swiftly to the mark—

Mom, what is that?

Come away, Paige. Now.

—and then nothing.

What lay on the beach before her was no more than rock and seaweed. The man with the lantern was nowhere, and her mind was trying to make mincemeat of her resolve. She backed away in haste and fell over a piece of driftwood. The flashlight flew from her grasp. With a strangled cry, she crab-walked in search of it and located the instrument by the beam half-buried in the sand. Snatching it out, she jumped to her feet. Something huge and dark and solid blocked her way. With a scream, she launched the light at it, which hit with a noise like rock on stone.

"Shit, Paige, what the hell are you doing?"

Paige reeled in shock relief. "Who is that?"

"Dan. It's Dan Stauffer."

Paige brushed sand from her pants and arms, retrieving her flashlight once more from the ground. "Sorry," she said. "I hope that didn't hurt too much."

"I'd be charging you with assault if it wasn't so damned funny."

Mouth twisting, she shone the light on his face, checking for bleeding. "Could be a bruise cropping up. What are you doing here?"

"I saw a light and came to investigate."

"So you saw him, too? Good. I need to—"

"Him? I saw you. Was there somebody else here?"

His gaze darted back to her from the direction of the jetty as he held up a hand to block the light.

"Yeah," Paige said. "There was a guy with a lantern. You didn't see him?"

Dan's hand dropped. A fleeting confusion passed across his features. "I didn't see anyone but you, staggering like a drunk. Have you been drinking?"

Lowering the flashlight to her side, Paige raised her other hand to her hip. "I had half a beer. Not even. I lost my balance for a second, but I'm fine. Just where were you that you 'saw' me?"

He jerked his thumb toward the ridge. "Up there by the cottage. I came to talk to you—"

"I didn't give you the address."

"I'm a cop, remember?"

For the first time she noticed he wore street clothes, his size diminished by the missing bulletproof vest beneath his dark T-shirt. She needed no reminder of his occupation, but she found the fact that he'd been able to locate her unsettling. "How'd you do it? Find me, I mean?"

"I'll be honest. It wasn't such a feat. The woman who rented you the place happened to mention it to me in passing about a half an hour ago. And I figured I'd stop by for a chat."

Paige shifted her weight from one foot to the other. "It's after nine o'clock at night, Dan. Bit late for a chat."

"Your lights were on, so—"

"No, they weren't."

He stepped aside, affording her a full view of the rental cottage. Sure enough, every window in the bungalow glowed with the distinct cast of incandescent lighting. The door stood wide, illumination seeping into the night like yellow dye.

"Did you go in?" Paige asked.

"I did *not*."

Paige lurched into a run up the hill.

Chapter 6

"Stay where you are. I'll check it out," Stauffer ordered as he passed her, keys on a ring jangling from his belt loop. Paige ignored him. She'd never been one for listening. That behavioral trait had earned her a reputation as an intractable student in school despite her straight-A status. She pursued Dan doggedly up to the cottage and arrived on the walkway only a few seconds behind him.

An elongated shadow undulated across the lit squares of stone. "Wait here," Dan commanded again, and vanished over the threshold.

Paige followed.

"Paige?"

She skidded to a halt. Liam stood in the room's center. Beside her, Dan, who had been extending an arm to stop her, dropped his open palm to his denim-covered thigh with a slap.

"Do you know this man?"

Paige circled around Dan. "Liam, what are you doing here?"

Liam moved to the left, as if trying to keep both of them in his line of sight. His gaze kept straying to Stauffer. Dan glanced frequently at him, too. Something odd inhabited the exchange.

"Do you two know each other?" Paige asked.

Neither man spoke.

"Do you?"

The two men employed another silent exchange, as if gauging each other's size and capabilities.

"No," said Liam.

"I've seen him once or twice," said Dan. "Don't know him, though."

"Oh, for crying out loud," muttered Paige, swinging the door closed. "Liam, this is Dan Stauffer, an officer with the local PD. Dan, this is Liam Gray."

Both men grunted in greeting. Paige sat down in the room's only chair and pulled off her left shoe to shake out a pebble. Sand stuck to her jeans and hands like glitter from a grade school project.

"What happened to your head?" Liam asked. From the corner of her eye, Paige saw Dan touch his bruised forehead.

"She threw her flashlight at me."

Liam laughed. To Paige's surprise, Dan chuckled, too. Paige lifted her brows. "Well, ha-ha. But I need you both to tell me what you're doing here. Which one of you is going first?"

Both men maintained a stoic silence.

"Okay, I'll pick. Liam?"

Crossing the floor, he stopped at the small section of kitchen counter and leaned his hips against it. He folded his arms across his chest. "I came looking for the cat. Your door was open. Again."

"I shut it," Paige said, more to herself than to either of them. Still, they exchanged a look. "What?"

Liam shook his head.

"So," Paige went on, "you found the door open and the lights on and walked in."

"Lights were off. I turned them on when I realized you weren't here. If Shadow was inside, he's gone now."

"Do you think Shadow nudged the door open?"

"Doubtful," interrupted Dan. "Not if you closed the door properly."

Paige shrugged. "Maybe I didn't."

Dan shook his head. "Then you should take better care. Is anything missing?"

"Missing? A cat's not likely to—"

"You don't know it was the damn cat," Dan said.

Paige looked from Dan to Liam, whose expression had gone stony. "I don't have much worth stealing," Paige advised them both.

"Check your purse."

From where she sat, Paige could see that her bag on the bedpost hadn't been disturbed, but she rose to check it, slipping her foot back into her shoe. On her way across the floor, she gave a wrinkle in the area rug a shove with the toe of her sneaker. She felt something hard beneath. "What's that?"

Without waiting for an answer she expected wouldn't be forthcoming, Paige grabbed the rug's edge and peeled it back. A curved iron handle stuck up at a slight angle from a recess in the floorboards where it normally rested, meaning it had been moved. She stepped back, searching each man's face. "What is that? A trap door? Do you think someone might have—"

"I'll check," said Dan. "Paige, give me that flashlight of yours."

Liam held his hand out for the flashlight at the same time, ignoring the fact Paige had extended it in Dan's direction. "It's only a crawlspace," Liam said. "Every cottage along the beach has one. Still, it's worth a look."

"Why don't you just let a cop do his job?" Dan demanded with a touch of sarcasm.

At the change to Liam's demeanor, Paige dropped the instrument onto his palm instead of Stauffer's and moved away. She didn't care which man did the checking. It wasn't out of the question that a rambunctious cat could have shifted the handle in a battle with the rug, but she needed an assurance that no one lurked beneath the cottage.

Paige pulled the rug back a little more. "It couldn't be the man from the beach, could it? I can't see him moving that quickly."

Liam paused, the ring for the trapdoor gripped in his hand. "The one you said you saw earlier?"

"I saw him again, right before I ran up here."

Liam looked at Dan. "Were you out there on the beach?"

"Yeah, and I didn't see anyone. Anyone but Paige, that is."

Sand ground between Paige's fingers as she stretched them in agitation. "I followed him. Or tried to. He disappeared when I was climbing off the rocks."

"I didn't see anyone," Dan repeated. "And that's a stupid move, trailing some unknown guy alone in the dark like that."

Paige remained silent. Liam shot her a fierce, unfathomable glare before yanking the trapdoor up, rusted hinges creaking. He shined the light down into the darkness. Paige stepped forward to peer into the hole from behind him.

Dan grabbed her arm. "Just do me a favor and stand over there."

Mutely, she complied. From a man's viewpoint, it made sense to have a woman out of harm's way. But as the woman in question, one who'd always maintained her independence, free from reliance on any male in her life, the request grated. Still, she was grateful not to have to deal with a possible intruder alone.

"Do you see anything?" she called down to Liam, who had descended into a crouch at the bottom of the decrepit stairs.

Dan wagged his head. "I think we would know if he did."

Hunkered over his heels, Liam shuffled forward. The light went with him, blocked from the crawlspace entrance by his shadow. A tremor shook the floorboards beneath Paige's feet. Dan felt it, too, and ducked toward the entrance.

"You okay down there?"

Liam appeared in the open square. "Sorry, bumped the joists. I want to check something farther back. If I yell—"

"I'll be right there," Paige said at the same time Dan spoke similar words. Blushing, Paige retreated to the chair and sat. Stupid thing for her to say. She folded her hands between her thighs. Dan lowered himself to his knees next to the trapdoor.

"Is he talking down there?" Paige asked.

Dan waved a hand. "Shhh. To himself."

She heard Liam say something else, louder this time. Dan shoved his upper body into the opening. Paige tensed. Two seconds later, he was back out and rising. Liam appeared a moment later. He climbed up, brushing cobwebs from his hair, and then flipped the door shut. The crash of wood on wood echoed through the room. He pushed the handle down into the depression. The two men pulled the rug back into place.

"Clear?" asked Dan.

Liam nodded in a manner that made Paige sit up.

"What was down there?"

"Spiders," said Liam. "Some discarded furniture. A few nests."

"Nests?" Paige echoed. "What kind of nests?"

"The kind that might be the reason Shadow keeps coming over."

Paige pictured a dank and dirty subterranean space filled with cavorting mice. Better than rats. And far better than a bearded man in a coat and a knit cap—because that was where her mind had traveled, despite the absurdity. "Thank you both," she said, "for checking."

Liam tossed the flashlight to her. Paige snatched it from the air above her head.

"I'll be heading home, then. You're safe." He shot a look at Dan. "I assume."

Paige stood. "I—"

"It's all right. I'll see you tomorrow."

Dan followed him outside after telling her he'd be right back. Paige frowned at the closed door, listening to their indistinct voices on the opposite side, Liam's gravel tones raised. Since she had no interest in an abrupt conversation between two strangers intent on pissing on each other's shoes, Paige went to the bathroom to rinse the sand from her hands. A few minutes later, Dan returned.

"Paige?"

She stepped out, towel in hand. "I'm assuming you have something to tell me? You came looking for me, after all."

"Yeah. You need to be more careful with your doors."

"It was shut—"

"I know it was. When I came around to knock before I saw you on the beach, the lights were all on but the door was closed."

Paige frowned. "What are you saying? That Liam is lying?"

"He said the door was open and the lights were off, didn't he?"

"Yes, but that doesn't mean he lied." Paige thought a moment. "It could mean that after you were at the door and before Liam came over, someone else came and went." A light chill fingered its way along her nape.

"That, too," Dan agreed.

"Why would someone come in here?" Paige heard the shrill intensity in her voice and knocked it back a notch. "I mean, does it look like a place where someone might be stashing big bucks?"

"Nothing's missing, right? Check your purse, now, will you?"

Paige hurried to the bed. She yanked her bag from the headboard. Her wallet was still inside, along with the cash and all her cards. Her keys rattled, glinting in the light from the bedside lamp when she tipped the purse's contents for a better look. "Everything's here."

Dan shook his head. "Then I don't know the answer. Use that lock, though, when I leave, okay? Lock it whenever you go out, even if it's only to the water."

"What are you thinking?"

"I don't know what to think. Except that Gray guy is probably full of—"

"No," said Paige. "He's not."

"Okay." Dan started for the door.

"Wait, you did have something to tell me. And not about keeping my door locked." Paige started after him and paused. "Isn't that why you came? Did you find out what happened with my father's boat?"

"Oh. Yeah," said Dan, turning around. "Got anything to drink? Water? I'm a little dry after that run up from the beach."

Paige yanked a bottle from the refrigerator and twisted off the cap. She handed the water to him, lobbing the cap into the sink. "Go on."

He drank half the bottle down before answering. "Yes, your father's sailboat went down in an unexpected storm. I'm digging into the details. Your father wasn't alone when the ship sunk. He had crew members. All in all, there may be some things you don't want to know."

"Like what?"

"Drowning can be pretty gruesome."

"Is there something to mark his passing? Like the stone cross on the headland? His name's not inscribed on the one here in Alcina Cove. I checked."

"I told you, Paige, I don't know much yet." Impatience roughened his tone. "It wouldn't be, though, if he wasn't living here anymore."

Paige lowered her lids, studying him from behind her lashes. "You're not telling me everything. There's more you know already."

Dan finished off the water and lowered the empty bottle to his hip. He exhaled through his nose. "One of the older guys at the station remembered something…about your dad. Remembered going out to your house." He jerked his head toward Paige's old home next door. "Responding to a call about a domestic dispute. Not the first time. Things were…not pretty. Your mom refused to press charges, though, and the responding officers left."

Paige stumbled over to the chair and lowered herself onto the hard wooden seat. Crap.

"And nothing else? Nothing about any other kind of trouble?"

Dan frowned, tilting his head. "What are you asking?"

Paige shrugged. "Bea Hunt implied my father was involved with people she referred to as 'objectionable,' so I just wondered."

"I see."

"Plus my mom…she said some things before she died. I only want answers, you know?"

"Sometime in the next couple of days, I'll go down to the archived reports and see what I can find. If you want me to," he added, taking a shuffling step toward the door.

Compressing her lips between her teeth, Paige gave a quick nod.

"You all right?"

She nodded again.

"I'm going to go. Lock the door behind me."

Forcing herself to her feet, Paige followed him and threw the deadbolt once he'd stepped outside. Eyeing the rumpled rug, she went over to the bed and yanked the heavy iron frame a few inches at a time until she'd centered a leg over the trapdoor. She threw herself belly first on the mattress, ignoring the sand spattering from her jeans across the coverlet. Dropping her head onto her folded arms, she began to cry.

Chapter 7

The keyboard's clatter filled the room. Liam kept his office sparse. No soft surfaces to deaden sound. No personal mementos. No tennis ball to bounce off the wall when thought processes had stalled. He had his desk, his laptop, an external hard drive for photos, and a stack of books on the floor near the window. He preferred the barren workspace to a place cluttered with distractions. Because the types of distraction he would have chosen would elicit memories, and memories could do nothing at this point but renew guilt and pain. He'd been learning to release in stages the scorching culpability haunting him. Avoidance helped. His unexpected attraction to Paige Waters did not.

In the monitor's lower right-hand corner the digital clock read three-forty-five. Liam pushed his fingers through his hair and then rubbed his hand down the side of his face, feeling beneath his palm's calloused flesh the raised cicatrix along his jaw. Paige had asked how he'd received it. Not one to hold back, that woman. Something on her mind, out it came from her mouth. Presumably unedited, but he could be wrong. She might have a lot more rolling around in interior dialogue she didn't bother to voice.

Liam leaned back in his chair, stretching his arms above his head. When he brought them back down, he tapped through the shortcut on the keys to save his work and shut the laptop, waiting a moment for his eyes to adjust to darkness before rising and moving to the window.

The quarter moon had been a sickle in the sky late in the afternoon but had set some time ago, leaving the sky as black as a crow's wing spangled with dew. The shipping lanes were empty, making it impossible to discern the sea from the dark dome above. Liam could barely make out the spume against the rocky shoreline. He pressed close to the windowpane, the glass cooling the healed, ridged skin, and recalled how he hadn't known he'd been cut, how he hadn't felt the pain, how he had mistaken the blood pouring from the wound to soak his shirt as salt water and sweat.

He thought of Paige then, wondering if her insomnia had worsened after the incident at her cottage two nights ago. He hadn't seen her, not even a glimpse, and he'd been watching. Did she keep her door locked now? It might not even matter. Her curiosity and all she wanted to know could prove her undoing. The truth would destroy her. It might very well destroy him.

* * * *

Paige had taken to sleeping with the light on over the stove. Before dawn, she rose from bed and crossed the floor, smacking the switch to the off position in defiance. Whatever had taken place the other night, she didn't understand it, but nothing had been stolen, nothing disturbed. She would much rather forget the whole thing, yet she didn't plan to move the bed from its position over the trapdoor.

Returning to the mattress, she sat in the gloom with her feet tucked up and her arms around her knees, listening to the first stirrings of songbirds in the bushes outside. When the sun peeked over the horizon, they would be in full form. By that time, she hoped to be climbing into her car and heading north. Dan had called last night with the name of the harbor from which he believed her father's boat had sailed on its last trip into the wide, blue sea.

Her stomach knotted as she thought about unearthing that part of the puzzle. After what she'd learned about the long ago visit of the police to her home, she wasn't sure she should bother to try. The fact the authorities had been called only confirmed what she'd always understood about her father's predilection toward violence. She would be better off not discovering any more. She had been better off not knowing him, hadn't she?

She ground her teeth together. With effort, Paige relaxed her jaw, drawing and releasing several long breaths through her nose. Her eyes stung with unshed tears. She leapt from bed and snatched clean clothes from the tiny wardrobe. After dressing, she ran a hasty comb through her hair and pulled the curls back into a loose ponytail. No doubt by the time she reached her destination, she'd have to arrange it again since she liked driving with the windows open.

Deciding she would stop along the way for breakfast, Paige grabbed a granola bar and shoved it into the recesses of her purse. On the doorstep, she double-checked the lock three times. The action might be obsessive-compulsive, but the last thing she wanted to do was doubt herself an hour down the road.

In the car, Paige hesitated before turning the engine over, her fingers wrapped around the keys dangling from the ignition. Although it was light enough to see shapes in muted colors, the sun had not yet risen. Looking toward her father's house, Paige realized she could see the structure from the cottage driveway. The second floor with its steeply pitched roof peeked above the rhododendrons and pines between. Beneath the soffit overhang, a rectangle of radiating light indicated that an upstairs lamp had been turned on.

Paige exited the car. She hadn't seen Liam since the night she'd found him in her cottage. The hour was too early for visiting, but she found herself walking in the direction of the house anyway. She certainly wouldn't knock on the door, but if he was up and about and noticed her, she'd make up some excuse for being there. She had wanted to talk to him, to measure his reaction to her since the "event." Dan had implied Liam had lied to her, to both of them. She only wanted the truth…but perhaps only her version of the truth: the man who'd sparked her interest was a man she could trust.

Fat chance, she thought, coming to an abrupt halt. If she had an interest, that meant she'd already recognized a fatal flaw in him. Such was her *modus operandi*.

Pivoting on her heel to return to her car, movement in the window caught her attention and she ducked behind the evergreen branches. Illuminated from within, Liam passed the glass panes. From her vantage point, the view of his naked back and his tousled black hair caused an embarrassing flush to heat her skin. Still, she kept her eyes on him for a few seconds longer. Long enough to see a shadow pass along the wall behind him. He wasn't alone.

Paige hurried back toward her car and slid into the driver's seat, where she gripped the wheel with both hands and stared through the windshield at the clapboard wall before her. What more fatal flaw could there be than a previous commitment? "You're a fool, Paige Waters," she muttered, and started the engine.

As she headed north on the main highway, Paige wondered if everything about her quest would prove to be a blunder. If she had any sense, she'd turn the car around and head back to Nashville. She had a life there. This…this was someone else's life, not hers. Not anymore.

* * * *

By the time Paige reached her destination, she'd calmed down considerably. The first thing she noted about the town was the tourist factor. That made sense. If her father had earned a living by taking people out on his sailboat, no better place than where vacationers sought a thrill. After parking her car in a five-dollar lot, Paige smoothed her unruly hair back into the band and climbed out, intending to head first to the expansive dock. If she could get the boat owners to open up, they might be a source of decent information. She'd only gone a half-block, though, when she spotted a sign for a local newspaper above a shop door. She walked in expecting to purchase one, but instead found herself in the establishment itself. Through an open doorway in the back, she heard the clatter of printers and smelled the scent of ink.

"Well," she said to the woman behind the counter, "this is a welcome sight."

The woman arched her brows.

"So many papers have gone out of business," Paige explained. "Most people want to read their news online. I like a paper in my hands."

"Gotcha," the woman said with a grin. "Can I help you with something?"

"I was planning to buy a paper to check out the local spots, but I have to ask, do you archive old editions anywhere? The library, maybe, or…?"

"Something in particular you're interested in?"

"A charter boat went down. A sailboat. In high seas, I believe. In October, year before last."

"A charter out in October?" The woman shook her head at what she obviously viewed as an imprudent undertaking. "What was the name of the ship?"

"I…I don't know. But the owner, the captain, would have been Edwin Waters."

With a nod, the clerk began to type something on the keyboard at her elbow. After several minutes, she shrugged apologetically. "Are you sure he operated out of this harbor?"

"That's what I was told," Paige said. "Or just sailed from here that day."

"Wait one sec." The woman resumed typing and read through the results that popped up after. "Here's a charter went down. Not much of a story. Just a paragraph. The sailboat capsized in heavy seas during a storm. Never should have been out there, if you ask me," she added in an aside. "A couple of commercial fishing boats made an attempt to aid the ship when the SOS came, but without success. It's not even mentioned here how many went down with the ship. I would assume he had a crew, passengers? Doesn't say. We picked this up from another paper. Not one of our stories."

Paige craned her neck in an attempt to view the monitor. "Did the ship operate out of your harbor here?"

"Can't tell from this, but I doubt it. We would have been all over that if it had. I'm sorry. Is this someone you knew?"

"Not well," Paige said, and then left with a thank you and no gazette.

Locating a bench down the block, Paige confiscated it from a child with an ice cream cone whose parents were calling him anyway and planted her rear end in the middle. Masts with sails furled bobbed from side to side in the near distance against a bluebell sky. Between whitewashed buildings, Paige glimpsed sailing craft and motorized boats, but no commercial vessels. Not surprising, since the town appeared to be a playground of the moneyed crowd and sightseers. She would head toward the docks in a few minutes, though she didn't anticipate receiving any hard facts. For now, she needed to think. Sit and think about what she had ever hoped to gain from her search.

"Excuse me, I think you dropped this."

Paige glanced at the hand extended before her face. Calloused and hard. A working man's hand. She looked up.

For a fleeting moment, she thought she knew him from somewhere, but then she realized he possessed what she and her friends at home had dubbed "the everyman face." The high cheekbones and chiseled jaw advertisers used to grace ads by the hundreds in glossy magazines. The kind of man women wished they knew. The guy standing in front of her, however, hadn't looked like that in a while. One too many battles had shattered his handsome countenance, and time had healed it in ways it shouldn't have. The expression on his face made Paige draw back.

"I don't know what that is," she said with a nod at his hand, "but it's not mine."

"Are you sure? Take another look."

She frowned at the folded cardstock printed with a colorful, wrinkled depiction on the inner side. "I'm positive."

"Take it."

"I beg your pardon?"

"It belongs to you."

"I'm going to call the police." Paige reached for her cell phone and pulled it from her purse. With a laugh, the man flung the object down at her feet and strode away. Clutching the phone in her fist, Paige watched until he was safely out of sight before bending to pick the article off the sidewalk. She grabbed the edge of paper with her fingernails, setting it down on the bench at her side, afraid something might fall out. After a moment, she used the edge of her phone to spread the cardstock flat. Her heart skipped a solid beat.

She hadn't dropped this. Not here. The last time she had seen this particular item had been three nights ago, where it had marked her place in her book on the nightstand.

Chapter 8

Dan observed Paige's entry into the diner with a clinical eye. She walked with an irate stride. He supposed that was good. When he'd spoken to her on the phone, she hadn't been angry. She'd been afraid.

She stomped over to where he sat and dropped down into the booth on the opposite side of the table, plunking her purse onto the bench seat beside her. "Are you eating?"

"Waiting for you."

"I just want a coffee."

The waitress was already writing down the order. "And you, sir?" the girl asked.

"Same. And a piece of that blueberry pie."

Dan waited until the girl left before speaking again. "Were they any help? The uniforms up there?"

"Not really," said Paige. "I gave them a description. They took the damned bookmark."

Dan grunted. "What's the problem with that? Does it have some kind of sentimental value?"

"No. But I thought perhaps you could get fingerprints from it."

"So can they, Paige. That's probably why they kept it."

She exhaled loudly and began tapping the fingers of her right hand in a rolling rhythm across the laminate before glancing in an agitated fashion over her shoulder. "Where's that coffee?"

"Is it possible you've already had enough?"

She threw herself forward with a hiss like a steam locomotive. "Are you freaking kidding?" she demanded in a loud whisper. "How long was I back in Alcina Cove before some psycho broke into my place and stole a goddamned bookmark? Then he trails me two days later for an hour and a half without my ever noticing the same car in my rearview, only to give it back to me. Who the hell is this guy? What does he want?"

Dan shook his head. "And you didn't recognize him?"

"No!"

"All right. Calm down." Dan leaned back against the seat while the waitress deposited the coffee and his pie on the table. He was grateful for the interruption as Paige got a reign on her hysteria in the interim. He shoved a forkful of pastry into his mouth and took his time chewing while he mulled the situation over a little longer. "Did you piss somebody off?"

"In three and a half days?"

"Right. Although, I've seen you in action…" He rubbed the bruise on his forehead with a knuckle.

Paige choked on a mouthful of coffee. "Not funny."

"Understood."

"And I'm sorry." She jerked her chin in the direction of his head. "About that."

Dan released a discreet sigh, digging into his pie again. He'd looked her up in the high school yearbook and realized why he'd had difficulty remembering her. They hadn't run in the same circles, and she'd been rather non-descript in both looks and mode of dress. It was a pity she'd turned out so damned good-looking all these years later. She wasn't his type at all. He liked his women… well, he liked his women. But in particular, he liked them a wee bit more relaxed than Paige. He was fairly certain she could be a handful. For any man.

"You married?"

She straightened, lowering her coffee mug to the table. "Why? Do you think this is some estranged husband sending me a nasty-gram?"

Yeah. A handful. "Something like that," he said.

Lifting her mug again, she tipped back her head and swallowed the remainder of her coffee. As if on cue the waitress appeared behind her shoulder, brandishing the pot. Dan shook his head. The girl retreated.

Paige shifted, reaching into her purse. She pulled out a tin of mints and offered him one. He declined. "The guy I saw today and the guy I saw on the beach the other night are not the same."

"All right," he said. "That's…something, I guess."

"I just thought I would mention that. Liam suggested the fellow on the beach might be a ghost."

The blueberry pie withered from the sudden spurt of acid in Dan's stomach. "Your neighbor said that, did he?"

"What do you think?"

"I think…I think I have no opinion on that matter."

She eyed him from beneath lowered brows. "I don't believe in ghosts, either."

That's not what I said, Dan thought, but kept his mouth shut. He had a reputation and a job to keep safe. "What I do think, though, is that you shouldn't return to the cottage."

"I paid for the entirety of the summer in advance."

Good God, and stubborn, too. "Considering your safety is an issue, you could probably get your money back."

"I'll think about it." She glanced around for the waitress, who was fortunately nowhere in sight.

"You'll think about it?"

"Yes."

"You'll think about it."

"Yes." She began to drum her fingers lightly on the table again.

"How many cups of coffee have you had?"

Folding her other hand around the offending one, she dragged them both into her lap. "Point taken. They kept bringing them to me at the station up there, and I kept drinking. By the way, my dad's ship didn't operate out of that harbor. The only report anyone had was a nameless sailboat going down in a sudden storm, nothing about captain or crew or recovery of any part of the ship."

"I'm sorry."

"Did you get a chance to check the archives?"

"Not yet."

"Doesn't matter. I'm not sure I want to deal with any of that right now."

"Can't blame you." He nodded at the server, who deposited the check on the table. Paige reached for the paper, but he beat her to it.

"Maybe you could come back with me," Paige said, "for a couple of minutes only and check the cottage again before I lock myself in?"

She wasn't coming on to him. No, she was serious. But a return to the cottage could prove problematic. "I have plans."

"Oh." She gathered her purse. "Okay. The guy would be stupid to come back, right?"

"I would hope. But you can't count on that. I can get one of the on-duty officers to accompany you. Or you could call your neighbor. Liam...Gray, is it?"

"Yes. Liam Gray."

She sounded odd. He frowned. "Would that be a problem? You should talk to him about this."

"Why?"

"Because you should." Dan slid to the end of the bench and stood. "He's the closest neighbor. He should know."

"I thought you didn't trust him."

"I was obviously wrong, unless he's a master of disguise. And in the meantime, I've also requested an increased patrol of the area. You need anything, 911, got it?"

Paige thanked him at the register while he was paying and headed for the door. "I want to get back before dark."

"Sure. And talk to Liam."

She didn't answer. He watched her through the glass as she crossed the parking lot to her car. She looked around before she got in, including checking the back seat. Good. And she needed to talk to Liam Gray. That guy had some explaining to do.

* * * *

Paige turned off the ignition and leaned her head back against the headrest but didn't remove her seatbelt. Something about the containment, snug across her hips, her chest, felt safe for the moment, comforting. The doors had automatically unlocked upon putting the car in park. She hit the button that secured them and heard four locks click into place with a satisfying thump.

Next door, the setting sun glazed the upstairs windows in gold. Paige tried to recall the good times she'd had in that house. They had to have existed. She hadn't been an unhappy child. Not always. But she should have stayed away.

Who was that guy today? Some unstable individual she'd passed on the sidewalk in Alcina Cove who, in his lunacy, chose to fixate on her? If so, she reckoned he would be more dangerous in his unpredictability than if it had been someone she had once known but didn't remember.

Understanding she couldn't stay locked in the car all night, Paige removed the keys from the ignition, steeling herself to get out. In one movement, she removed her seatbelt and threw open the door, scrambling out and upright beside the car, purse in hand, heart beating in her ears.

Inhale. Exhale. Close door. Lock it. Move.

Years ago, she'd seen a movie in the theater about dinosaurs in a park who had escaped to rampage, stalk, and try to eat the few people on an island. She'd only been seven or eight years old, but still mature enough to recognize the people were actors and the dinosaurs not real. But that night, coming home, walking up to the front door beside her parents, the bushes had rattled, from the wind, perhaps, or a small animal. The fear she'd experienced, no matter how irrational, had been genuine. She felt that way now, standing beside her car with the cottage door key in her hand. Exposed and vulnerable and filled with the certain knowledge something far beyond the realm of reality was about to gobble her whole.

In short bursts, like a mismanaged puppet, Paige sped across the open expanse toward Liam's front door. She faltered on the walkway. With the clarity of the immediate, she recalled the night of flight more than sixteen years ago in every detail, seeing herself and her mother stumbling with the weight of the suitcase between them toward the car. The urgency, the devastating confusion, mingled with her fear in the present. Overwhelmed, she sat down hard on the huge white rock beside the walkway—the one her father had placed there long ago as a centerpiece for Debra Waters' planned garden that had never come to fruition—and wept.

A hand dropped gently on her shoulder blade. Paige rocketed up and away.

"Paige? What is it?"

Paige spun to face Liam on the other side of the rock. "Nothing. I'm sick and tired of crying."

"Paige."

"What?"

"Your... your friend, Dan Stauffer. He called me."

"Why would he do that?" Paige demanded, beginning to pace on the walkway. "And he's not my friend. Not really. I suppose he is. I don't know what he is! Does he think I can't handle this on my own?"

"You shouldn't have to. And you did call him. You must have decided you needed something from somebody."

She stopped, fists clenched, staring at him in challenge. "I would have called you if I'd had your number."

"I'm not the police."

"I don't care. You're the one I would have called."

"Paige."

Paige Waters, you always charge in before thinking.

I know, Mom. I know.

"Do you have someone in your life, Liam?"

As she spoke, her nipples hardened within her thin bra. All he needed to do was look and he would see. But he held his gaze steady on hers.

"I don't. Not anymore."

Paige marched across the walkway and onto the white boulder glistening in the dying day. This is how she would reach his mouth. Just like this.

Chapter 9

Liam opened in shocked but eager willingness to the heat and hunger of her questing tongue. She had unexpected strength in her arms, pulling him solidly against her body. He lost his breath and clear thought as blood plunged into his groin. Inside his boxers, his penis sprang up hard against the rough denim of his jeans.

He slid his hands beneath her blouse, wanting skin, naked and warm and responsive, against his palms. Yanking down a soft bra cup, he grasped her stiffened nipple between his fingers. She moaned. He maneuvered his other hand past her waistband, cupping her buttocks, pressing her against his straining cock. A shock ran though him, like a static charge. He wanted in. Now. He shoved her pants down farther, the waistband expanding to accommodate his search, and slid his hand into her underwear, fingering the soft, slick places, feeling her shudder.

Conscience and self-preservation took his libido in a strangle hold. He released her, backing away. "Paige, I'm sorry."

"I—what?" Paige stepped down from the stone, shoving her hair off her face. Her ponytail had come loose in a mass of tangled curls. He reached for her hand.

"Oh, God," she said. "I'm so sorry. I shouldn't—I need to go."

He grabbed her fingers before she got away. "No, Paige, you don't need to go anywhere. I don't want you to go anywhere." Recognizing the truth in his last statement nearly floored him. A couple of deep breaths were in order. "Come inside and sit for a minute. We'll go get a few things from your place that you might want for the night. You can have the couch. Or we can finish what we've started."

She shook her head. "Not tonight."

"That's fine. It's up to you. But you're not staying at the cottage. There's no guarantee of safety there."

"And you're sure there's no one—that I haven't just—that—"

He smiled. "I've never seen you at such a loss for speech. Not since the night I met you, anyway. And I'm positive. There's no one." His heart contracted with a hollow, remembered pain when he spoke those words.

Leaving Paige on the sofa, looking like an animal ready to chew her paw off to escape a trap, Liam climbed the stairs to the upper hallway to shut down his computer. He hesitated at the attic door. Twice last night, while he'd been working, he thought he'd heard a weighted step on the timbers. He hadn't gone up, as he'd gotten used to these occurrences. Now, in light of what had happened to Paige, he figured the attic warranted an examination.

Liam yelled down the stairs for Paige to help herself to whatever she might like from the fridge. He received a mumbled reply that at least assured him she hadn't left. Reaching for the attic doorknob, he paused to eye the heavy doorstop in his office, gauging its use as a weapon. After a moment's debate, he picked it up.

Hefting the weight in his hand, he understood his fists, his strength, might not be enough because sometimes people had other plans, ways and means of doing bodily harm that had nothing to do with the limits of human endurance. And he feared that the man who had been in Paige's cottage, who had followed her north and likely back again, was such a person.

* * * *

Paige returned to the couch with water in a tumbler. She sat, gazing at the lowering night through the bow window. Suddenly the lamp on the end table clicked on. She jumped, splashing liquid on her knee. Spotting a timer hooked up to the cord, she relaxed and sat back, taking a sip from the glass. Her actions, the room around her, were reflected in the curved expanse of the window. She turned the lamp off. Anyone could be out there, able to see in. She'd rather sit in the dark.

Liam was taking a lot longer upstairs than she'd expected. Recalling those few heated minutes outside, the abandon with which she threw herself at him, her underwear's condition right now, Paige vacillated between longing and a niggling anxiety. But she wouldn't go back and undo it. Despite her babbling behavior immediately following, what had occurred was exactly what she'd needed. She only hoped Liam's long absence wasn't due to regret.

Five minutes later, she heard him coming down the stairs with a quiet, hesitant tread. She bit her lip. In spite of his ability to hold himself utterly still, she'd noted his energetic locomotion from place to place. He liked to pound up the steps two at a time. Perhaps he'd noted the darkened living room and hoped she'd gone. Well, no reason to keep him in suspense now that he was nearing the bottom. She turned the light back on.

The stairs were empty. Paige shot up from the couch.

"Liam? Liam! Where are you?"

He gave a shout from somewhere up above. A scant minute later, his footsteps sounded across the ceiling and down the stairs to the first landing. "Sorry," he said, "I was having a quick look in the attic." He came down and crossed the floor to pull the drapes.

"I thought I heard you on the stairs. When I looked, no one was there."

Liam paused a moment in his adjustment of the curtains and then continued, his back to her. "You really never noticed anything like that when you lived here?"

"Hearing footsteps and finding no one? Not that I remember. Are you going to try to tell me this house, the house I grew up in, is haunted?" She moved to stand between him and the curtained window. Even now, his nearness caused her blood to heat.

"Yes, that's what I'm telling you," he said.

"I don't believe in ghosts, Liam. But tell me, why wouldn't it have been haunted when I was a kid?"

Liam twitched a shoulder. "Recent catalyst?"

"Like what?" She considered a moment, eyes widening at the implication. "Not my father dying?"

No matter what her father had done, who he'd hurt and who he'd abandoned, Paige had no wish to see his spirit, his soul, whatever energy survived after the body had failed, trapped in some kind of limbo. Because that's what people said, didn't they? Ghosts had unfinished business, couldn't move on, whatever claptrap believers touted.

"I didn't say it was your father," Liam murmured. "This house is nearly a hundred and twenty years old. It was built around the turn of the last century, but you knew that, I suppose."

Paige barely heard him. Her thoughts had returned to the morning, when she'd looked up at the window and witnessed a shadow converge with and pass over Liam's, moving faster than he had been. "Liam, don't misunderstand me when I ask this. It's not the same question I asked earlier. Was there someone with you when the sun was coming up?"

"No." Quickly. Maybe too quickly.

Paige narrowed her eyes at him. His expression remained bland as he faced her with the curtain still in his fist, giving the material one final tug. His blue eyes looked black in the lamplight.

"I need to know," Paige said. "Please tell me."

Dropping the curtain, he came to her and took her hand, pulling her down beside him on the cushions. He shook his head. "No. No one was with me. Why?"

Turning her fingers in his warm grasp, she realized how cold her own had grown. "I was outside and I looked up. I saw you in the window. I saw someone, or something, with you. I saw what I thought was their shadow moving past."

He remained silent for a small time, finally rubbing his free hand across his eyes. Releasing her, he stood. "Thank you for telling me. Are you hungry? I know it's late, but I'll make us something to eat."

Paige rose beside him. "That's all you have to say?"

"That's it."

"You're not surprised."

"Surprised? No. But confirmation troubles me in ways I can't even begin to explain."

She frowned. "I haven't confirmed anything."

He turned a condescending expression on her. Unreasoning anger shot through her veins like boiling water. She opened her mouth to speak, but closed it before a word escaped. Loosening her curled fingers, she flattened her palm against her thigh. She knew this scenario. She'd played it out many times before. Sex, pick a fight, move on. Most men were happy to have it that way. But she and Liam hadn't had sex yet. And she held a deep suspicion Liam Gray wasn't most men. "Can I help with dinner?" she asked. Reasonably, she hoped. "What are you planning on making?"

Scratching his head, he gazed at the ceiling in thought. "I have leftover beets. Three or four eggs. Enough ham and bread for a single sandwich. Think we can make something out of that?"

Paige snorted. "If we skip the beets? Definitely."

* * * *

Though attentive and shockingly kind, Liam kept himself at a distance. She couldn't blame him. He'd invited her into his house for her protection. If he slept with her, the night and however many days that followed could get complicated pretty quickly. She wasn't even sure he wanted to. Not emotionally, anyway. The erection he'd pressed against her was pretty solid evidence his body had a different idea.

Liam went alone to collect her things from the cottage and returned with a puzzled expression on his face. "What was the point of placing the bed over the trapdoor?"

"I don't like mice," she said, and left it at that. It didn't matter he'd found nothing beneath the floorboards. Blocking off the dark province under the cottage had eased her mind, however foolish. Microscopic, icy feet tiptoed up the ridges of her spine in memory. Suppressing a shiver, Paige grabbed her toothbrush and comb from her suitcase, along with something suitable to wear while sleeping, and put a foot to the bottom stair tread.

"Bathroom's upstairs, first door on the—"

"I know," she said.

"Forgot." He smiled apologetically. The scar almost disappeared in the deep creases created by his grin. One day, if she didn't blow it, they might reach a point—as friends, if nothing else—when he would feel comfortable telling her about the injury. Of course, that one day would have to come soon, or she'd be gone. She'd given herself until the Saturday prior to Labor Day before heading back home. The way the last two days had panned out, she might not make it that long. If somebody didn't find the creep who'd broken into the cottage, her departure could be much sooner.

Upstairs, Paige made her way slowly toward the home's only bathroom. On her way, she glanced toward the room that had been her parents' and, finding the door open, paused in the hallway to look in. She experienced no guilt over her study since it had nothing to do with curiosity about Liam and his lifestyle, whatever that might be. Nope. For the briefest of moments, she thought she might be able to feel her parents there, perhaps recall tenderness, a display of affection, some small proof of the love they must, at one time, have shared.

She'd sensed nothing downstairs while sitting on Liam's sofa. She felt nothing of them here, either, gaze lingering on Liam's large and tumbled bed, his dark, masculine furniture, a handsome, brightly-colored area rug upon which a book lay open to a page marked by what appeared to be discarded junk mail. She backed away and crossed the hall.

She paused in the middle of the cracked tile floor of the bathroom. Liam had only made a rudimentary attempt at renovations in this room. It looked almost exactly as she remembered. Paige sank down onto the closed toilet, shutting her eyes to block out the burden of recollection prompted by wallpaper bits still stuck to the plaster walls, the fixtures with their yellow light beside the outdated mirror, the familiar curve of the sink. Images circled in her mind like flotsam in a whirlpool.

Mom, what happened to your face?

Don't ask questions, Paige.

In time, the influx passed enough for Paige to perform her nightly routine, washing up, brushing her teeth, combing her always hopelessly tangled hair. Changing her clothes, she tucked everything under her arm and exited the bathroom, breathing a sigh of relief in the hallway. Here, the walls were freshly painted, and a runner on the floor covered the age scars on the wooden floor. She found herself wondering again about the footsteps on the stairway, the shadow dancing past Liam's. Pressing her personal items close to her breast, she held her breath and listened.

Nothing. Why would there be? Nonsense, all of it. Utter nonsense.

An abrupt creak of the joists in the attic caused her to jump and then chuckle at her foolishness. The door at the base of the narrow steps leading up beneath the roof stood slightly ajar. Paige walked toward it. "Liam?"

"Paige, what are you doing?"

Paige whipped around toward Liam's voice. He stood with a foot on the uppermost stair, his dark brows raised.

"I thought you had gone back to the attic. I heard—"

"No ghost," he said with a laugh. "The wind's picking up. I probably left a window cracked up there."

She made a face at him. "So you're going to pooh-pooh me now, after all your talk."

"This time, yeah, I am. Come on downstairs."

Paige trailed him back to the lower floor and found he'd been in the process of making up the couch with sheets and a thin blanket. He tossed a pillowcase and pillow at her, nearly causing her to drop everything else on the floor. Tucking the pillow beneath her chin and tugging the case over it, she eyed Liam's body with unrelenting avarice as he worked. Disgusted with herself, she tossed the pillow back in his direction before turning away to her open suitcase to slip her toothbrush and comb into the small cosmetic bag.

"Paige."

"Hmm?"

"Don't allow me to give you the impression you're easy to resist, because you're not."

She straightened, faced him, folding her hands before her abdomen like a schoolgirl awaiting punishment from a nun for impure thoughts. Her stomach furled into a molten knot. She cleared her throat. "Really."

"Really." Spine like a rod, he clutched the pillow in his fist. She wondered if he had the same urge to fly in her direction as she did in his. Fortunately he possessed restraint, and she possessed shame to keep her rooted where she stood. "There are multiple reasons why, not the least of which is what happened outside."

The fire in her belly rushed along the gasoline of her blood to her limbs. And to her face. She knew her cheeks had gone as bright as cherries.

He dropped the pillow onto the couch. "But as you said, tonight is not the time."

The flames receded a tad. She breathed again. He smoothed the blanket over the fully made sofa. Paige hurried to the water she'd left standing on the end table and drank half in one gulp.

"Do you want me to put the television on? It might help you sleep."

Paige nodded at him over the tumbler's rim.

"I've locked all the doors and windows. The outside lights are on."

Lowering the glass, Paige admitted to him his litany of the security precautions had only served to unnerve her more. "Not that I'd forgotten, but…"

"I'm sorry, but they're necessary." He headed across the room and paused at the stairs. "I'll be up for quite a while in my office. I have work to do. You hear anything, get frightened, sing out, okay?"

"Okay. I'm not much of a singer, though."

He stood a moment longer, his dark gaze intent. "God, Paige, I want…I want to kiss you. And a kiss is a simple thing, really. But not the way you do it."

Paige closed her eyes on an expulsion of breath. "Goodnight, Liam." When she opened them again, he was gone. She snatched up the remote and clicked on the television as she threw herself down on the couch. It was going to be a long, sleepless night.

Chapter 10

Out over the water, lightning shimmered in the belly of rolling, gray clouds, too far away for the thunder to reach Raleigh's ears. Soon, though. He could smell the storm in the air, sense it on his skin. He watched the lightning through the smoke curling around his head from a glowing cigarette. He sucked in another lungful, blew it out, made tiny rings of it like his granddad used to do. Long time ago. Too long ago to really think about. More pressing issues weighed on him. No use looking back.

After several minutes, he stubbed the butt out beneath the sole of his shoe. Ground it with his toe right down into the sand to hide it good. Wouldn't want anyone to know he'd been standing out here. Already had to duck from sight once when that cop car came cruising by. Checking for him, he knew that, but it didn't much matter. They weren't going to find him.

Staring across the road at the blank window, the glittering television glow dancing at the curtain's edge, Raleigh thought about her sleeping on the couch, open-mouthed, the remote clutched in her hand. He'd seen her through a slit in the curtains after he'd unscrewed the light bulb by the door. That pretty little piece baffled him, she did. Couldn't figure out her game, why she'd come back unless to play her hand. And what the fuck was she doing holed up with Gray? Gray ought to know better. Taking chances that might blow the whole deal. Unless she'd told Gray something he'd decided to hold close for use at the right time.

Opening his fingers, he narrowed his eyes at the photo on his palm. Small, dog-eared, a date in ink smeared across the back. He liked to take a few chances himself. Should be precious, a photo of one's mama. But just like that bookmark, she hadn't even missed it.

Chapter 11

Thunder's first rumble vibrated the window at Liam's back, followed by a cool breeze wriggling into the worn fabric covering his torso. A moment later, he heard rain drumming on the roof. With a sigh, Liam rose and crossed the floor. He lowered the sash. In the glass pane, movement reflected behind him.

"Paige, did the storm wake you?"

He shut the window and locked it before turning slowly to face her. She had come halfway into the room and paused, frowning at the monitor's glow on his desk. Sleepily, she raised a hand and pushed curling strands from her eyes.

"I had a dream," she mumbled.

"About what?"

"My dad."

His indrawn breath caught. He said nothing.

"You know how you dream you're awake, only to realize you're not awake yet?"

Liam nodded. He saved his work, shut down the computer, and straightened some papers on the desk while he waited for the screen to darken.

"In my dream, I woke up and found him standing over me."

A single printed sheet fluttered to the floor. He bent and picked it up. Taking his time, he replaced the article on the pile. "How did you feel?"

"What? About seeing my father? I didn't really even see him, but I knew it was him. And then I realized I was still asleep. One of the crazy dream-world things. I hate that. You feel so disoriented afterward."

"I've had some of those myself."

"Who'd you dream about?"

He shook his head. "Another time."

Alerted by her prolonged silence as he finished straightening his desk, he glanced in her direction. The single lamp cast her shadow across the wall and highlighted the amber hue of her round gaze, her mouth partially open, as if she'd started to speak and held her tongue. She looked vulnerable to him, a direct contrast to a woman who tended to count her victims on both hands, which was how he'd begun thinking of her in the long, dark hours. After knowing him for all of three days, she'd climbed up on him in an attempt to initiate what might have been stunning sex, and though he'd been more than willing to follow her down that rosy path, he'd found he couldn't. Being left behind as nothing but a chalk outline on her headlong flight through life didn't suit him. He wanted more. Finally. And he wanted more with Paige Waters. His timing sucked.

She'd warned him. Without realizing, she had warned him a couple of nights ago, out on the porch. She'd said she couldn't get beyond her past. She was haunted by what had happened in her life all those years ago. As was he, by what had happened in his, and by what waited now in an altogether different form, threatening explosion. That alone should force wisdom and a wide berth around Paige and her desperate search. That alone would make her hate him if she ever learned the truth.

He clicked off the lamp and took her by the arm, ignoring the chemical heat at the touch as he led her from the office. He continued past the open bedroom door, down the steps, his hand slipping from her arm to her fingers, circling them, tightening, aware of her skin's texture, the slenderness of each digit, the strength. At the bottom of the stairs, he let her go.

Lightning flashed through the darkened house. Thunder throbbed along the floorboards beneath their feet. Paige put a hand to the wall.

"It's just a storm, Paige." He hadn't meant to sound so short. Or maybe he had. She shot him a look of amused tolerance.

"I know what a storm is. We had them in Tennessee, too. What time is it?"

"I don't know. Three-thirty? Four?"

"Do you always stay up all night working?" She headed to the sofa and seized the blanket. Wrapping herself in it, she dropped cross-legged onto the cushion. He lowered himself into the nearest chair, his gaze on the blank television screen.

"Not always."

"Are you angry with me, Liam Gray?"

Lightning continued to illuminate the room at intervals, thunder a persistent rumble. "I think I'm angry with myself." He'd made so many decisions in this past year that had entangled him in deeper and deeper complications. He'd never expected Paige to come strolling into his life right in the thick of his difficulties. Making them worse because…well, because he cared.

Paige shifted on the sofa. "Maybe it would be better if I didn't stay here, if I went back next door."

"You can't do that."

He heard her sigh through a brief lull in the cacophony of the storm. "I'm not your responsibility, Liam. You know that."

He did know she wasn't his responsibility. But that recognition existed in a place other than his heart. There was no point in saying that aloud. Placing his hands on his knees, he heaved himself from the chair and stretched. "That's a bit of an insult, your statement."

"No, it's not. It's the truth."

He went to the window and peeled back the drapes to view the storm raging outside. He wanted nothing more than to strip off those oversize clothes and press her naked body into the soft cushions with the weight of his own, sliding an erection into her, deep and hard. He knew she would receive him with infinite pleasure—at least in the physical sense.

His breath escaped in a rush, forming a damp circle on the rain-spattered glass. There were many reasons why he shouldn't follow through with his inclinations. She could never learn all the truth she sought, no matter how hard she looked. And mysteries like that left scars as evident as the one on his face. They both had their secrets. He'd admitted as much to her. Paige's belonged to Paige, wrapped up in her family's dysfunctional life, but his extended beyond his solitary existence. They could even reach her if he let them.

She rose from the couch behind him. A moment later, her suitcase snapped open. He turned to find her repacking the few items inside. "What are you doing?"

"It's late. Or early, depending on your perspective. You need to get some sleep. I need to get back to that uncomfortable bed next door."

"Paige."

"Walk me over if you like. See me safely locked inside. You will have discharged your gentlemanly duties."

"It's a deluge out there. Wait until it passes."

Through the parted curtain, a distant, brilliant flash of silver and white lit her face. Thunder followed belatedly in a low, rumbling growl. "I can't wait," she said. "You can't afford to have me wait. I understand that. I've disrupted your routine more than necessary. And disturbed you. I can see how much I have every time you look at me."

"It's not that, Paige. I just—"

Paige hiked the suitcase up under her arm and slung her purse over the other before yanking open the door and heading out into the downpour. She ducked her head against the onslaught and another flash of lightning. Adopting a similar position, Liam followed, pulling the suitcase from her grasp. "Gentlemanly duties, remember?" He held the case over her head in a semblance of protection from the pounding rain as they ran for the cottage.

* * * *

Paige stood at the kitchen sink with her arms extended like a vulture in the sun, laughter bubbling uncontrollably. Water ran in sheets from her clothing to puddle on the floor. In no better shape, Liam tossed her suitcase onto the chair, his hair plastered to his head. He hadn't bothered with shoes and was better off without them. She wriggled her toes and watched the liquid force its way out of the canvas.

"Son of a bitch."

"Paige, your mouth…"

She glanced up in time to witness his smile. Without another word, he went into the bathroom and returned with two towels, lobbing one in her direction. She slipped off her shoes and hurried to the room he'd vacated and shut the door. She stripped off her wet garments and toweled dry, then tugged her bathrobe on. Upon exiting the bathroom, she found Liam still shirtless, wringing water from his T-shirt into the kitchen sink. The towel lay beneath his feet, absorbing the spillage on the floor and drainage from his jeans. At the sound of a bird outside the window despite the fearsome weather, he lifted his head to listen.

"'Wilt thou be gone? It is not yet near day: It was the nightingale, and not the lark, that pierced the fearful hollow of thine ear,'" Paige quoted quietly.

Liam glanced over his shoulder. "What?"

"Never mind." She had no intention of revealing she'd quoted Shakespeare to him. He already thought her brazen and strange. It occurred to her Liam Gray might be more conservative than his appearance suggested. Grabbing fresh clothes for bed, she went back into the bathroom and dressed. Upon her return, Liam still had not put on his shirt. The garment hung over the sink edge, no longer dripping but crinkled and translucent. Palms planted on stainless steel, he leaned toward the window, not looking through the glass but at her reflection in it.

"Liam?"

"I'll lock the door."

"You can't. You need a key. It secures from the inside."

"I'm aware of that." He strode to the door and turned the deadbolt, standing a moment with his body inches from the wood panel, immobile except for his breathing.

Paige studied his long, lean back, the solid structure of his arms, and could barely catch a breath, causing her voice to come out as little more than a whisper. "I figured you'd be going right home."

"So did I, but I need to talk to you."

Ah. Okay. Talking. Paige cleared her suitcase from the chair so Liam could sit. She climbed up onto the mattress, situating herself in the center, legs bent and tucked into a position to support her arms across her knees. She lowered her chin onto a forearm. He took his seat.

"Go ahead," she encouraged him when he hesitated. "Whatever you need to say, I'm a big girl. I can take it."

A run of his fingers through his hair sprayed droplets on the wall behind and over his shoulders. His nipples rose in chilled response. She looked away.

"It's not anything you might imagine. I'm not even sure where to begin."

"I can imagine a great deal," she said. "And begin at the beginning."

Grunting, he turned his head and folded his arms over his bare chest, casting about the room in mute search. She went and rummaged through the small dresser until she found a shirt and handed it to him.

"I like to wear loose clothing to bed." Not waiting to witness how he responded to her statement, she returned to her comfortable roost on the mattress. He slipped a large T-shirt on without comment.

"Okay, so what is it you want to tell me?"

He pushed his hair back again. Paige watched the water spray across the borrowed shirt in a random pattern. In the gloom, his pupils widened, darkening his eyes to jet. A sense of premonition stole over Paige. Something bad was coming.

"About nine months ago," he began, "I had the trawler out, more than forty-five miles off the coast in deep water. Cod and haddock were running like I'd never seen them. The crew, well, they were willing to stay out despite a storm approaching because it looked to be the best haul yet. Promised to be really good money. I figured we could race the weather in, beat the worst of it. And we would have, even when the seas got high and the wind started keening."

Paige stopped looking at him. She studied the blanket's weave in front of her bare feet, fighting the urge to hide. She managed to push two words out, hardly recognizing the shape of them. "What happened?"

"A distress call came in. We were the closest ship under power. So we responded."

Paige squeezed her eyes shut, biting down on her lip until she tasted blood.

"It was your father, Paige."

* * * *

Paige paced the cottage from one end to the other. Every time Liam opened his mouth to speak she raised a hand to silence him. Before he clouded the issue with any sort of explanation for why he'd kept this from her she wanted to formulate the proper questions to ask, ones he couldn't skirt around with counter questions and more deception. Liam Gray had lied to her. He'd lied by omission, but it was a deceit nevertheless.

She went to the door and flung it open, breathing in storm-fresh air before reminding herself that danger lurked outside. She slammed it shut, throwing the bolt.

"Paige…"

She shook her head. Not yet.

"I didn't lie to you. Not really."

She strode to the dresser and back to the kitchen, Liam's gaze trailing her movements. He sat very still, hands clasped loosely between his knees.

"You know exactly where my father's ship went down."

"Yes."

"You know when."

"Yes."

"You lied when you said you knew nothing."

His head moved from side to side. "You have to understand."

"I don't have to understand anything."

"I didn't say I knew nothing. You were asking about when I bought the house, whether I knew your father, and I said I hadn't known him. I said there were other people better able to answer your questions. And there are."

She stopped within an inch of his bent knees. He lifted his head to meet her eyes. She could feel his breath against her shirtfront. "How did you think I would feel when I found out the truth?"

"Like this."

"Like this." She backed up and sat on the mattress edge, nearly missing it. "You let me run around town asking questions, when all the while you could have provided me with the answers I sought."

He brought his hands up onto his thighs as though he were about to rise. She shook her head at him. "Stay there."

He did, relaxing his spine against the chair's ladder back. "I won't be able to make you understand, but believe me when I say I'm sorry. The facts surrounding your father's death weren't the only answers you were looking for, Paige. In fact, based on what you've told me, that is the least of what you need. You want to know more than what happened out on the ocean. You want to know about your father's life."

Damn it, his understanding was putting a real damper on her anger. She needed to stay mad. Something was missing from his story, and she couldn't follow through with the right questions if he turned the focus back on her. "If everything happened as you said, why was I unable to find out sooner? Nothing in the papers. No one willing to say a word. Not even you."

"Paige, please."

"What is the mystery?"

He shook his head. "I don't know. I wasn't aware there was a mystery. I didn't go looking for news stories, never asked about it in town. I had no idea. I'm sorry."

"Don't act like you did me a favor, Liam, by keeping this to yourself. Yes, I want an understanding of my parents' lives, but I planned to start with the one solid fact I knew. My father died. I needed the when, where, and how, and all that information was yours to tell me."

He said nothing.

"I've had so much trouble finding out the smallest details, and you kept quiet. I don't understand."

"I know you don't."

She frowned. "Then help me to." There was a reason for his omission, an explanation that would make sense. It couldn't have been cruelty. He didn't *know* her, for crying out loud. Unless pathological, a decision to lie was usually based on the dynamics of an intimate, long-term interaction between two people. "You're leaving something out. What?"

He lowered his head against his hands until his palms ground into the hollows of his eye sockets. "I…I don't want to."

"Please."

"It's not a day I care to relive. Perhaps it would have been easier to tell you right away, when I still didn't know you, rather than now."

Paige slipped from the bed and onto her knees. She circled his wrist with her fingers. He raised his head.

"I lost two of my crew that day, and your father's crippled ship went down beneath the waves with his own crew still inside. There was no saving them. And the fire—"

"Fire?"

He nodded, closing his eyes. The pain in his voice tore at her. She turned his hand until his fingers lay in hers.

"Yes. The ship burst into flame before it went down. But the worst... the worst hadn't happened yet. When I got home I found out I'd lost them. No one had radioed me. I guess I should be grateful for that, but somehow I'm not."

"Lost who?" He didn't mean his crew, surely. He already would have known.

"My wife. Our unborn daughter." The cartilage in his throat bobbed as he swallowed. "Placental abruption, it's called. I should have been there with her. I couldn't have stopped it, I know, but I should have been there. She must have been so damned scared."

Tears stood out along his lashes, dripping onto her hand as he bowed his head. Shock stilled her tongue. She couldn't imagine what it had cost him to reveal this to her. Anything about that day had to have been terrible to recall. His hope she would discover her facts elsewhere and not force him to dredge up the past was a motivation she understood. Straightening, she took his hand, tugging him toward the bed.

He pulled back. "Paige, I can't."

"I'm not asking you to. What do you think I am? You shouldn't be alone right now, so kick off those wet pants and get beneath the covers. I've slept well. It'll soon be dawn. There are other things I can do beside crawl into that bed next to you, okay?"

His lips twisted into a crooked smile. Disengaging his fingers from hers, he yanked his pants down past his ankles and handled them off to her. "Thank you," he said, and shimmied beneath the covers. Trying not to gawk at the tight curve of his buttocks in damp boxers or the burn scars covering his long legs, Paige carried his jeans into the bathroom and positioned them over the shower curtain rod to dry.

Taking a few minutes to gargle, put on deodorant, and otherwise ready herself for a very early start to her day, Paige thought about what he had told her. She'd had a right to her anger, but he possessed more rights to his secrets. Liam had risked his own life to save a man he did not know and then suffered the most horrific, unexpected loss. Paige hadn't had a relationship with her father for many years prior to his demise, and her mother's illness had been long, yet even so, she didn't often barrel into conversations about the particulars with people she'd just met. She couldn't blame Liam for his hesitation, either. He'd hoped she would find

Celia Ashley

out what she needed to know elsewhere, keeping him from having to revisit that tragic time in his life. She would have to accept that.

By the time she exited the bathroom, rosy light traced across the walls, shining through the windows. She clicked off the fixture above the stove and went back to the bed to peer down at Liam. Hair tousled in dark strands across her pillow, he'd already fallen asleep. She bent, careful not to bump the mattress, and pressed her mouth in a light kiss on his brow before grabbing her book from the nightstand. She then opened the door and sat on the threshold.

Storm clouds had blown inland, leaving the sky above the ocean streaked with thin, high swirls of pink and gold and azure. She could see all around, clear enough to make out anyone approaching. She opened the book on her knee, searching for the place once marked with her absent bookmark. This morning she wouldn't let fear, or regret, or any of the numerous puzzles in her life trouble her. Because this morning, despite everything, she had recognized a singular emotion she hadn't ever thought to experience for a member of the opposite sex: tenderness.

She had no idea, however, what to do with the feeling. The challenge made her smile.

Chapter 12

Liam opened his eyes, gazing around in confusion as he struggled awake. He had no idea where he was. Somewhere nearby, though, he heard a tapping noise. "Who is that?"

"Sorry. I didn't mean to wake you. I was getting hungry."

He lowered his lids again. Paige.

"I made a sandwich for you, too, if you're awake enough to eat it. Otherwise, I'll stick it in the fridge for later."

He sat up on her mattress and pushed the tangled sheets away, realizing his disorientation might be partially related to the bed's odd positioning. He narrowed his eyes against the glare through the open door, trying to pick out from Paige's silhouette whether she faced him or was looking the other way.

"Was that groan supposed to signify a yes or a no?" she asked.

He cleared his throat. "I don't know. What time is it?"

"Ten-thirty. Maybe a little early for lunch."

"No. That's fine. I'll take it." He extended his hand and she deposited a plate on his outstretched palm. After a moment's dithering she sat down next to him and balanced her own plate on her knee. He curled back the bread on his sandwich and peered underneath. "What is it?"

"Turkey. Did you get enough sleep?"

Taking a bite, he nodded. His bladder was painfully full, but he didn't want to get up. The result of that type of pressure would be all too evident in his boxers. "Thank you," he managed around a mouthful. "For letting me stay here. I slept better than I have in quite a while."

"I'm glad." Her tone remained carefully neutral. "And I'm sorry for getting angry at you last night. I understand how hard it was for you."

He shook his head in dismissal of the subject. "Why is the door open?"

"For fresh air," she said, as if that fact should be obvious.

"You know what I mean."

She swiped at a drop of mayo and then licked it from the back of her hand. The act appeared unconscious, not designed to entice or arouse, and yet he found the brief flick of her tongue across skin produced precisely those results. He took another bite from his sandwich, concentrating on chewing.

She tossed her head, shaking hair back from her eyes. "I figured with you here, I didn't have to worry so much. Plus it's a beautiful morning."

Liam set the plate on his knee. "I do have to go home, though. I have work to do."

"And I have to go into town."

Liam questioned the wisdom of an unaccompanied trip to anywhere at that point in time, but he didn't think he'd win that argument. A warning would have to suffice. Not that she needed one. He found her independence particularly appealing. However, her unnatural reserve this morning made him feel guilty as hell. He wondered what she felt after his confession. Betrayal? Anger? Even if she'd set aside the fact he'd hidden what he'd known about Edwin's death, he didn't want to be treated as if he might break based on the latter admission. He didn't want her believing he'd gifted her with insight into him as a man, either. He'd spoken because he trusted her, because he hoped to make her understand his motivation and his reluctance. But he wanted nothing from her in return because, goddamn it, he'd only given her half the truth.

"Liam, what's wrong?"

"Nothing." He shifted the plate from his leg and started scooting toward the mattress edge beneath the sheets. "Are my pants dry?"

"Not yet," she said, standing. "I went next door and grabbed you a clean pair, though. I spotted some folded laundry on the dining room table last night when I—"

He froze. "You did what?"

"I didn't go anywhere but straight into the dining room. I wouldn't be nosy about your private life."

"That's not the point."

Paige came around the bed. "Are you worried about me going over there? I assumed it would be safe. That psycho wasn't after you, and it is broad daylight—"

"It was broad daylight when he accosted you in the street, wasn't it?" He could tell he'd confused her by his confrontational tone. Though he had every reason for concern, he had none for anger. Not an iota for which she was at fault, anyway. "I'm sorry, Paige. Ignore me." He stood up, remembered he wore nothing but his boxers, and sat down again. "My jeans?"

"Here." She handed them to him with her eyes averted and wearing a look of impatience. "I saw you in your underwear last night. No need to be shy all of a sudden."

He shoved his legs into his pants and stood, jerking the waistband up over his hips. "Look, Paige, I—"

"No, it's all right. Truly. I understand. I get it." She turned back to him and, with a snort of amusement, tugged the sheet out he'd inadvertently shoved down his jeans along with the hem of the T-shirt.

"I'll get this back to you," he said, pinching the soft fabric of the T-shirt between thumb and forefinger.

"No rush, Liam. And I do get it. Basically, we're strangers—"

"Hardly that."

"Hardly more," she argued.

Despite all the reasons piled up like cordwood against pursuing her, she touched him, reached him, in a way no one had since Alice died. In a way no one could. The leaping of his blood in chemical response to her was the least of it. And yet…yes, and yet.

He thought of the frigid January evening almost three months to the day after he'd lost Alice and their daughter. The evening Fate had strolled up to him with a casual greeting and tendered an offer he'd decided not to refuse. It hadn't been the money. He could have resisted that. Sometimes the possibilities of opportunity were enough. He'd viewed it as a win-win situation. But now, people were going to get hurt. Well, not people. One person. Paige.

"I'm sorry, Paige."

"You apologize one more time, I'm going to kick your ass all the way down to the tide line and leave you for the gulls." Handing him his half-eaten sandwich, she set his plate and her own in the sink. "Take that with you. Go do whatever it is you have to do, and if you decide later you want to invite me to drink a disgusting beer again, we'll do that, and if not, I'll be right here, locked up and safe and reading my novel."

His grin felt like it began in his stomach. He wanted to put his arms around her and laugh into that curly, wild hair of hers. He didn't deserve her kindness, her understanding. God knew, he didn't. But he wanted it. Oh yeah, he would have given anything to deserve what she offered.

Paige grabbed a band off the counter and wrapped it around her hair, bringing it into questionable submission. She hooked the strap of her purse over her shoulder, looking at him with raised brows.

"Oh," he said in comprehension. "Leaving right now. Thanks for the sandwich."

Outside, he watched her turn the key in the deadbolt lock and then walked her to her car out front, where he gave the back seat the onceover before opening the door for her. "You keep your eyes open in town, all right? And call if you need anything. Because despite your threats to kick my ass—which I'd like to see you try, since I think it would be pretty entertaining—I will be there in a heartbeat if you call."

Although her eyes had become a narrow, honey gleam at his comment, her mouth twisted into a smile. "I don't have your number, Liam."

"How about a pen?"

In silence, she plucked one from the front pocket of her bag. He grabbed her hand, pulling her arm straight. Beneath his fingers, he felt the pulse in her wrist, rapid and light, like a bird's tiny heart. In swift strokes, he wrote his number on her forearm and handed the pen back.

"Blood poisoning? I'm flattered."

"It'll be right where you can see it. No hunting for a piece of paper."

She nodded. He saw the reason for immediacy sink in as she glanced again at the phone number he'd inked onto her skin. "Thank you," she said. "911 is easier to remember, though. Hopefully I won't need either."

As she climbed into the driver's seat, her gaze went to his house and widened. She quickly turned her attention to inserting the key into the ignition. He looked over his shoulder, wondering aloud what had caught her eye.

"It's nothing," she said, swinging the door shut. "I thought I saw movement in the end bedroom. Is that your office? Used to be my room."

Without further comment, she pulled out and headed down the road with a wave. He waited until her car had disappeared over the rise in the road before hurrying over to his house and up the stairs to the second floor. He found the doorstop wedged between the office door and the jamb. Pushing the door open, he stepped into the room and halted. "Where have you been?"

With a chirp, Shadow crossed the floor to leap into his arms. Holding the cat against his chest, Liam walked to the window, looking to the weathered cottage roof next door. There were no ghosts here today.

Not today.

Chapter 13

"Thanks for coming in, Paige. How are you doing?" Dan spoke as he walked away from her, moving with a rapid stride down the hallway. Paige loped to keep up. Her stomach felt as if a fish were flopping around inside.

"In here."

He paused outside a door before shoving it open. With a jerk of his head he indicated she should enter. Dan followed her inside. He set the folder he'd been carrying onto the laminate table top. Sitting in the nearest chair, Paige clutched her purse on her knees.

Dan dropped into another chair and scooted it over the gray institutional carpet and nearer to the table. He flipped open the folder to withdraw a photograph, which he slid across the table toward her. "This the guy?"

The agile fish jumped into her esophagus. She swallowed it back down as she leaned forward for a better look at the photo. Closer examination didn't help. The photo was pixelated and ill-focused. She lifted the printout for a different angle. "It could be. The build looks right. Possibly the clothes, too. This photo is from what? A security camera?"

Dan nodded. "I know the image quality isn't there. We got it from a bank down the block and tried to pull the details in. Not much luck."

Paige narrowed her eyes in an attempt to find definition in the face. She glanced up at Dan. "Do you think you might know who this is?"

"Have you noticed anyone following you, anything suspicious, since your initial run-in last week?"

The fact that he'd avoided an answer with a question of his own wasn't lost on her. She supposed, as an officer of the law, speculation would be frowned upon. "Nothing," she said. "Funny, though, I think the night you were at the cottage wasn't the first time someone had been in there. The night before, I found Liam's cat inside and couldn't imagine how he'd gotten in. If someone had entered the cottage and left the door open for a time, Shadow might have wandered in then."

Dan tapped his fingers on the tabletop, considering, then snapped the photo up and returned it to the folder. "You stay in the cottage?"

"I did." He didn't need to know about last night. She would be in the cottage tonight and every night thereafter until she left. Returning to stay with Liam would be a mistake. He'd become skittish and she'd developed a premature affection, and those things together were not a compatible combination.

Dan rubbed his eyes. "I would feel better if—"

"I don't have anywhere else to go. I'm fine."

Dan subsided with a scowl. "Anything happens, you call. Anything you remember, you call."

"I will." She stood up, assuming the interview finished.

"Do you remember anything about your father's associates?"

Paige sat again. "Associates" was a strange term to use. "No. Not really. Why?"

"Did this guy look familiar to you at all?"

"A bit, but not like I knew him. I only saw him for a few seconds from the front, and then he walked away. Why on earth would someone my father had known be stalking me? Besides, he looked too young to have been a friend of my dad's."

Dan spun the folder with his fingertip. "I said associate, not friend, but it doesn't matter. I'm just trying to get a handle on why someone would zero in on you right after your arrival. You've been gone for quite some time."

"Look, Dan, I don't know much about my father, but obviously you have some inkling. Why else would you be thinking a man who'd commit burglary—even if he only stole an object of no value—might be someone my father associated himself with?"

"That's not what I said."

"Yes, it is. At least from where I'm sitting it is. Is there something you're not telling me?"

"No. There isn't."

She eyed his bland expression with distrust, yet to accuse him of outright lying seemed out of hand and, well, a teensy bit paranoid. He was a cop, after all, trying to help her. This whole business was making her anxious. With good reason. "You'd tell me if you found out something, wouldn't you?"

Dan shifted his body, his vest creaking beneath his shirt. "Paige, why would you think I wouldn't?"

"You know, you men in this town have an irritating habit of answering questions with questions."

His lip curled, a small puff of air escaping his nose in amusement. "How old do you think this fellow was?"

Paige thought a moment. "I don't know. It's difficult to tell. Not even fifty? Looked like he had a rough life, as though he got into a lot of fights or something. I guess if I'd had my wits about me, I would have taken his picture with my cell phone."

"Don't do that."

"Take his picture?"

"Blame yourself for not thinking of something in the moment. Your head doesn't go there. You're not trained to it. And also, yes, don't take his picture. Not if he's standing right in front of you. An action like that could provoke an attack."

"You're right, of course," she said. The guy hadn't been physically threatening, but she could understand how her snapping something as damning as a photo could cause a switch to flip. The guy had some serious psychological issues. He'd entered the cottage not to rob her of valuables, but to steal a memento, trail her, and then confront her with it. "Anything else you need to tell me? Did they find fingerprints on the bookmark?"

Dan slid the folder off the table and tucked it close against his chest. "Nothing worth a damn. Yours, of course, and some smudges that couldn't be lifted. Real investigations aren't like the crime shows. There are more unsolved cases than you'd believe." He rose. "Are you going to the fireworks Saturday night?"

The abrupt change to chit-chat threw her for a second. Preceding him to the door, she answered as she passed him. "I'd forgotten about the Fourth, actually, but yes, I think I might."

"Alone?"

She hesitated, wondering where he might be headed with the question. "If I go, that's the likely scenario. As you pointed out, I don't really know anyone around here anymore."

He reached past her to turn the doorknob. "Be careful, then. It'll be dark, and there will be crowds. If you stay at the cottage, since you insist, and watch from the windows, you might be safer."

"Thanks for the warning. I can always hope the guy was a random sicko and he's gone far away." For good measure, she rapped her knuckles against the wooden doorframe as she passed.

"Maybe," she heard him say behind her in dubious agreement. "Unfortunately, it doesn't usually work that way."

He didn't walk her out, leaving her to find her way to the front of the building and outside. She descended the steps to her car, looking to either side as she did. She'd been careful to check the traffic on the road behind her and hadn't noted anything suspicious, but she eyed the interior of her car before sliding behind the wheel.

She sat a few minutes, contemplating all that Dan Stauffer had told her and, more importantly, what he did not. She had no real reason to suspect he hid anything. After all, if an officer of the law intended to safeguard somebody, wanted someone to be able to protect themselves, he'd arm them with the facts, plain and simple. She knew that.

By the time she put the car into gear, she had considered the headway she'd made in her search for information about her father's life. She hadn't gotten far, that was for sure. She'd discovered more about her mother, and even that was limited. Paige didn't like mysteries outside of a novel. She'd come to Alcina Cove with a purpose and had not only been unsuccessful in moving toward her goal, she'd been sidetracked by a lunatic with a fixation. Why was he obsessed with her?

Unless he'd mistaken her for someone else. She wouldn't wish this affliction on anyone, but if his behavior was meant for another, she wished he'd recognize his error and move on.

Paige decided to continue her day with a visit to Mrs. Hunt. Although she stood to gain nothing from further conversation with Bea, she had promised to come back, and the poor lady did give the impression she was quite lonely. Paige could stop by for a quick tea and possibly get names of friends her mother had when she'd lived here—women her mother's age and not Mrs. Hunt's—thereby killing two birds with one stone.

Beatrice Hunt, however, was not answering the door. Hearing a noise inside, Paige leaned over a bush and peered in through the lace-covered window. She found the woman standing behind the sofa, staring right back at her. Subduing her initial astonishment, Paige tapped on the glass.

"Mrs. Hunt. Bea! It's Paige. Paige Waters."

Paige wondered if the woman had experienced a medical trauma. Her eyes remained on Paige as if unseeing. Paige drummed the glass again.

"Bea! May I come in?" Paige straightened. She yanked the screen door open again and applied her fist to the wood panel. "Mrs. Hunt, are you all right? Open the door so I can be sure."

After a minute she heard Bea's shuffling steps on the other side, saw the doorknob wiggle as the woman fumbled with the lock. Bea opened the door a couple of inches. "Paige, dear, what is it? What do you want?"

"I came to see if we could have our tea, but now I'm worried about you. Don't you feel well?" Paige tried to peek around her and into the house.

"I'm fine, dear," the woman said breathlessly. "I'm just not up to company today."

A cold suspicion entered Paige's mind and proceeded across her skin with a soft, glacial tread. "Bea, is someone in the house with you?" She reached for her cell phone as she asked the question, her other hand moving to the knob.

"No. I'm alone, like I always am."

"Do you mind if I check?"

"What? I don't—"

Careful not to knock the elderly woman over, Paige pushed the door open and stepped inside. She grabbed a heavy ceramic duck off a nearby table. With enough of a swing, an object like that could yield some serious damage.

"Paige, what are you doing with Charlie? My neighbor's daughter made that for me."

Holding Charlie and her phone at the ready, Paige hurried through the house, announcing her intention to call the police. She realized she shouldn't be broadcasting her objective, but performing it. By that time, though, she had determined the house was empty with the exception of herself and Beatrice Hunt. She returned to the living room and placed the duck back on the table. Bea watched her, thin arms folded.

"Bea, why wouldn't you answer the door?"

"What is wrong with you, Paige?" The woman's wheezing tones had taken on strength in her indignation. "How dare you burst in here?"

"I'm sorry. I thought…I thought something was wrong. Are you sure you're all right?"

"Positive."

Paige sat in the nearest chair, the vanished rush of adrenaline leaving her drained. Bea eased over to the sofa and perched on a cushion. "I don't really want to talk to you."

"Why not?"

"I can't say."

"You can't say?" Paige thought about the manner in which their last discussion had gone so awry.

"You have no intention of taking me seriously."

Paige briefly closed her eyes. Not this again. "Maybe we don't talk about things like that. We can talk about the flowers lining the walkway. I'm rather envious of them, you know. Perhaps you can tell me your secret."

Bea bestowed a stony glare on her, lips tight.

"So, no tea?" Paige said.

"No tea."

Paige wondered at the absence of courtesy. Normally, women her age held decorum above hurt feelings. "Okay, then, if you don't want me to visit, could I ask you a quick question? And then I'll go."

The woman remained silent, saying neither yes nor no. Paige plunged ahead.

"Do you know any of the names of my mother's friends? Her other friends?" Paige added to avoid any further insult.

Bea clenched her bony fingers together in her lap. "I really shouldn't be talking to you."

"Why?"

"It isn't a wise thing to do."

Frowning, Paige leaned forward. "Once again, why?"

The woman turned her head, studying Paige from the corner of her eye.

"Bea?"

"You have to go."

"I don't want to."

"This is my home, and I have every right to demand you leave." Bea's voice resumed its tremulous quality. Paige stood.

"Just one," she said. "Just one name of one friend, and then I'll be on my way." Watching the woman's mouth work, Paige longed to yank the words out of it.

Bea spoke with obvious reluctance. "Andrews. Felicia Andrews. Or that was her name a long time ago. I'm sure she's been married since then, but I can't help you any further."

Paige stepped closer to Bea, who flinched. Paige shook her head. "Bea. Mrs. Hunt. I apologize for upsetting you. I really would like to come back for tea if you'd consider asking me. I'm going to leave my number right here on your end table, and you can call me if you want, okay?" Pulling Dan Stauffer's card out, she wrote her cell number under his name, with her own beside it. She'd saved his number to her phone, so didn't need the card anymore, but if Bea might require a police officer's number, Dan's was a good one to have. "And thank you for the information. I'll see if I can track down Felicia Andrews."

Bea remained mute. Paige exited the house, bewildered and concerned, and locked the doorknob before pulling the door shut. She wavered a minute or two on the walkway, pretending to admire the flowers, but her thoughts were on Beatrice Hunt's strange behavior. The woman had acted afraid—not of Paige herself, perhaps, but possibly of being asked questions. Did Bea think Paige would blame her for anything discovered based on her reports? Damn, the residents of this town could be a strange lot.

Chapter 14

A trip to the library to check the high school yearbook for the year her mother had graduated garnered Paige more pertinent tidbits of data than she could have hoped for. She found her mother's senior photo and shed a few tears over it, and nearby, the photo of Felicia Andrews. In a candid shot of students on Alcina High School's grounds, she located a picture of the two friends again and a young man holding Felicia's hand, identified as Billy Woodward. In a town like this, Paige suspected people often married their high school sweethearts, so she searched the files in the computer for the local paper, looking for older wedding announcements. Sure enough, Felicia Andrews and William Woodward held their nuptials right here in Alcina Cove. Whether they remained married to this day, Paige couldn't ascertain, but she had a place to start.

Woodward's Garage lay right outside town. The owner was a William Woodward, Sr. Paige thought it more likely this William would be Felicia's husband rather than a father-in-law, who should have retired long ago. Pulling into the lot, she passed two gas pumps, numerous cars jammed into parking spaces along the blacktop, and an open garage where a sedan hovered in the air on a lift. She parked the car and got out. She walked into the garage and waited while a man finished his task in a wheel well. Not William, Sr., surely. The fellow who turned and spotted her was about eighteen.

"May I help you?"

"Is Mr. Woodward about?"

The young man wiped his hands on a rag from his pocket as he came toward her. "My name is Woodward. People around here don't call me 'mister,' though. Chance you mean my dad?"

He stood a moment, arching his spine backward as if it ached. Stuffing the oily rag back into his pocket, he faced her.

"Probably," she said. "Is he William Woodward, married to Felicia?"

"Was. They split about five years back. Who are you?"

"My name's Paige Waters. My mother and your mother were friends back in high school, and probably after, I would think. I've come back for...for a visit, and I thought I'd look her up. My mother passed away, and I wanted to ask your mom a few things."

He studied her with a critical, narrowed eye. "All right."

"All right?"

"She's not far. I'll give you her number and address. Won't do you no good today, though. Not until next week. She went away visiting for the holiday."

Paige tamped down her frustration and thanked him, following him into the shop where he wrote the information on a blank receipt. Noticing some photos tacked to a corkboard, Paige pointed in that direction.

He spoke before she did. "The bubbler? Help yourself."

Taking him to mean the water fountain directly beneath, Paige grabbed a cup and filled it halfway, using her time drinking to study the pictures on the wall. She glanced back at him before jerking her chin toward a picture of a woman who resembled the high school photos. "Is this your mom?"

He came up beside her. "Yuh. That's her there." He pointed a stained finger. "And there. You never met her, then?"

Paige shook her head. "Not that I can remember."

"She's wicked funny, my mom. I think you'll like her."

He handed her the paper with his mother's contact information. At his words, Paige experienced a rush of affection for the young man and his "wicked funny" mother, as well as a certain amount of longing for a relationship she no longer possessed. She threw the cone-shaped paper cup into the trash pail and turned to shake his hand.

He yanked his hand away from hers with a laugh. "Don't think you want to be doing that. You'll be marking everything you touch for the rest of the day."

She conceded his point and walked back outside. He followed to stand next to her.

"My mom, she's caretaker for Alcina Nature Center. The naturalist, I guess you'd call her. That got built about twelve years back, I think. She lives there now in the little stone house. You've been there, to the nature center?"

"No," said Paige quietly. "I've been away a while. No nature center existed when I left."

"Some university professor uncovered a circle of standing stones, like they got in England, you know? Not as old or as big, I hear. Somebody's idea of a joke, maybe, way back in the sixteen-hundreds. But that's where Alcina Cove got its name originally, from those stones. Some legend or something. Anyway, the center got built up around them."

Paige arched her brows at him. "You're a font of information, aren't you? Thank you."

He waved away her gratitude. "You ought to check it out, even before Mom comes home. Nice day for exploring. Just stay on this road."

She thanked him again for his help and got back in her car. She found the idea of adventure solely for enjoyment very tempting. And like he'd said, it was a nice day for that type of excursion. By the time Paige left the parking lot, she'd made her decision and turned right rather than returning to town.

The landscape to either side quickly turned wild, full of windblown pines, rocks, and scrub trees. Paige kept an eye on her rearview to make sure no one followed. The precaution struck her as surreal, like something from a movie, but she was determined not to be caught unaware again.

Within a mile of the change in scenery, a wooden sign in burgundy with gold lettering announced the entrance to Alcina Cove Nature Preserve. She turned in and drove along the graveled road until she reached a parking lot with a dozen cars. She pulled her car into a space and got out. She opened the trunk and rummaged around. Locating her baseball bat, she yanked it out and hefted it in her hand. A group of women in matching shirts was exiting a nearby mini-van. She tossed the bat back in and walked in their direction. Safety in numbers and all that.

At the far side of the lot, a broad sign beneath a narrow roof cover showed a map of different trails. The women headed in that direction, Paige close enough behind to read the inscription across their shirts: *Lazy Day Ladies – Book Club and Hiking Group*. Based on the name, she immediately wanted to become one.

Hearing her footsteps on the gravel, the two women walking at the rear turned and smiled. "Beautiful day," said one.

"Have you been here before?" Paige asked.

"Nope," said the other, "first time."

"Me too."

"Feel free to tag along, then. And ignore Sylvie," the woman said loudly enough for another up ahead to turn and flash the finger. "She's got a mouth like a trucker."

To one side of the map was a brief history of the finding of the stones, the development of the park, and a bit about the mythology of Alcina, a sea nymph who acquired mortals as lovers and afterward changed them into rocks and trees. The women took turns reading portions of the history aloud, making raunchy jokes about taking stones as lovers. Afterward, they all headed down the indicated trail.

Breathing pine resin and salt air, Paige followed them up the brief ascent to a place where the woods gave way to a rocky crest. She stopped, open-mouthed. Obviously, much time had been spent clearing the area, which, according to the signage, was deeply overgrown. The once-tumbled circle of standing stones had been righted and stood tall against the evergreen backdrop beyond, looking both prehistoric and breathtakingly lovely. Far smaller than the grandeur of Stonehenge, the gray, striated stones made an impressive circle, like crooked teeth in a giant's open mouth. Paige estimated most stood about fifteen feet tall.

"Amazing," announced one of the group. Another released a low whistle of appreciation. Then, as one accord, they all marched forward in hushed reverence. Paige followed, overwhelmed. She'd never seen anything like this in person.

Inside the circle, they walked from stone to stone in clockwise progression. Paige placed her hand against the surface nearest. A sharp, sudden chill coursed along her body, and the flesh tightened between her shoulder blades. She noticed several other women had similar, shivering reactions. They all laughed in an attempt to dismiss the sensation. Except Paige. Beyond the sunlight shining down into the ring's heart, she spotted movement in the shadow of the stones.

Several seconds passed. Her breath whistled out. It was only a raven alighting on the ground. She observed its bobbing momentum across the grass to be certain before continuing on her way.

"You okay?" asked one of the Ladies.

Paige nodded. "This is quite the experience."

"I've heard of sounds coming from this ring at night, almost like singing. Don't think I'd like to come back at night."

Paige smiled in agreement, although she couldn't help thinking that if people heard singing in the stones at night, it probably was a human group of singers, not something fantastical.

Another shadow passed across the ground inside the circle. Paige looked up to find a second raven floating overhead with wings spread to land on the grass beside the other. Breaking into abrupt chatter, the Ladies moved on toward the path at the other side, a trail leading, so the sign said, to a small pond farther in the woods. Before Paige could reach the worn path at the edge of the ring, a dark silhouette undulated across the stones. Paige shot a quick look toward the sky, seeing no bird. The shape was that of a man, anyway, tall and thin. Spinning, Paige searched the circle, looking for a point of origin. She found none.

"Hello?"

The Lazy Day Ladies had gone on without her, joyfully oblivious. When the shadow appeared again to her left, Paige's heart exploded. Adrenaline forced her legs into action, jerking her into a ground-eating race away from the stone circle. Blood pounding in her ears drowned out the distant, laughing voices of the Ladies as Paige ran along the path toward the parking lot, refusing to look back, filled with terror that the shadow would come after her. This wasn't anything human, not the sinister thief of bookmarks, but something in Liam's jurisdiction—a specter, a ghost, a thing in which she didn't believe.

She skidded in the gravel beside her car and went down onto one knee. Scrabbling upright, jabbing the lock release on her key fob, Paige managed to yank open the door and throw herself inside. She slammed the button to lock all the doors and shoved the key into the ignition. Stone spurted from beneath her tires as she wheeled the vehicle around in reverse. Jerking the gear into drive, she sped forward with a last, fearful look in the rearview mirror. Nothing. Thank God, nothing.

She returned her attention to the road ahead and slammed on the brakes.

A hollow, breathless cry tore from her throat. Three hikers were crossing the road in front of her car. Although affronted by her careless driving, they waved, possibly in appreciation of the fact she hadn't run them down. Something about the incident struck her as both comical and so very mundane in terms of a world where ghosts did not exist, she found herself succumbing to a nervous laugh in the midst of her apology. Clamping her lips tight against hysteria, she waved back at the three men and continued driving. Having been negligent before, Paige checked the backseat in the rearview mirror when she reached the main road. Her eyes were underscored by the dark half-moons of shock in a face as white as paper.

Remembering Liam's number on her arm, half hidden beneath the lightweight, three-quarter length sleeve, Paige pulled out her cell phone and dialed. After several rings, his voice mail came on.

"Liam," she said, "nasty-tasting or not, I could really use one of those beers right now."

Chapter 15

Liam pulled the door shut and checked the lock. He held a twelve-inch square wooden box under his arm, a dripping bottle of beer in his hand. He'd gone out and bought a six pack of something he thought Paige might find more appealing, but he wasn't having one himself. Now was not the time.

Crossing between their two houses—if the cottage could technically be called a house—Liam thought about what Paige had told him on the phone. All of it. He'd talked to Dan Stauffer about part of the conversation afterward. He didn't like where the investigation was heading. Not the course it appeared to be taking and not what he feared might be its ultimate outcome.

And then, there was the whole ghost story. Paige didn't believe in apparitions, but skepticism did not preclude having an encounter, whether a person accepted it or not. If he'd known where she was going, he might have warned her. He'd filled half a book on the tales of the stone circle, although he hadn't experienced anything for himself when he'd gone out there to take photographs and gain a feeling for the overall ambience. Stories of hauntings had been told for years, even before Dr. Columbus had located the stones shrouded in forest growth.

Liam knew the occurrence had frightened her worse than the break-in to her cottage and the later appearance on the street of the man in possession of her bookmark. A *bookmark*. To steal such an intimate item with no monetary value had nothing to do with greed and everything to do with a personal campaign. But Paige had not recognized the man. Liam had asked Stauffer if there was a possibility he might view the photo he'd shown Paige. As far-fetched as the notion might be to some, Liam's association with Paige might have made her a target. He needed Stauffer to recognize that fact. Liam had made arrangements to stop by the station the next day.

When he came around to what was, essentially, the front door to the cottage, despite its position facing the ocean rather than the road, Liam set the box and the beer down on the stone step. At the tide line, Paige stood gazing out to sea. Liam observed her for a minute, wondering at her stillness. Paige Waters was nothing if not a ball of energy. He rarely saw her sit still for longer than it took one thought to move on to another.

Honestly, though, how well did he know her? Sometimes he forgot they'd only met a few days ago. He didn't know if forgetting was a good or a bad thing.

"Paige!"

She didn't hear him. Not surprising. The tide's roar at close range could easily drown out any noise. He trotted down the stairs to the rocky beach and crossed over to her. "Paige," he said again when he got closer. She remained unaware of his presence. Not wanting to startle her, he walked in a wide semi-circle toward the water so he'd fall into her peripheral vision first. She turned to him slowly.

"Hi."

"Hi," he said. Stepping in, he leaned forward and kissed her on the side of her head. The gesture felt significant, as if they'd crossed a boundary. He was in deep shit. "Everything okay? God, Paige, your hair." He ran his fingers through the locks behind her temple, careful not to tug on any tangles.

She brought both hands up to grip the curly mass. "What about my hair?"

"It's adorable." Had he actually said that? What had happened to "Keep an eye on her, Liam, and keep your fucking distance"?

She rolled her eyes. "If you say so."

His stomach churned with the knowledge of how much he meant it, and that transported him right to something resembling panic. "I brought you a beer." Voice sounded normal. Good.

She glanced down at his hand.

"It's up by the door."

"Oh."

"I brought you something else, too."

"What?" Her gaze lost its distance and lit up with curiosity.

"Something I found in the attic."

She didn't wait to hear any more, but began a brisk walk up the beach. He watched her with an idiotic smile on his face. About thirty feet away, she pivoted to look back at him. A burst of wind blew her curly chestnut mop into a shape like a dandelion seed puff around her head. Lifting her arm, she held out her hand.

"You coming?" Her fingers curled in, beckoning. He closed the distance and slipped his hand around hers, her slim digits fitting between his like the pieces of a puzzle. He didn't want to let go.

"God help me," he whispered. Fortunately she didn't hear.

Paige had locked the deadbolt when she went down to the beach and handed him the key to open it while she gathered the items he'd left on the doorstep. Liam noted that the cottage had been rearranged yet again in a way he found charming. The bed was back against the wall, but angled. She'd placed the low chest on the rug over the trapdoor and set the chair beside it, like a sitting area.

"I can drive a few nails into that trapdoor if it will make you feel better," he said.

She picked up a hammer from the kitchen counter and wagged the tool at him. "Already done. I stopped in town to grab a few things once my heart stopped racing. I have dinner if you'd like it."

"We'll see. First, you want to tell me again what happened today?"

She twisted the cap off the bottle and took a tentative sip of the contents. Her right eye scrunched in a lopsided squint as she took the beer's measure. "Better," she said with a distinct lack of conviction.

"Not everybody likes beer."

"In general, I don't really like alcohol." She shrugged. "I just thought I'd give it a try. People rave about how wonderful a beer is in the summer heat."

He shook his head. "It's not all that hot today."

"No."

"Did you think it might calm you down?"

"I guess."

He reached out, took the beer from her, and swallowed several mouthfuls before setting the nearly full bottle in the sink. "Don't like it myself," he said.

"Did you buy that for me?"

"I did."

"Liam…"

"Tell me again what happened at the standing stones."

Her demeanor altered with his request. She dragged her fingers through the mop of her hair and began to pace. "You've talked about these things in such a matter-of-fact manner, as if they were true. As if you'd known them to be true. Before today, Liam, I didn't believe you at all."

He took a seat in the single chair and crossed his arms over his chest, following her movements with his eyes.

"When you said this town had been referred to as Haunted Alcina Cove, I had all I could to do to keep from laughing." She paused, facing him with an earnest expression. "I didn't want to hurt your feelings."

"Go on."

"But what I saw today… There was no human present besides me. I was alone. But I wasn't alone. I had no doubt of that. That's never happened to me before."

On her third pass, he grabbed her hand and pulled her down onto his knee. She didn't seem to notice where she'd landed. He could see her remembering the event, eyes darting from side to side, not quite focused, pupils dilating.

"Don't be afraid, Paige."

"Easy for you to say."

"I've never seen you afraid, not even facing me in the dark when we first met."

"Well," she said, leaning her forehead against his, "you're a man."

"And as a man," he answered, "I could have done a lot more damage than a ghost ever could." He hadn't realized he'd put his arms around her, but he felt her ribcage beneath his hands, her torso expanding and retreating in slow respiration. Her face pivoted until her mouth was a bare inch from his own, the warmth of her breath passing from her lips over his. He tasted the sweet-bitter flavor of hops in the moist passage of air.

"Paige."

"I know." She rose, moved away. "This can't happen. Like I said this morning, I get it. And I do."

That wasn't what he'd meant at all, but he let it go. What he wanted to tell her was how much he craved her, every inch of her, what he wouldn't give to lose all memory of himself deep inside her for as many minutes, hours, days as she would grant him. Sighing, he lifted his chin toward the box he'd carried over.

"That was in the attic. I think it was…well, I think it was your father's."

She jerked around with a small jump, staring at the box as if she thought the lid might pop open and pull her in like an element of some deep, dark magic. "What's in it?"

"I have no idea. I only know it's not mine. But I did see there are photographs in there."

Her brow puckered. Still, she wouldn't touch it. Liam rose to stand beside her, eyeing the wooden container.

"Pick it up. You need to lift the lid to find out what's inside. That's how it works."

"Maybe...maybe I don't want to know what's in there."

"You told me you were looking for answers from your past. I can stick the box back in the attic if you'd like." He made to reach for it, hoping to motivate her to action. She took the bait, snatching the box from the edge of the bed where she'd set it down.

"You're right, of course." Climbing up onto the mattress, she kicked off her shoes and sat cross-legged, contemplating the box settled against her calves for several minutes more. Liam lowered himself onto the other end of the bed, waiting. The ancient box didn't possess any quality and might fall apart once opened. He'd delivered it, and that was all he could do. The rest was up to Paige. He didn't enjoy lying to her. In fact, he would have preferred all the honesty she deserved. But certain falsehoods were created to protect her. He'd been forced to recognize that fact from his very first conversation with her.

Teeth set in her lip, Paige pulled her hair away from her face, circling the length of it up into a self-contained knot behind her head. She placed her hands to either end of the lid, palms flat, fingers stiff, and slowly drew it open. For what seemed a very long time, she gazed into the box without touching anything. Lashes lowered, her hooded eyes remained unreadable to him.

"Paige?"

She shook her head. With shaking fingers, she grabbed one, then another, then a whole packet of photographs, spreading them like cards on the bed.

"They're me."

"Yes."

She shot him a look.

"I saw some of them, like I said. I didn't mean to, but I did open the box. I had no idea where it had come from or whom it belonged to." He had a sudden vision of his sister when they were children, dancing around him, chanting, 'Liar, liar, pants on fire!' He closed his eyes.

"They're all photos of me. And not only from when I lived here. There are some more recent. And this—this is me at my high school prom with that dork, Ashford. Who names their son Ashford?"

He knew she was crying without looking up. He kept his gaze on the floor below his knees. A moment like this shouldn't take place in front of someone who was little more than a stranger. He should have acknowledged that, walked out the door the moment she took the box into her hands.

"I don't understand. I don't *understand*. Why would my father have these? Why? Where did he get them?"

She didn't appear to expect an answer, and he had none to give.

"I don't understand," she said again, quieter this time. With a flurry of motion she snatched up the photos from the bed and threw them back into the box. She shoved the container toward him. Without a word, he moved it to the floor.

Rolling, she landed on her side on the mattress and buried her face into the pillow. Liam scooted closer, curving his fingers over her upper arm. "I can go. I'll take the key with me and lock you in."

"No."

"But—"

"Stay."

The timbre of the single syllable dug like a swift, sharp knife into his abdomen. "I can't make this go away for you, Paige." But hadn't he been thinking that very thing? Losing himself and all he wanted to forget in the fierce, heated act of sex with a woman he'd begun to realize meant more to him than he had any right to expect.

"You can."

"Not—"

"For a few hours."

A few hours. Fire rushed, molten, to his groin. He lay down, curving his body to fit around hers and pulled her close. "Paige…"

"Take off my clothes, Liam. Let's pretend for a while that we're real lovers."

He stilled beside her. "For the love of God, Paige, if we do this thing together, what is it you'll think we'll be?"

She shrugged. He thought she might be crying again, but he couldn't see her face. When she spoke, her voice was hushed, distant, as if she'd slipped away. "I don't know."

He stroked her unruly hair back from her face in an effort to see her better. "You don't know?"

"Lovers are—people who hold each other's hearts. Otherwise, it's just sex."

His lips curved. He understood now, or was starting to. It was a matter of trust. Leaning over her, he kissed her ear.

"I'm broken, Liam. That's what I tried to say the other night. I came back to try to fix me, who I am."

Grabbing her shoulder, he pulled her around until she lay on her back. He positioned himself over her, one arm to either side, looking her in the eye. "Sweetheart, you can't fix the past. You can make amends, but you can't repair what's gone. It's not tangible. The past is not a physical object. You can, however, reshape what it's done to you. You can take what you have in here"—he lightly touched a finger to her breast in the vicinity of her heart—"and here"—and then moved his fingers into her hair, cupping the shape of her skull in his palm, feeling the warmth of her scalp—"and remake it."

Tears glittered on her lashes in the steep angle of the sun through the window. He pressed his mouth to one eye, then the other, and pulled away, tasting salt on his lips. "And you can rebuild trust. I promise you."

Even as he said those words, he experienced a sickening, guilty wrench in his abdomen, and yet he believed them with his whole heart. To stop the pain that had begun to flood his veins, he kissed her again, on the mouth this time. Hers opened beneath the pressure with a tiny moan that rushed against the tide, pushing culpability and anguish back into that dark cubbyhole he'd created inside him for its keeping.

"So," she whispered against his scar. He doubted she even noticed it. "It's not just sex?"

He closed his eyes and shuddered at the touch of her tongue along his jaw, his throat. "It's not just sex, Paige," he said, struggling to manage coherent thought for words. "We might be undefined right now, but just sex it is not."

"All right, Liam. I'm going to do my best to trust you." She breathed warm and oddly effervescent air against the hollow below his ear. Guilt flared once more in a brief conflagration and vanished as she did something to him that made him cry out and forget everything but the moment.

Chapter 16

He had remarkably sensitive earlobes. Every man possessed some point of contact from which he could not return. Paige heard his cry and let it rush over her skin like water. She tugged his T-shirt out of his jeans and closed her thumb and forefinger on the rigid nub of his nipple as she continued her prior ministrations. The sound he made then proved more delightful than the one before. He seized her hands in a sudden flurry and jerked away, gazing down at her with eyes as dark as midnight.

"Good God, woman, I think I should tell you it's been a ridiculously long time since I've...well, you know, done this. How about letting me set the pace?"

She heard herself purr like a cat as she arched her body toward his against the gentle restraint he maintained on her wrists. He slid back on the mattress, pulling her up onto her knees.

"Stay there," he said. "Don't move."

Perfectly willing to be compliant, she lowered her buttocks onto her heels and waited, observing him with a fascinated eye. First he pulled off his shoes. Not the work boots she was used to seeing him wear, but a pair of canvas deck shoes. His socks followed. He set both aside and stood. He yanked off his shirt and tossed it. She watched the blue-striped fabric flutter and land somewhere beyond the chest, and then she snapped her gaze back to him. He had a long spine and a back marked by lean muscle and strength. Paige found her breath coming in short bursts and forced her respiration to lengthen, to restore oxygen to her brain. She failed miserably when he turned to face her and her breath caught again at the expression on his face, the contours of his chest and arms, the clear and present danger evident behind the fly front of his jeans.

She held her arms out to him.

"Not yet," he said. "Your turn."

Her blouse had a deuced amount of buttons down the front, and it took her forever to unfasten them. When she neared the hemline, she opted for expedience, and went to pull it over her head. His voice stopped her.

"There are only three more. Take your time. There's no rush."

She nearly broke the last one in frustration when she couldn't push the button through the hole.

"Let me."

Placing one knee on the wrinkled bed linens, he bowed his head to the task, his dark hair brushing across her cheek, and then her breast as he bent closer. She could smell his shampoo, something with coconut, and the fresh air. His fingers grazed her belly as he pushed her blouse back and straightened. He slid the sleeves from her arms. She followed the trail of his gaze down her body, saw him pause, nostrils flaring.

"Look at you."

"I don't, very often," she said.

Placing two fingers into each cup of her bra, he pushed the fabric down, popping her breasts free. Her nipples hardened in the air, in the intensity of his gaze. She reached behind to unfasten the confining garment.

"I've got it." He raised her arms above her head and left them there, then slid his hands behind her back to work the triple hook and eye. His breath drifted across her skin, causing the rosy flesh of her nipple to pucker more. He placed his lips beside it, and then under it, pushing softly against her breast. She wanted to scream out for him to take her into his mouth, but she waited, barely breathing. He unhooked her bra and stood.

Circling her upper arms with his fingers, he urged her upright, helping her to find her balance on the mattress. He pulled her unfastened garment off her body and dropped it at the foot of the bed. "Jeans next."

Paige unzipped them and pushed the denim down past her hips, wriggling them to her ankles. Taking her hand, Liam placed it on his shoulder for stability and removed her pants himself. They went the way of his shirt, flying onto the floor. She started to ease back down.

"Wait," Liam whispered.

Standing on the bed in nothing but her panties, she crossed her arms over her breasts, suddenly timid. He uncrossed her arms, holding them away from her body. "You're beautiful."

"No, I'm not. I could—"

"What? Be perfect? Perfect is a flaw in itself. It's not perfection but who we really are, every imperfection of form, every element of personality, every quirk of insight and opinion, that captivates and enthralls."

As he spoke, he slid aside her soaked underwear, parting and exploring with a touch as light as air.

"Oh God, Liam…"

"Shhh."

With a small ripping noise, the material of her panties parted at her hip and slid down her thigh. His mouth closed over her, the flat of his tongue moving in inexorable strokes. She shoved her fingers into his hair, drawing him in, widening her stance, feeling his fingers on her buttocks in an effort to keep her upright, to prevent her toppling off the bed. His tongue's movement accelerated, focused, circling and suckling as her nipples hardened to stone on her breasts and heat flashed like flame over every surface of her body.

She cried out in wordless ecstasy, and he still did not relent. Her knees buckled and he caught her, dropping down with her onto the bed. She had no idea at what point he'd shed his jeans, but his boxers followed as he spread her legs. He kissed her thigh, the curve beneath her ribs, and then he latched onto her nipple. He didn't linger. His urgency was palpable in the goose bumps on his flesh, his labored breathing, the turgid position of his penis, tight against his belly. She took him in her hand and guided him in. She didn't need hours. She needed this now, the enveloping blindness of yet another climax while he thrust himself into her, hard and without control, two bodies in passionate, abandoned consummation, quick and frenzied and on fire.

Were they lovers by her definition? She didn't care. She would sort that out later.

* * * *

Liam lay with his head on his arm on Paige's pillow. Her wild mane curled across the linen and onto the bend of his elbow. He pondered her breast in its rise and fall beneath the sheet, calm now, steady and rhythmic. Her mouth had parted about fifteen minutes ago, showing the pearly edges of her teeth. No other sound issued from her mouth but soft, raspy breath.

He wished he had some way of looking into her mind, stealing into her thoughts. Although she had curled against him after lovemaking, craving physical closeness, he'd witnessed her emotions close to him. She'd made small talk, avoiding any mention of the photos, her experience at the standing stones, the fact they'd made love without restraint in this damned cramped bed more than once. He refused to refer to what they'd engaged in as sex, even though technically, it was no more than that. He didn't want what they'd shared to fall into such an inadequate category.

But so what? In the morning, or whenever he chose to leave Paige's bed, would what he wanted really matter? And, honestly, did he have any right to expect it should?

Lifting his right hand, he curled a chestnut lock around his index finger, studying its color, the texture in the darkness. What would she say if she knew not all her secrets were hidden? Would she hate him for that?

God, he hoped not. He didn't think he could take it.

After another fifteen minutes of watchfulness, he required fresh air, a stretching of his legs. Deep down, he understood what he really needed was familiar surroundings, a tether to the life he knew. He exited the tangle of sheet and blanket with exaggerated care and climbed into his jeans, followed by the shirt he finally located under the foot of the bed. He listened for any change in Paige's breathing, but she slept on undisturbed.

He'd laid the keys on the kitchen counter earlier and they remained there, gleaming slightly in the darkness. Although he didn't intend to be gone long, he planned to lock the door, and scooped the keys quietly into his palm. He had no way of knowing what Paige's reaction would be when she woke up and found him gone, but he certainly wouldn't leave her unguarded.

Outside, he strode several yards away from the cottage door. Standing beneath the stars, the flags of silvery clouds, he listened to a nightjar calling in the stand of pines across the road. Sometimes the nighttime occupation of Alcina Cove's establishments reached him out here, but when the wind blew off the ocean it snatched the noise away, driving human clamor inland, and then he might as well have been the only human in the world. He welcomed those nights more than he cared to admit.

Thrusting his hands into his pockets, Liam headed down to the beach. He heard a radio blare as a car sped by on the road, then fade quickly into a tinny melody. He thought of the soft places on Paige's body and increased his pace, falling into a pattern parallel with the water surging toward the shore. Several times an energetic wave flooded across his bare feet, soaking denim. He changed direction, striding away from the tide toward the jetty with its huge, black boulders. As he approached, a shadow rose up.

Shock jerked him to a standstill. He yanked his hands from his pockets. "Who is that?"

A second shadow broke away from the inky darkness surrounding the stones and moved to stand beside the first. "Who the hell do you think it is?"

* * * *

Paige sat bolt upright. It took a second to remember she hadn't been sleeping alone, and then another to figure out her bedmate had gone. The noise that had woken her was a scratching, like metal at the door. Her heart hammered up her throat and into her temples, nearly drowning out the sound. Throwing herself from the bed, she fell to the floor, tangled in the bedclothes. She yanked the blanket free as she struggled upright, tossing it around her naked shoulders. Hurrying across the floor, she headed to the last place she'd seen her cell phone. She tried to snatch it from the dresser, nearly knocking it through the air. Catching the phone as it spun across the wood, she prepared to dial the police. At a muffled murmur, she flew instead on bare feet to the light plate beside the sink and flipped on the outside light. A key rasped into the deadbolt and the door opened. The beer bottle from the sink missed Liam's head by a bare inch as he stepped inside. The bottle didn't break, but tumbled to the floor, rolling in a wobbling ellipse. The remnants of yeasty liquid sprayed across the boards.

"Shit, Paige, you could have killed me."

"That was the plan," she said, grabbing several paper towels. She tossed them down to soak up the beer. "How was I supposed to know who was coming in?"

"I know. I'm…I'm sorry."

Crouching to sop up the fluid, Paige paused, staring up at Liam's ashen face. Abruptly, she straightened, flipping the trailing edge of the blanket around her hips and tucking it under her arm to keep it in place. "What's wrong?"

"What?"

"What's wrong?"

He shook his head, striding across to the bed. "I didn't mean to worry you. I just needed some fresh air." He sat. Heavily. Paige frowned.

"Are you…are you ill?" She glanced at the bottle, still rocking a little on the ground. "Are you drunk?" She didn't see how he could be, but he could have gone home. She hadn't any idea of the time and not a single clue how long ago he'd left. Heck, he could have gone out to a bar somewhere. Although, spotting his bare feet, she decided he probably hadn't.

Paige took a couple of steps toward him. "Liam, is this all just a little too strange for you? Are you feeling, I don't know, regretful?"

He lifted his gaze to her, dark eyes shadowed with sleeplessness, jaw tight. "Regretful seems a mild term."

Her stomach turned over, and she sucked in a breath. She felt as if she'd been slapped. "You could have said no."

"What do you mean? In response to your question?"

"No. In response to the sex. You could have said 'no' and gone home while the sun was still shining."

Wearing an odd expression, he shook his head a couple of times. "I don't regret it, Paige. Not at all. I was only remarking on the fact that regretful was a mild way to express what people sometimes feel after getting together. And, once again, I'm not saying that I have any regrets."

She made a face, uncertain how to respond. His voice sounded strained, his commentary rambling.

"Do you, Paige? Have regrets?"

She sat next to him, taking his hand. "No."

He closed his eyes. The color still had not returned to his face.

Paige stroked hair back from his brow. "Something is not right with you, though. I can see it."

Liam slipped his arms around her, pulling her down onto the bed as he stretched out across the mattress. "I'm fine. I promise. Let's try and get some sleep."

"I'll turn the porch light out first." Paige attempted to get up, but he held her tighter. Not in a manner she would consider arousing, or even alarming, but as though he didn't want her far from his side.

"Leave it," he said. "Leave it on."

The way he uttered those words worried her. "Liam—"

"It's nothing, Paige. Really."

"Do you want to take your pants back off?"

"I'm good."

Even that concerned her. He appeared shaken, uneasy, but she couldn't imagine why. Releasing the edge of the blanket, she threw it over them both against the draft of the overhead fan. In time, she relaxed against him, but didn't sleep. Neither did he.

Chapter 17

Paige fell back asleep sometime before sunrise, having witnessed the dark window turn pale. By that time, Liam was snoring lightly, his arm flung across his eyes and his head turned away. But when Paige awoke he had gone, slipping from bed and covering her back up without disturbing her. He did, however, leave a note. One of the sticky notes from the pad hanging on the wall beside the kitchen counter was affixed to her face. After her initial confusion upon awakening to a tacky, crinkly object clinging to the curve of her cheek, she smiled at the image of him placing it there. When she turned the page toward the sunlight to read the penned words, her smile faded.

I will only be locking the doorknob since I don't want to take the key to the deadbolt. I have to go away for a couple of days. I wanted to be here to keep an eye on you, but since I can't, please, please be careful and don't hesitate to call the local PD. Shadow will need looking after if you don't mind. I'll leave his food and bowl on your doorstep. He's good company if you want to let him in. I'll see you soon. ~L.

Something *had* happened last night. As she bounced out of bed, she wondered if he'd received a call. Perhaps something had happened to a family member? Why hadn't he told her? But why would he? She headed into the bathroom to shower. One toss about in bed didn't make her his confidante. She didn't know what it made her. The *see you soon* in his note signified some kind of promise, though.

"God, Paige, you're an idiot," she chastised herself in the mirror as she applied her facial cleanser. There had been a time when she hadn't worried about such things. What made Liam different from the other men she'd known? What made her want him to be different?

Because maybe you've fallen a little in love with him, her inner voice whispered. Paige frowned at her reflection. And how much hurt would that bring if it were true? She'd fallen in bed with him, not in love, damn it. In like, perhaps, but she'd never been willing to wager on the positive outcome of love. She knew better. Love…well, love just wounded people.

Even her mother spent all those years alone after fleeing Alcina Cove, not even dating another man. Or at least not one Paige knew about.

Making a deliberate decision to not consider the complications of emotional connections, at least for a while, Paige climbed into the shower. At the far side, pasted to the tile wall, the ink running a little from the splash of water, hung another sticky note, the three words large and clearly legible.

MISS ME YET?

Paige laughed, her heart suddenly ten times lighter.

* * * *

Around midday, Paige sent Liam a text asking if he was all right and received a quick reply of *yes, talk to you soon.* Okay. She'd accept that. She turned to Shadow, who'd appeared at the door at nine-fifteen in the morning and had since shown no inclination to leave. "Your father says hi." The elderly cat looked at her with full recognition of the lie and returned to licking his tail in the middle of her bed.

"I had a cat once. I don't remember much about him. Or her? See? I don't really remember anything. Except I don't think I let it sleep on my bed."

Shadow ignored her, managing to turn himself three times in a circle without fully rising before dropping his head to her pillow. His yellow eyes closed. Paige continued to straighten up the tiny cottage around the cat, all the while moving the box Liam had found in her old attic from place to place in the room. Eventually, she set the hinged wooden container on the mattress. Shadow lifted one lid at the disturbance but then returned to slumbering.

Sitting on the far edge, Paige folded her hands in her lap. She gazed at the box for several long minutes. She'd come back to Alcina Cove looking for answers. Instead everything she'd discovered had only unearthed more mystery. If her father had been keeping tabs on her for some reason, these were not the types of photos he would have collected. The few she'd seen had been intimate family keepsakes from events in which he'd never been involved. They certainly hadn't been taken by any private detective. She couldn't imagine her parent doing such a thing.

Sliding the box closer, Paige flipped back the lid.

Be brave, Paige. Yes, her mom had said that to her so many times in those final days, exhorting Paige to bravery when she herself faced the great unknown. If that hadn't already been Paige's mantra, she would have been shamed into accepting it by the very dichotomy of life events, hers and her mother's, and how courageously her mother had accepted it all.

Digging into the photographs, she pulled out handful after handful, spreading them beside her on the white blanket. Here, Paige's high school graduation, Paige standing among a dozen other students. And here, Paige in her cap and gown. She flipped the images over, looking for handwriting on the back and finding none. She performed the same on a dozen more, locating no date, no note, nor markings of any sort. Digging deeper into the box, she uncovered older snapshots—photos likely abandoned, given the haste with which her mother had left everything behind—early days of school, a series of her hunting for shells and sea glass along the beach, a shot of Paige holding a dark-colored kitten on the living room floor next door. She took a closer look at the last one, eyeing the single white paw on the kitten, the other three feet of the kitten tucked close and not visible in the image. She glanced at Shadow's two white paws stretched across her pillow. Could it be?

Turning the photo over, she found a caption in her mother's writing. *Paige with Spooky at ten weeks.*

She'd been forced to leave Spooky behind only a few months later. She hadn't totally forgotten him, despite what she'd said to Shadow. She'd been heartbroken. Holding the photo up, she compared it to Shadow's sleeping form. A seventeen-year-old cat wasn't unheard of, but would her father have kept Spooky around after she and her mother were gone? What had Liam said about Shadow? That he'd found the cat when he moved into her father's house.

"Shadow?" The cat meowed and peered in her direction, twisting his head in a flirtatious move. "Spooky?" He meowed again, which, she knew, meant nothing but a response to her tone. Besides, if he was her old kitten, after sixteen years he wouldn't recall the name he'd gone by for a few short months.

But that wasn't exactly accurate. If her father had kept Spooky, he would likely have maintained the name as well. Scooping up all the photos, Paige flung them back into the box and secured the lid. With the advent of recall, she knew her kitten had possessed another telltale marking, one she'd vowed was unlike any other. It was the reason she'd picked him out of the litter.

Careful not to startle the cat, Paige slid across the bed and began to pet his belly. Once he got to purring full bore, she slowly turned him over, catching a glimpse of white fur. A surge of excitement swept through her and she rolled him all the way onto his back to get a better look.

Bitter disappointment burned through Paige's veins when she didn't find the half moon bib of white fur. She blinked tears from her lashes. Had she really expected to find Shadow and Spooky were the same cat? After all these years? How could she be so foolish?

Shadow, confused by her sobbing, leapt from the pillow to the floor. Unable to set her distress aside, Paige put her head where his had been, stifling the noise of her perplexing sorrow into the mound of foam and cloth. Why should it matter? Why should it freaking matter? Spooky had vanished with her childhood, and Shadow belonged to a man who confused her. To have thought for one moment she'd found her long-ago pet had been irrational and infantile. And yet, if they had been the same cat, she would have found a connection between past and present that brought joy and not pain.

The type of rollercoaster emotions she'd been experiencing, not just since her arrival in Alcina Cove but for many months before, were doing her no good. What she needed was the type of distraction that didn't involve a man in her bed or the solving of mysteries. She loved fireworks. They thrilled her in a way few entertainments managed. Tomorrow night, with all due precaution, after treating herself to a meal in town, she was going to stand beneath the sky and be diverted.

"So there," she announced to the room in general. Alerted by her change in tone, Shadow crept cautiously back. She cuddled him close to her chest and, since he appeared he would tolerate the attention, decided the next course of action was a nap with an innocuous warm body.

* * * *

Liam lengthened his stride as he traversed the street between passing cars. He smoothed down the hair along his neck, stemming the sensation of eyes observing him. Nothing he could do about being trailed or watched. Nothing he could do about any of this except follow through. He headed with determination toward the drugstore.

Anxiety and an outlandish excitement coursed together through his bloodstream, heightening his senses. Anger, too, which served to temper the rest in a way that made him think clearly, almost concisely, of the events rushing to a head. He darted through each action and possible reaction in search of any flaw, but so far he'd found none.

That didn't mean defects wouldn't pop up. Dangerous errors. He was only one cog, not the entire mechanism. A great deal existed beyond his control. All he could do was his best to protect those he cared about.

Even if she ended up hating him.

Chapter 18

Driving along Main Street, Paige passed the various shops and people thronging the sidewalks. Dan Stauffer hadn't been wrong about the crowds. Apparently they began to congregate early for the Fourth of July display. She had to break continually for pedestrians in the crosswalks. Many of the shops displayed flags and banners as wells as signs in red, white, and blue proclaiming holiday sales. While waiting for two families to traverse the crosswalk by the drugstore, Paige perused the items listed for sale on the sign in a huge plate glass window. In her side mirror, she caught sight of a man in a distinctive purple shirt crossing between traffic close enough to the back of her car that her brake lights emblazoned the khaki covering his legs. He continued past with an aggressive swagger onto the sidewalk to her left. Paige gasped and lowered her window, leaning her head out.

"Hey!"

He didn't turn in response, but she knew it was him. The Bookmark Man. She kept her gaze on him as he continued across the street until the driver behind her tapped his horn. The crosswalk had cleared so she shot forward, trying not to lose sight of the man in the oblong of the side mirror, and made a quick left into the angle of an open parking space halfway down the block. Throwing the car into park, she got out and hurried as fast as she could manage along the crowded sidewalk, making her way back toward the drugstore. She was certain he'd gone in there.

As she wove a path between people with everything from packages, chairs, and coolers in hand to children in tow, Paige pulled her cell phone from her purse in anticipation of calling Dan or snapping a photo at a safe distance. Reaching the drugstore, she pushed her way inside. It appeared they were giving everything away, if the jammed aisles were any indication. "Excuse me. Sorry. Would you let me through, please?"

She rose repeatedly up onto her toes, hoping to see farther into the store over the display shelves.

At the building's back end, she spotted a flash of purple on a patron making a beeline toward the pharmacy counter. As Paige reached the end of the aisle, one of the store employees stepped out in front of her wheeling a laden cart for restocking the nearest shelf. Paige put out both hands to keep from being run over.

"Sorry, miss!"

"No problem," Paige said, trying to ease by without success. "Could you move this, please?"

"I'm trying."

"I'm in a hurry."

"So's everyone."

Paige half climbed over the cart to get around it, ignoring the young girl's comments about rudeness. By the time she reached the pharmacy window, there was no sight of the man. A bright red Exit sign indicated a door at the back, but she didn't think he'd gone out that way since it wasn't standard egress from the store and would probably have set off an alarm. Determined, she paced the ends of each aisle, taking a moment to study the customers down each one.

A hand closed around her wrist. Paige jerked free, her head snapping up as a familiar, rumbling voice spoke her name.

"Liam," she cried, "when did you get back?"

"A little while ago. I haven't even gone home yet. I had an errand here at the pharmacy. What's wrong?"

"He's here. The bookmark guy is here."

Liam's face blanched white beneath his dark hair, the scar standing out like silver twine. Half-circles like pale bruises marked his eyes from sleepless nights. "Stay where you are. Point me in the direction you saw him."

Lifting her arm, she complied. "He's wearing khakis and a purplish shirt. His hair is a mixture of blond and gray, I think."

"Stay put," he reiterated, and rushed off. Paige took two steps after him and stopped. She clambered up onto a step stool for sale in order to obtain a better vantage point. Liam, easily visible because of his height, headed straight for the far wall where she'd pointed. Although she could no longer see the other man, she hoped Liam would be able to spot him soon enough. When Liam strode quickly toward the front, Paige jumped off the stool and headed in that direction, hoping to reach the entrance before either man did.

What she found was Liam coming back in the automatic door with a look of frustration. Spotting her, he shook his head.

"Did you at least see him?"

"I saw someone dressed as you described. He went out the front door, but I couldn't find him outside. You're sure it was the same guy?"

"Yes." She rushed past him toward the exit. Outside, she visually searched the sidewalk in both directions, and went so far as to step out into the street in case he'd already crossed. Liam followed, taking a few steps north, peering into cars. He returned.

"I'm calling Dan," she said when he neared. "Maybe they have cameras in the store."

"Good idea." Liam waited beside her as she made the call. She hung up after Dan promised a car would be out to check the area.

"Liam," she said, "what are you doing here?"

"I shop here."

"I mean, you left a note saying you would be gone for a couple of days. Although you did send me that text saying you would see me soon, I had no idea when you were coming back. Is everything all right?"

"It will be," he said.

Paige studied him with a frown. "Even though I haven't said anything, I do still have a couple of questions from the other night. Whenever you're ready," she added.

"Okay." He didn't appear too sure but was putting a brave front on it.

Paige nodded as an idea came to her. "And right now, you weren't following me? Not keeping an eye on me?"

His lips curled. "I'm pretty sure you ran into me inside the store, not the other way around."

"No. You grabbed my arm. I hadn't seen you yet."

"I'm not following you. I swear." He put an arm around her shoulders and pulled her close. She stepped right up against him, breathing in his scent, amazed at how familiar she found it, how much she'd longed for it. Liam's mouth pressed down on her hair. "I've missed you."

She smiled. "I got the note. I've missed you right back." The rush of closeness, of pleasure, made her feel exposed and defenseless, but she couldn't quell the genuine happiness.

Liam lowered his arms to his sides. "I had a few things to take care of. They came up rather suddenly."

"I understand."

"Paige."

She smiled. "Liam."

Celia Ashley

He bent slightly from the waist so that his face hovered near hers. "I would kiss you now, but you'd probably melt like an ice cream cone all over the sidewalk."

With a snort, Paige took a step away, fitting her fingers into his. "You hold yourself in pretty high esteem, do you?"

His laughter turned her insides to pudding. She wanted to throw him in her car and take him home, do things to him for which pudding was a very good consistency. Instead, she released his hand and hiked her purse back up on her shoulder.

"Do you have any interest in fireworks, Neighbor Gray?" she asked.

He twirled a skein of her hair around his finger and let it go. "Besides the kind you make?"

"Yes," she said, suppressing an urge to kick him in the shins for the reference. "The kind that are generated for public display. Tonight. Here. Well, somewhere in this town."

"So, this is like a date?"

"Exactly like a date."

"Perfect. We'll have dinner first?"

"Those were my plans, all by my lonesome. It will be so much nicer with you."

Liam turned solemn. "Everything will be better, I promise you."

She squeezed his fingers. "Don't make promises like that. Blanket assurances in life don't usually work out."

"Okay. We'll be better. How's that?"

She heard the hitch in his voice and knew he had reservations. Fine. So did she. But this time, unlike any other, she was willing to take the chance.

A police unit pulled up in the street, followed by a second one. Paige dropped Liam's hand and went to the nearest car to speak with Dan, Liam at her heels.

Dan leaned from the window, peering over his sunglasses. "Did you get a better look at him this time?"

Paige shook her head. "I only saw him from behind. But I recognized him. The way he moved. His body shape. The cut of his hair. You have to remember, I watched him walking away from me for quite a distance before I picked up the bookmark. Liam might have gotten a better look than I did today. He was in the drugstore when I went in. He saw the guy leave."

Dan gave Liam the once over. The two men then nodded at each other like wary dogs.

"Stauffer," said Liam by way of greeting. No handshake. None of the other civilities people normally engaged in. Their strained interaction was excessive. Teaching eighth grade kids should have educated her to the way of male tactics, but perhaps the kids needed to grow up a bit more to start behaving so immaturely.

"Gray. Did you see which way he went?"

"If I did," Liam said, "I'd be on him already."

The look Dan shot him was frankly disapproving. "Not your job."

"Maybe not. But if the opportunity arises, I'm not letting him walk away."

A muscle in Dan's jaw twitched. "Did you get a look at him?"

"Just what he was wearing. Khaki pants, hole in the right rear pocket. A dark violet T-shirt with a logo across the shoulder blades. Said 'Victory' or something like that. I never saw his face."

Paige's eyes widened. She hadn't even noticed the logo. "You're observant," she said.

"I've learned to pay attention."

Dan surveyed the exchange. His eyes, barely visible to Paige behind his sunglasses, flicked back and forth between them to finally rest on Liam. "You saw all that, but you didn't see which way he went once he got outside."

Paige heard the swift intake of Liam's breath at her shoulder. He didn't bother to answer.

Dan picked up his radio, giving the description to the officer in the other vehicle, who began to cruise slowly down the street. "Did he look familiar to you?"

"No," said Paige. "I told you that. I've never—"

"I was talking to your boyfriend, Paige."

Paige shut up, too shocked to be offended. She turned to Liam. She could see Dan's antagonistic behavior had affected him. Liam met Dan's gaze in a steady, smoldering contest.

"Not at all," he said.

Dan drummed his fingers on the steering wheel, shifting his focus to the crowd on the sidewalk. "I'd like you to come into the station, Gray, and talk to someone there. You might be able to add to Paige's description so we could get a better overall sketch."

To Paige's surprise, Liam simply asked, "When?"

"The sooner the better."

"I could be there in an hour or so."

With a nod at both of them, Dan pulled away into the Fourth of July congestion. Liam took her hand and gave it a brief squeeze. "We'll eat first? It's a while until the fireworks start."

"Sure," she agreed, a little taken aback by his agreement to meet Dan at the station. She assumed he wanted her to go with him when the time came. "I've got a chair and a blanket in my car. Wasn't sure which I was going to use."

"You were really going alone?"

"Who do you think I would have gone with? Dan?"

He appeared to contemplate that for a moment, a mocking comment playing on his lips, but his expression changed, sobered. "No. I'm not worried about him. It's the alone part that concerns me. You need to be careful."

He kissed her then, as he'd promised, and she did nearly melt like frozen confection in the hot sun.

Chapter 19

Paige sat in an uncomfortable blue plastic chair in the police station lobby. Her folded hands rested on her thighs, left thumb stuck inside the fist of the right. Dan had promised to keep Liam no more than a quarter hour. The minute hand had long ago passed the half hour mark and was moving up the left side of the clock face on the wall. Photos flanked the utilitarian timepiece on either side, community events at which the police had played a part. She recognized Dan in one and the dedication of the stone circle at Alcina Cove Nature Preserve in another. As the photo was filled with people and held a caption beneath, Paige rose and crossed the small foyer to see if any of those pictured might be Felicia Woodward.

Left from center, beside Alcina Cove's mayor, stood the woman identified by the legend beneath as Felicia Woodward. The teenage girl of the yearbook photo remained evident in this older version, smiling as she shook hands with the professor who had discovered the standing stones beneath the encroaching forest. Paige could tell by the shot that Felicia had said something humorous because everyone but the three of them faced the photographer's lens, both the mayor and Columbus gazing at Felicia with open laughter.

What had the woman's son said? That she was wicked funny. Knowing her mother had possessed such a friend, a companion who had provided her joy and alliance, made Paige's lips curl in a fondness as dear as if she already knew the woman. She would definitely return to the nature center to speak with Felicia Woodward—avoiding the stone circle, of course.

Remembering, Paige's gaze strayed to the stones rising in eerie formation from the earth behind them. The photographer had captured a cool air mist circling around the rocks, floating low to the ground, drifting up and around the upright boulders here and there in a foggy caress. Paige reflected on the mythology of Alcina's lovers transformed to stone by her once she'd finished with them. Paige had been a little like that. Not turning them to stone, of course, but turning them away, pushing them from her life, often without plausible explanation.

Paige, I worry about you.

I know, Mom. I worry about me, too.

Paige blinked to clear her vision of a memory overlapping the photo before her. She blinked again, slowly, deliberately, and stepped closer to the framed image. Coiled by fog and pressed against one of the stones, a dark figure stood, nearly blended into the myriad shadows of trees and undergrowth beyond the circle.

Footsteps sounded on the linoleum behind her. "Paige?"

Paige lifted her hand and tapped the glass with her fingernail. Liam stepped up to her shoulder, leaning close.

"Holy shit," he whispered. "Is that—"

"Not a ghost," said Paige. "It's my dad."

* * * *

Liam watched Paige pick at her nails in the front seat of his Jeep. An uneven color splotched her cheek like a hand slap. "I guess that was a shock," he said. "You've probably been carrying him around in your head a certain way, and then to see him in everyday context threw you for a loop." He waited. She didn't speak. Liam turned the key in the ignition.

"Where are we going?" Paige asked.

"Over to the ball field. Or don't you feel like staying for the display now?"

"No, I do. Sorry." She straightened, turning to look out the side window and then ahead. "It'll be fun."

"You don't quite sound like you believe that."

She surprised him with a bolt of laughter. "Don't mind me. I'll snap out of it soon enough. Soon as those boomers start going off for sure. What do you think he was doing there?"

Liam steered around a man pulling a folded stroller out of the open door of a car. "I'm assuming you don't mean the creep in the drugstore right now."

"You assume correctly."

"I don't know. Came for the ceremony?"

"He looked like he was hiding."

"Maybe he was, maybe he wasn't. That photo is a snapshot of an instant in time. He could have been checking out the circle and something the mayor said caught his attention and he came closer to listen. Paige, you can't judge anything about your father's character through that one photograph."

"I'm not."

She spoke with particular emphasis. He wondered how much she remembered about her father from when she was young. Enough, he supposed. But sometimes people weren't quite what you thought they were. Memories could be colored by misperception, by interpretation, by the influence of others.

"We can avoid the crowds if you'd rather. There's a place we used to go… People will be there, but not like at the ball field. We could even watch from the comfort of the Jeep. What do you think?"

She agreed, reaching into the small cooler she'd transferred over from her car. With a smile, she handed him a bottle of water, twisting the cap off before she did so. Once she'd grabbed her own, she drank thirstily for several seconds before speaking. "So, were you any help to Dan with his sketch?"

Liam set his water in the pocket on his door. "I suppose."

She shot him a sideways glance. "Does he have ideas he's not telling me about?"

"He has ideas not worth telling you about."

Paige snickered. "Suspicious of everything, that guy."

"That he is. Nature of the job, I guess."

"Diligence."

"Whatever."

Paige squeezed his arm. "He suspects you of something, I'm guessing."

"What makes you think that?"

"He told me I should talk to you about all of this."

Liam's hands tightened on the wheel. "That makes no sense. Did he think I broke into the cottage?"

"No," Paige answered. "He thought you were less than truthful, though. I, however, trust you implicitly."

Liam experienced a sudden tug of tension at the base of his skull. "Do you really, Paige? Even with all my secrets?"

She shrugged. "Let's say I'm starting to. And we all have secrets."

He wasn't ready for that degree of trust. Didn't deserve it or want it. Because he knew how much more she would hurt if he failed her. If? When.

"Liam?"

He said nothing, swinging the Jeep left and off the road up a dirt track. Sentinel Hill was more like a wide knoll rising unexpectedly out of the surrounding landscape and providing an unassailable ocean and town view from its peak. The crown had weathered over millennia to a plateau, making a perfect spot for camping or parking a vehicle to stargaze or indulge in the types of things one did in the dark with another person.

Although not exactly around the corner from his hometown, he'd driven up for parties with his buddies on weekends as a teenager and with high school dates. Those times had been on his mind when he suggested the spot to Paige. Driving at a snail's pace up the worn lane, he thought of Alice.

Not a place for intimacies with another woman. He hadn't been expecting Paige to leap into the backseat with him as if they were sixteen, but there'd been a passing fantasy. It was gone now.

As they drove onto the hilltop, Paige looked around. "What is this place? I don't think I ever knew it existed."

Liam lowered his eyes as he pulled up the brake on the Jeep, studying her hand still lying on his arm. Somehow, with that statement, he felt infinitely better. The idea she might have been here engaging in the same type of activities he'd once enjoyed had, ridiculously, made him jealous.

* * * *

The first rocket went up about half past nine, shooting brilliant white stars across the sky. Paige forgot she'd been about to pass the bag of chips back to Liam and clutched the crinkling paper sack to her chest.

"You were really going to eat all this stuff you brought by yourself?"

"Yep," she said, "I really was."

In the dark, she heard her own *oohs* and *aahs* echoed by the watchers gathered on the hilltop. She settled back against the angled seat with the intent of not looking away from the sky until the finale. When the second, screaming whistle rent the night, Liam leaned across and kissed her on the mouth, pulling away with the bag of chips in his fist.

"You taste like barbecue," he said, "and salt."

"So do you. Funny how that works. No surprises later, then." She grinned at him.

He left her to her enjoyment after that, the fingers of one hand entwined around her own, the other firmly engaged in finishing off the barbecue potato chips with the occasional pause to fish the water from the door. Every boom reverberated in her chest. The sky above the small ballpark rained color and transformation in dazzling pyrotechnic skill. Paige didn't anticipate the grin leaving her face before morning, especially when Liam's hand tightened around hers. She glanced over at him for a second. His focus was not on the display or on her, but caught by something outside the Jeep's passenger side. With a catch in her throat, Paige swung around to her open window.

Someone stood right beside the door. Liam moved like lightning beside her, reaching past out the window and grabbing shirt in his fist. "Who the fuck are you?"

"Wait. Liam, wait! I know him." Paige pushed back in her seat, giving Liam room to withdraw. The man next to the car tugged on his shirt front to smooth it down. He bent from the waist, peering in at Paige.

"I'm sorry," he said. "I didn't figure on scaring anybody. Did I hear you say you know me?"

"Yes," Paige answered, moving closer so he could see her. "We met the other day. I was asking about your mother. I'm Paige Waters."

"Yeah, right," the younger Woodward said. "I remember that. How're you doing? Enjoying the show?"

Liam leaned forward again, an arm across the dashboard. "Did you want something here?"

"What? Oh, yeah, forgot."

Paige wondered if Felicia's son had been drinking. She was sure of it when he stumbled a bit, digging around in his pocket. Not drunk, but having himself a good time on the Fourth. Paige wondered if perhaps he had spoken with his mother and she'd given him a message for her. How he'd known to find her in Liam's white Jeep was a mystery unless, of course, he'd seen them pull in. It hadn't been dark then.

But no, that couldn't be right, either. When she'd spoken to him a few seconds ago, he hadn't known her. "Billy? It is Billy, right? I think that was on your name tag."

"Yep," he said, "Billy. Hold on, I've got it right here."

"Got what?" Paige wriggled closer to the door edge, squinting at his antics in the dark.

Billy pulled something small from his pocket with a flourish. "Here. He said to give this to you. I didn't know it was you, though. He just said, 'give this to that lady in the Jeep over there.'"

Taking her hand, he pressed a square of thick paper into Paige's palm. Before Paige could say anything in response, he strode away into the dark with a wave. Paige dropped the door to the glove box open for light and unfurled her fingers.

"Who was that?" Liam asked.

"Billy Woodward. The third, I guess. And someone Dan needs to speak with."

"Why is that?"

Paige held up her shaking hand. "This is a photo of my mother. A photo which, up until the night the bookmark went missing, I'd wager resided in my wallet."

Liam swore, a string of words all in keeping with the one he'd uttered in his recent demand for Billy's identity, and then he flung open the door.

Yanking his keys out of his pocket, he tossed them in her direction. "Lock it up. I'll be back."

As soon as he vanished into the night, Paige secured the doors to the Jeep and closed the windows, barely leaving enough space at the top for circulation. She clasped the photo to her breast, teeth firmly entrenched in her lip. Damn it, damn it, damn it.

Outside, the fireworks continued unabated, the revelers unaware of the drama that took place in their small corner of the field. She had convinced herself the bookmark theft was a sick quirk. Pilfering her mother's photo indicated, as Liam had once suggested, a far more personal involvement. A vendetta, perhaps. But why? Could this be something to do with her father? Was that why Dan had been asking her questions about his associates? What in heaven's name could her dad have been involved in?

In her anxiety, Paige had begun rocking in the car seat. She forced herself to count to ten, out loud and slowly. Hysterics would do no one any good. Panic was not her usual method of coping. Disbelief? Loads. And rage? Yeah, that too.

Reaching for the door handle, Paige noted a flaring light stabbing into her peripheral line of vision. Well beyond the harbor, a party boat had sent up a rocket in private celebration, orange sparks spreading in an umbrella in the sky above. She recognized the reflected beauty on the rippling water despite her agitation, but summarily dismissed her admiration. She needed to find Liam. She wouldn't have him hunting through the people on the hilltop on her behalf by himself.

Another rocket went up over the water. The car to her left started its engine and rolled out of place. People standing beneath the sky moved aside. She heard another car and then another, headlights coming on all around. Liam appeared at the door, sliding on the grass. She let him in.

"Why are people leaving?"

"Buckle up," he said. "That's a distress call out there."

Chapter 20

Paige couldn't tell what Liam thought or felt. Concentration had settled over his features like a mask. The knuckles on the hand wrapped around the wheel were the color of bone. With the other, he shifted through gears in rapid succession. Paige's fingers dug into the seat on either side. She thought about her father.

"Liam?"

"I have to do this, Paige. I've seen these signals go up numerous times since I've moved to Alcina Cove, and I've ignored them. It's killed me, but I can't help thinking—"

"About that night you tried to save my father? Coming home and finding your family gone?"

"Yes."

Liam slowed the Jeep as they neared the harbor. Red and blue strobe lights cut through the night, reflecting across the onlookers' faces in a jarring hue. Paige's heart leapt with the same rhythmic intensity as the shadows jumping like animation across building fronts. The area was already a mass of activity, mostly official from what she could tell, with the Marine Patrol in the forefront to keep the growing crowd cordoned off and under control. Liam swung the Jeep into what wouldn't have been a parking spot on a normal day and propelled himself from the vehicle before he'd fully opened the door.

"Stay here."

Paige was getting a little sick of those words and, as usual, did not heed them. She snatched the keys he'd left dangling from the ignition and clambered out, locking the Jeep behind her. She had to sprint to catch up to him.

He glanced down at her as she appeared at his elbow. "I told you—"

"Yeah, I heard you. Word to the wise. Don't give me orders. They tend to backfire."

He said nothing but she glimpsed a flicker in the muscle of his jaw. She hoped it was amusement.

A man in a dark T-shirt with an emblem emblazoned across the breast and a radio to his mouth held up a flashlight as they approached, not shining the beam at them but indicating that he wanted them to stop where they were. Paige obliged but Liam continued forward, speaking close to the man's ear in a rapid exchange. Paige couldn't hear a word of it, but twice they glanced back in her direction. Not waiting for the third time, she joined them.

"We can go on," Liam said. "Are you sure you want to do this?"

"Are you?"

His brows lowered in a brief frown and then he squeezed her upper arm. "Yep."

He took her hand and tugged her forward through the turmoil. People ran back and forth shouting into radios, yelling across open space, coordinating the rescue effort. Floodlights lit the docks. Paige saw small boats cutting slowly through the water, searchlights on their bows that slashed a direct beam across the rippling, dark harbor for employment, she supposed, in seeking survivors if the ship went down. Farther out, a larger vessel—a Coast Guard search and rescue craft —had already reached the signaling ship. She and Liam were stopped again, this time by a man in uniform.

"If you're short-handed, I can pilot a boat." Releasing her hand, Liam pulled his wallet out of his pocket and displayed identification for the man standing by the barrier. The uniformed official nodded in response.

"You can go down," he said. "Might not be necessary, but the help is appreciated. You, miss, will have to stay here."

"Understood," Paige answered and stepped back. Liam passed a grazing kiss across her forehead before moving with a long, swift stride toward the far end of the dock. "Take care, Liam," she whispered at his departing back. He was a brave man, choosing to face his fears this way. At least the sea wasn't choppy. Whatever had disabled the ship, it wasn't something likely to threaten the rescuers.

With a nod at the official, Paige moved from the main activity. No need to be in the way. She couldn't do anything to help. She only hoped Liam would be all right. After what he'd told her concerning his attempts to save her father, this scenario had to be dredging up some troubling memories.

She, on the other hand, had nothing to compare it to, despite the circumstances of her father's demise. She hadn't been there, hadn't sat by his bedside. Sometimes it seemed less than real because of that. An orphaned adult. No parents, no brothers or sisters. She did have an aunt out in California and planned, perhaps next year, to visit, but in the meantime, with the exception of her friends left behind in Tennessee, she was alone. "Good God, don't start feeling sorry for yourself on that account." The sound of her own voice startled her and she glanced around. From about a dozen feet away a man nodded in her direction. The cigarette in his mouth smoldered with a deep ruddy glow in the shadows. "Sorry," she said. "Sometimes I talk to myself."

He gave a short laugh and went back to gazing toward the water, smoke drifting up into the bright light beaming over the fence at his back. Paige reached into her pocket to fish out the photograph Billy Woodward gave her. She suspected he would be found blameless in this whole thing once Dan spoke with him, but Billy might be able to provide a more complete description of the perpetrator. Of course, a description, even a sketch, would be worthless if they didn't come up with an identity to attach to the face.

Holding the photo close, Paige was able to make out Debra Waters' features in the tangled crossing of shadow and light. Her mom hadn't been one for photos. But this one the woman had liked. The picture had been taken in July, the year before her mom had gotten sick. At a barbecue. And the laughter had reached Debra's eyes in a way it rarely did. Paige had always imagined her mom as the stronger one of the pair of them. Lately, she'd begun to wonder if Debra hadn't just been good at hiding her weaknesses. Maybe that was all anyone could hope for, really. Not revealing to others your fragility, your fears.

"You believe in ghosts?"

"Bloody hell," Paige cried as she recoiled, the photo fluttering from her fingers. She bent and snatched the snapshot back as she sidled away from the speaker. She smelled the cigarette smoke and realized the man she'd apologized to had moved up next to her without her knowing it. She had to be more careful. Liam would be pissed, and rightly so.

"Why do you ask?" She shoved the photo back into her pocket, taking a moment to collect herself. The stranger stood with his back to the floodlight, his hair in a halo around his shadowed face.

"Because I've seen them. I see one now."

Paige glanced toward the water where the boats were running in slow formation like geese in flight, perhaps with Liam manning one. Although not a believer in any sort of mystical occurrences before her arrival back in Alcina Cove, she now felt she had reason to reassess her beliefs. Had the man at her side some uncanny knowledge of death out on the sea this night? She asked him as much. He laughed, startling her. She whipped around to face him.

"Something's funny about this situation?" she demanded.

"You probably don't see it, I expect."

The fine hairs shifted at Paige's nape beneath her ponytail. She shivered. "What? The humor or the ghost?"

"You never look in the mirror. See what's staring back at you?"

"I see myself in the mirror. Nothing else." Paige started walking backward in the direction of the uniformed man at the barricade. "Whatever you see is your business."

The man lifted the cigarette from his side and took another drag, the ember flaring. Smoke curled above his head. "We're talking about you. What you see. Don't you see your dead mama? You're the spitting image."

A sudden, searing rage surged through her. Paige clenched her hands into fists and took two steps toward the man. "Who are you? Tell me. Tell me who you are and what you want."

He sniggered. "You don't seem much scared right now. But you will be."

"Of you? I don't think so."

"I can make you scared. I can hurt you, Paige Waters. Don't you ever doubt it."

Paige launched herself at the man as he turned away. She landed on his back with one arm around his throat, knocking him to his knees with the impact of her body against his spine. Aiming a punch at the side of his head, her knuckles slammed into his skull with a sickening crunch as a finger snapped. In the next instant, she was sailing through the air, crashing up against the fence, bouncing to the ground. His foot came down, hard, on the bone of her hip near the small of her back, causing sharp pain to shoot down her leg. Blood and agony whistled in her ears as she tried, without breath in her lungs, to move, to defend herself. Pounding footfalls bounced on the earth beneath her grazed cheek. She heard the man above her snarl as one last kick caught her in the thigh before he ran.

* * * *

"Jesus, Paige, what were you thinking?"

Paige looked from Liam, who had spoken, to Dan, who had not. "I wasn't," she said. "Not for one second." She touched the ace bandage on her hand. Her finger hadn't broken, only jammed.

"You know I can't charge him with assault if we find him," Dan said. He almost sounded amused. "You attacked him, and he could, reasonably, claim self defense."

"He kicked her on the ground!"

"Liam," said Paige quietly. "He knows that. I think Dan is only trying to make a point."

"No better look at him this time," Dan commented, not as question, but in reiteration of a previously stated fact.

"No," Paige said. "I'm wondering if he stages it that way. If he does, that makes him creepier than ever."

"He knew her name, Stauffer. He knows who she is."

Paige raised her gaze again to Liam, finding him and Dan in the middle of some kind of eyeball showdown. Shifting on the hospital bed, Paige grimaced at the pain in her hip. "He knew my mom, too, apparently. Let's not forget that. I'm sure they weren't buddies, but he knew of her. Maybe there was some kind of obsession there?" Paige blew out a sudden breath. "Again with the looks? What gives with you two?"

"We're both worried about you," said Liam.

"Dan doesn't know me that well, so I doubt he's worried except from a case standpoint. There's a lunatic out there. For that matter, you don't know me all that well, either." Liam's subtle change of expression brought instant remorse. "I'm sorry. I hurt and I'm cranky and I want to go home. None of which is any excuse for what I just said. Dan, I apologize to you, too. You both have gone above and beyond, and I appreciate it. I really do. But I want the doctor with the damned paperwork so I can get out of here."

Paige caught another mute exchange out of the corner of her eye before Dan excused himself, saying he would check for the doctor. Liam sat on the bed beside her. He slipped both hands around her undamaged one and lifted her wrist onto his thigh.

"You do need to go home," he said.

"Liam, I didn't mean to hurt your feelings. Don't ever tolerate that from me."

"You need to go home," he repeated, "to Tennessee."

Her stomach muscles tensed as if anticipating a blow. What he said made sense, was logical, and obviously discussed with Dan, if she read the last eye contact between them correctly. "I don't want to."

"I know you had a plan to find out about your father and mother, the life you left behind, but—"

"That's not the only reason." She tightened her fingers in his. "That is not the only reason I won't leave."

"You're a very stubborn woman, Paige."

"And I think you like that about me."

"One of the things I like about you. One of the numerous things." He kissed her, pulling her close, and she breathed an ouch into the hollow of his mouth, but she wouldn't let him back away. After several moments she did, though, leaning her forehead against his chin.

"We're going to have to be careful until you feel better. No acrobatics," Liam murmured against the hair curling up from her loosened ponytail to snag in his stubbled beard. "And we'll come up with a plan—a plan you need to stick to—to keep you safe."

She nodded against him.

"I wouldn't be able to live with myself if anything happened to you, Paige."

She had been about to say "not your responsibility," but she kept her sentiment to herself. Maybe, to some degree, it was his responsibility. Maybe his sense of duty, of accountability, fit in with her vague definition of what lovers should be to each other. And maybe she wanted that when she never really had it before.

Paige straightened at a short bout of throat-clearing near the door. She flinched at the movement, turning to find Dan watching them.

"Well?" he said.

Liam shook his head.

"Right. If you two weren't clinging to each other like furry little littermates, you might have been able to convince her otherwise."

Paige's lips twisted at his comment, a surge of ridiculous affection expunging her earlier anger at the man.

Dan nodded. "I'm heading out. We'll talk more on this subject over the next couple of days. Oh, and I have a visit planned to young Billy tomorrow. See what he has to say."

Dan departed without fanfare. Paige could see the doctor through the doorway at the main desk and figured he'd be in any minute. "In Britain, they call what we were just doing 'snogging,' I believe."

"Yes," agreed Liam with a hint of laughter in his voice.

"I like the sounds of that. It's homey and comforting and down-to-earth, somehow. Also, reminds me of food. I don't know why."

"All right. Snogging it is, then."

"And lots of it. As soon as we're somewhere not surrounded by Plexiglas panels."

"Deal," he said. The doctor came in and Liam rose from the bed. Paige took a deep breath, readying herself to fool the physician into believing she felt absolutely wonderful so she could get the hell out of the ER without argument.

Chapter 21

Flipping the ring in her fingers, Paige found the key for the deadbolt and inserted it. She turned the brass to disengage the tumblers.

Liam's hand fell across hers. "Hold on."

Paige pulled back with a start, thinking Liam had spotted something amiss with the door, but when she looked up at him, she saw his attention drawn to the waterline, eyes narrowed. Paige followed his gaze and sucked in a breath.

"Is that what you've been seeing, down there by the water?" he questioned.

In the same unwavering pace she'd witnessed before, the man with the lantern dangling at his side moved beside the surf. With the exception of certain details, portions of his body appeared almost translucent.

"Yes," she whispered.

"And it's not the same guy who—"

"No."

"Good to know. It's not who I thought you might be seeing, either."

"And who might that have been?"

"A neighbor," he answered with a dismissive shrug.

"So all that blather about ghosts and mirages was…?"

"Not blather."

Paige frowned. Her head had started to hurt along the route home. The doctor had checked for signs of concussion, but she hadn't hit her head. Not directly, although the back of her skull had come into brief contact with the fence after the rest of her body slammed into it. The dull ache was probably the aftermath of adrenaline flooding her veins. Driving had been difficult, but she hadn't wanted to leave her car in town. Liam had to satisfy himself with following close behind in the Jeep. When they arrived, they'd found an officer in a patrol car stationed on the shoulder across the road and had been informed, in no uncertain terms, that he, or someone else from the department, would be there all night.

With a sigh, Paige removed the keys from the door. "Since we've got a patrol car right out front, it's probably safe for us to go down and check."

"That's not necessary."

"Seriously, let's go." Paige limped forward a little, then paused when she realized Liam was hanging back.

"You don't need to be walking down that hill," he said. "Let's just go inside."

"Why don't we stand here a few minutes? We'll see if he disappears or comes close enough for us to know for sure." She went back to Liam and fit herself under his arm. After several seconds she found herself leaning all her weight against him in order to release the pressure off her left side. He slid his hand beneath the curve of her arm in support.

"There's a legend I've written about in several iterations, but I've never seen the apparition others have spoken of. Do I think this might be it? I don't know. Normally, spirits don't appear with such clarity or frequency. Do I want to find out? Sure, I do. But staying here is a better option than lugging you down to that beach and back."

She smiled against soft fabric, breathing him in. She loved his scent. It was like both balm and aphrodisiac. She wondered on an exhausted tangent if there was some way to bottle the stuff.

"What is it?" she asked. "The legend, I mean." Pressing against him, she watched the floating light. Prior to the occurrence at the nature preserve and her injuries, she would have bolted down to the beach to prove Liam wrong with all his ghost stories, but since then…

"An old seaman lost his daughter at sea and reportedly walks the beach at night hoping for some sign of her washed upon the shore," Liam said.

"Good God, that's a terrible story."

"I don't make them up. I just write them down. But he's rather solid, isn't he?"

Paige tightened her fist, the keys biting into her palm. "He's been pretty solid to me every time."

Another glow caught her eye, appearing close to the top of the jetty. "Look. Over by the rocks." Liam's body stiffened against hers, the muscles in the arm across her back like whipcord. As a light bounced over the rocks and onto the beach—clearly a flashlight held in someone's hand and not a lantern's glow—he muttered under his breath.

"What's wrong?"

"Nothing," he said.

"I know you don't like trespassers."

"I don't."

Paige stood immobile as a sense of déjà vu overwhelmed her. Had she witnessed something similar long ago? Probably. She'd lived in the house next door for thirteen years. People coming down to the beach uninvited wouldn't be anything new. Yet her gaze kept drifting to the tide beyond the lantern's glow and the approach of what appeared to be two people with a flashlight. To the place where she'd seen the gulls her first night back in Alcina Cove, and the memory, just out of reach...

Mom, what is that?

Sweetheart, don't. It's nothing.

Mom, no, I can see—

Come away. We shouldn't be here.

She saw again the mounded kelp and stone, the image of a body in her mind's eye, the flash of starlight...or was it metal?

"Paige, are you all right?"

Liam was suddenly in full support of her sagging body. In one fluid motion, he scooped her up into his arms. She wrapped her hands behind his neck, poking him in the ear.

"Sorry."

"Sh, let's get you inside."

"Wait. Liam, look!"

The two figures with the flashlight strode in a direct line over the sand toward the man with the lantern. As Paige watched, they converged with him and tramped straight through without pause, as if nothing existed there. An instant later, the lantern and the form holding it blinked out of existence. Liam's breath rushed out in audible release.

"You did see that, too, right?"

He nodded against the side of her head. "I did."

Carrying on the wind, laughter reached Paige and Liam where they stood. A couple strode hand in hand, nearly lost against the water but for the gaily swinging flashlight between them. Trying for humor, Paige elbowed Liam's arm. "Aren't you going to run down there and chase them off?"

"Nope."

"Maybe we should find out what they saw?"

"Obviously," said Liam, turning his back on the ocean and the now frolicking couple, "they saw nothing."

Paige wrinkled her brow. To Paige, this incident had been less frightening than the occurrence within the circle of stone. The comparatively small frisson of trepidation she felt now mingled with strange excitement. An exhilaration Liam didn't appear to feel. Liam, the man who made a living—of sorts, as he had said—writing about the supernatural acted more uneasy than elated, a reaction she would not have expected from him. After the night they'd both had, his uneasiness was catching. She had the key to the door ready in her fingers as he carried her back to the cottage

* * * *

Liam lit the burner beneath the battered teapot to make Paige some tea. Shock's aftermath had reared its ugly head. Paige lay on the bed curled in a tight ball, an ice bag lodged against the ugly black bruise on her hip. He'd given her two aspirin and tried to convince her to let him fill the prescription the emergency room doctor had written, but she'd refused. Searching the metal cabinets above the counter for the box of tea supposedly inside, he eventually located a nearly empty container of chamomile and prepared a cup once the kettle whistled. He carried the mug on a plate with a couple of cream-filled cookies beside it.

"You're a very nice man, Liam Gray," she said as she rolled a little to reach for a cookie. He set the plate on the nightstand and sat with care on the mattress so he wouldn't jostle her.

"Not really."

"Don't argue with a sick lady."

"You're not sick. You are, however—"

"Extremely foolish? I know."

"Not foolish," he corrected. "Reckless, though, I will admit."

"Yeah, I got that memo tonight. In boldface type."

He tucked her hair behind her ear. She'd ripped the hair band out and tossed it on the counter as soon as he carried her in the door, but the elastic had bounced off into a corner somewhere. "You might have been seriously hurt, worse than you are now. What stopped him, do you know? Don't get me wrong. I'm grateful to whatever caused him to run, but I know the officer at the barrier said the bastard was already gone by the time he got to you."

Paige shook her head. "I heard—well, felt, really—footsteps on the ground, running toward us. I don't have a real clear recollection of much after that until the ambulance came. It was probably the Marine Patrol guy at the barrier. He just didn't get there in time to catch him."

Liam nodded. "Do you—do you mind if I get into bed with you? I want to hold you. That's all. Nothing else."

Scooting closer to the edge of the mattress, Paige made room for him to climb over and stretch out behind her. He reached for the crumpled blanket and spread it across both their bodies before circling her with one arm, pressing as near as he dared with her injured hip. "Let me know when you want that tea. I'll help you."

"Maybe later. I don't mind cold tea. For now, I think lying here like this is good."

He kissed her shoulder blade through a shirt much stained from her battle, then lowered his head onto his folded arm on the pillow.

"If I felt better…" she mumbled.

"I know."

"At least you got to see the ghost on the beach. That's got to be one thrill for the night."

"Sure."

"You don't sound thrilled."

"You've seen one ghost, you've seen them all."

"Liam."

"What about you? You're not even scared."

She was quiet so long he thought she'd dozed off, but then she stirred. "People are far scarier than something that goes bump in the night."

He felt like he'd been stabbed, eviscerated, left to bleed in a silent agony of guilt. "Paige, if I'd known, I wouldn't have left you. I should have—"

"Liam, stop—"

"I should have been there."

"Liam, this isn't the same. I'm not your wife, your daughter. And even that wasn't your fault."

"But instead of staying with you, I ran off to rescue someone else. Someone who didn't need rescuing, but even so—"

"Helping people appears to be your nature. Don't condemn yourself for that. I'm sure tonight was hard for you and I'm, well, I'm proud of you."

Liam said nothing. His heart swelled with gratitude.

"Besides, half of what happened was my fault. More than half. I got out of the Jeep at the dock. I lost it and jumped on the bastard."

"You did do that, didn't you?" Liam smiled. "God, Paige, you are…are…"

"Insane? Yeah."

"Okay. Rather wonderfully, in fact. And if you ever do anything like that again, I'll borrow Stauffer's manacles and handcuff you to the bed."

Silence again. Liam leaned up on an elbow, peering around her hair. "Paige?"

"Sorry. Just picturing that scenario."

Groaning, Liam tossed the covers off and got back out of the bed. "Not fair, Ms. Waters. You're broken, remember?"

"Only parts of me," she said, "and they're merely dislocated."

At the renewed reminder, Liam's brief and ill-timed flare of arousal faded. He knelt down on the floor beside the mattress, bending to look into Paige's eyes. After a moment, he smoothed the riotous curls back from her face. "You know I'd like nothing more than to make love to you, don't you? I probably think about it one second out of every sixty."

She snorted.

"But you've had a rough night. I realize that's an understatement, but that's where we'll leave it."

Paige studied his face, the mask of calm hiding deeper concern. "Your night hasn't been easy, either."

"But you should sleep. I'll—" He glanced around the room, sighting the paperback on the nightstand. "I'll read for a while."

"What? My little mystery novel?"

"I've read worse. Hell, I've written worse."

"I don't like being scared, Liam."

He kissed her on the forehead and stood. "I know you don't. But you're the bravest scared person I've ever met." He tucked the blanket around her shoulders and retrieved the book. Pulling the chair closer to the bed, he sat on the hard wooden seat, stretching out both legs, ankles crossed on the end of the mattress. As he opened the novel, a piece of paper fluttered to the floor.

"Don't lose that," Paige said sleepily, pulling the blanket up around her face to block the light. "Call me sappy, but I thought your note was very sweet when I found it. It made me smile."

Sweet? After he'd penned the message on the Post-It, he'd felt the sentiment rather abrupt, considering the night they'd shared. Still, he wasn't about to argue. Stretching his fingers out over the floorboards, he grabbed the paper between two of them and dropped it on the open page of the book to smooth the edges. His heart nearly stopped mid-beat.

MISS ME YET?

He hadn't written those words. But he knew who had.

Chapter 22

Paige awoke in darkness with a scream careening around inside her head. She knew it had stayed there and not escaped her open mouth when she found Liam fast asleep beside her, undisturbed. She listened to his even breathing, his body warm and solid against her back. After a minute, she eased out from beneath the blanket—no mean feat with her limbs protesting every movement—and stood beside the bed. The floor was cold beneath her feet even though the small window air conditioner wasn't running. The temperature outside had probably dropped. It did most nights. And what with that damned mouse-infested crawlspace directly beneath…well, she wouldn't think about the area under the cottage. Not tonight.

She padded into the bathroom to use the toilet. After twisting off the faucet and watching soapy water swirl down the drain, she lifted her head slowly to the mirror.

Don't you see your dead mama? You're the spitting image…

Maybe she was. She'd heard it often enough. But she'd always had her father's hair. She didn't thank him for it. Not for the mess of it, not for the reminder. Right now, she didn't look much like either of them. Her cheekbone was blackened, the side of her face swollen and her skin had a pasty, sullen cast to it. She leaned forward, tapping a finger to the glass.

"Lovely."

Whoever that asshole was, he'd known her mother in her younger days in Alcina Cove. Paige's resemblance to her parent before their flight South would be the most evident, not what her mother had become through loneliness and illness. The likelihood of an association to her father had grown into the most plausible connection. And why not? A couple of bastards together. Buddies with a common theme.

She shouldn't have let her anger get the best of her. But what the hell did he want? Could be Dan and Liam were right. She should go back to

Tennessee. But she wasn't a runner. She figured some things you learned were contrary to what you were taught. Like standing your ground.

Hearing a noise, Paige turned her back on her reflection and flicked off the light. She opened the door and stood a moment on the stained marble threshold, listening. She heard it again. Not Liam. Creeping toward the door, she paused a couple of feet away and waited. As soon as she heard the sound repeated, she hobbled to the door and threw the bolt.

"Come in here, Shadow."

Black against black, Liam's cat whisked inside. Scooting past her, he made a beeline for the bed and jumped onto it, momentarily startled to find the mattress occupied. Recognizing Liam, the cat settled down, curling up against his waist. Paige started to shut the door, her grasp already firm on the deadbolt, but stopped, attention captured by movement on the ocean.

A few hundred yards beyond the breakers, a small vessel moved without lights, cutting across the waves and leaving a foaming silver trail in its wake. Frowning, Paige stepped outside onto the doorstep and watched the ship until it rounded the jetty and disappeared from view. She supposed enough starlight and reflected illumination existed by which to navigate, but it was a foolish undertaking, running dark like that, especially when the outgoing tide tended to expose rock precariously close to the surface.

Dismissing someone else's stupidity as not her problem, Paige turned on her bare heel. She caught sight of a light in one of the windows next door through the tree branches. With a startled gasp, her mind leapt ahead in a frantic scramble for her cell phone's last location, but in the next instant, she recalled the timer plugged into the lamp on the living room table.

"Right. Idiot." She needed to calm down. Really, what she needed was Liam. If not for her battered condition and his obvious exhaustion, she would have woken him up in a most satisfying manner and sought both solace and forgetfulness in his arms. Wasn't that what she did best? Used a man and then let him go? But she didn't want to let Liam go. She wanted to hold onto him tight, a desire that seemed, in the bare bones hours just before dawn, a craving more desperate than adoring. Liam deserved better. He deserved someone unscathed and unscarred. She'd meant it when she'd called him a very nice man earlier. That description was, to her, one of the highest caliber. So few of them existed, nice men, especially outrageously sexy nice men. With a touch of mystery. He had that, too.

Shuffling unevenly through the darkened room, she located her abandoned mug of tea on the nightstand and sipped the sweet room temperature liquid. Mug in hand, she made her way over to the side window and peered out between the curtains in the direction of her childhood home. As a breeze rattled long pine needles, the bulb burning brightly between the parted drapes at the side living room window appeared to leap from side to side. As soon as the wind settled, so did the light, returning to steady constancy. It was important to recognize how easily one could be fooled by variants. She needed to take more time, not be so damned reactionary. She needed to recognize certain truths about herself, about the people in her life, and accept them. If she never found out all she needed to about her parents, so be it. Life would go on.

As for the bookmark-photo-stealing lunatic—well now, that was a different matter.

"Hey."

"Is for horses," Paige whispered, remembering the aphorism much abused by her mom.

A rumble coursed in Liam's throat, like a growl or a fiercely contained laugh. The bed frame creaked beneath his shifting weight. "When did Shadow get here?"

"About five minutes ago."

"How long have you been awake?"

"About five minutes longer than that."

"What time is it?"

"The time?" she said, lifting the mug to her mouth again. "I don't know."

She heard him fumbling around, presumably in search of his phone. A few seconds later the screen lit up, illuminating the darkness around his face, revealing him sleepy-eyed and frowning as he read the time. "Come back to bed." He clicked the phone off.

Swallowing a last mouthful, Paige set the mug on the windowsill and climbed into bed as he slid over to accommodate her, his left arm wide and ready to wrap around her shoulders. She placed her head on his chest. His heart thumped beneath her ear in steady, comforting rhythm. Beside him, Shadow made a small sound and slid away.

"How are you feeling?" Liam asked.

"Sore. Stupid. Anxious. Angry."

His ribcage expanded and shook against her cheek. "So 'better' isn't in there anywhere?"

"No, better is in there. I feel a little better."

"Liar."

"That's me," she said.

He began to stroke her hair back from her crown in slow, easy movements, making her want to hum like a bee. She closed her eyes, maintaining a resolute silence.

"I care about you, Paige."

Paige's gaze shifted to the wall across the room where passing headlights out on the road described a diffuse, moving arc across the painted boards. "Okay."

"Don't sound so scared. For crying out loud, you leapt on the back of a stalker. I tell you I care about you, and you act like you stepped into a cage with a lion."

She pressed herself closer to the warmth of his body. "Well, it sounded like there was going to be a 'but' at the end of that statement."

"No but," he said.

She breathed, each inhalation bringing the scent of him into her nostrils, into her bloodstream, like an intoxicant. "And yet, you're afraid of caring, aren't you?"

He didn't answer, continuing to massage her scalp in long strokes.

"It's all right," she whispered. "I am, too."

"Do you think I'll hurt you?"

"Right now, or ever?"

"Both."

He deserved an honest answer, but she couldn't give it to him. Such a response could never be withdrawn down the line. It would always lurk in the background to haunt them both, subtly painting the relationship in miasmal hues. Thinking of what she and Liam had as a relationship, however, sent a small thrill through her veins that was its own hope. "Let's worry about now first, shall we? Like how you're going to avoid all these bruises when you put your hands on me."

"Paige we can't—"

"Too late." She lifted his hand and placed his fingers gently on the swell of her breast. "Done deal."

His groan turned into a rumble of laughter. "Oh, well, if I *must*."

"I do insist."

"Bossy wench."

"Gets the job done."

"Not if I refu—" The air rushed from his lungs as she stroked the length of his penis.

"I would say," she whispered, "that the whole business of an erection is like wilting in reverse, except you were well on your way to being hard. I don't think refusal was really on your mind."

"Take off your clothes, Paige."

"Now who's the bossy one?"

"I wear the pants, don't I?"

She laughed. "Not at the moment."

The only thing he had been wearing was his boxers, but she'd already managed to shove them halfway down his thighs. She trailed her fingers along his leg, sensing the shiver beneath her touch. Aware, too, not only of the ridges and hollows of his musculature, but of the scars she'd seen.

"Don't ask,' he said above her head. "Not yet. There will be time to explain everything to you."

Time. She liked the sound of that. Not the time kept by the ticking of a clock, by the movement of hands in constant forward momentum around a numbered face, but the time measured by events and growth and change.

She left off exploring the sensitive skin on his thigh, where hair follicles lifted in her fingertip's wake, and shifted her attention to the tightening flesh of his balls. His breath whistled in over his teeth as his belly expanded beneath her cheek. Remembering her thoughts about his possible conservative nature, she said, "May I?"

"May you what?"

"This." The moan, the shuddering tremor, was her answer. She ran her tongue over him again. He arched and sighed and said something she did not quite hear. Suddenly she felt his fingers circling her arms, pulling her up and away.

"Ow, ow, ow," she said, as she flipped onto her knees beside him.

"I'm sorry."

She kissed him. "Not to worry."

"No. I'm really sorry. About everything."

She let out a breath. "I don't like the sound of that."

He tugged the hem of her blouse. "Can I take this off without hurting you?"

"Yes."

With exaggerated care, he removed every stitch she wore until she sat naked on the mattress. He then stripped off his own garments and lay back down. "There's only one way we're going to do this, Paige. You can't move."

"That doesn't sound fun."

"Neither do cries of pain. Got it?" Placing a pillow beneath her hips, Liam helped her to lie on her back. "You know that expression, about the first two inches?"

"Mmm, maybe?"

"Liar. That's all you're getting, though. Those contusions on your hip are no laughing matter."

Paige ran a fingertip around his nipple. "If you don't want to…"

"Oh, I want to."

Taking her hands, he placed them on the headboard, curling the fingers of her left around the metal. "Hold on there and don't touch me. Control is going to be difficult enough without you doing the things you like to do. Understood?"

She nodded. Rising above her, he slanted his mouth across hers, his tongue moving in slow exploration. He then kissed her jaw, her throat, her breast. He licked her nipple, toyed with it, made her moan. Slipping his fingers inside, he tested her restraint, stopping every time she began to rock to the motion of his caress. Her grip tightened on the headboard. His thumb began a slow rotation on the slippery nub of flesh between her legs.

"Don't move."

She gasped as sensation rocketed from her core to every nerve ending in her body. He clamped her nipple between his teeth, lapping at it with delicate strokes. She released the headboard and took him in her hand, delighting in his rushing breath across her flesh, the way he liberated her breast from exquisite torture to arch back in a shuddering moan.

"Paige…"

"Liam."

"What?"

"Two inches be damned."

He plunged himself inside her, all pain forgotten as her pleasured cries mingled with the rumbling of her name. Tomorrow, she might awaken unable to move, but tonight—tonight she wanted to know she was his.

* * * *

Sauntering from Paige's cottage toward his home, carrying Shadow in one arm, Liam turned his head to watch the sun lift above the horizon. With its initial flicker the waves turned gold and in the next instant became striated with silver and orange across the deep gray-green waters. Despite everything in the offing, Liam experienced pervading contentment.

Until he stepped up on the porch and spotted the broken glass on the door.

* * * *

Paige pulled the shower curtain aside and leaned her head out. "Hello?" After a few seconds of listening, she turned off the water and stepped out onto the mat. Snatching the towel from the bar, she dried off as she went out into the main room, where she listened again at the window. Yes, they were voices she heard, quite a few, and a car door slamming.

Yanking aside the curtain, Paige peered out toward Liam's house— funny, how she had ceased thinking of it as her old home without any specific reminder—and glimpsed through the vegetation a police vehicle angled in the rough grass at the nearest side. Two uniformed men moved past.

With an exclamation, Paige struggled to pull clothes on over her still-damp skin. Grabbing her keys, she locked the door behind her and hurried as fast as she could manage across the space between the two houses. As she rounded the corner, she heard two familiar voices speaking, recognizing at once Liam's gravel tones and Dan's authoritative manner in counterpoint, somewhat subdued.

"You're certain?"

"Yes," Liam stated. "Quite certain."

"And so you think he broke in here. This could only mean...well, is there something he would find?"

"He didn't."

"Good God, where did he look?"

"Not here."

"What do you mean?"

"Paige," said Liam.

"Paige? But she doesn't—"

"Paige is here," said Liam.

Paige strode up to the two men. Liam watched her approach with a bland look, but Dan's expression was anything but calm.

"What about me?" Paige asked. "And what happened here, Liam? Are you all right?"

Dan cleared his throat. "Your boyfriend had a break-in last night."

She wished he'd stop calling Liam that. The grade school quality of Dan's utterance irked her. True or not, the way Dan said 'boyfriend' made it sound as if the designation could somehow sum Liam up in his entirety.

"Liam, are you all right?" she asked again. He nodded. She addressed Dan. "When I got out of bed last night, I saw a light in the living room over here. I thought it was the lamp on the timer."

"What time was that?"

Paige glanced at Liam. She had no idea, but he'd checked his phone.

"Just shy of four-thirty," Liam answered. "Paige, why didn't you say something?"

"Because I thought it was the lamp on the timer," she repeated.

"That goes out around one."

He didn't appear to be blaming her, but she felt responsible nevertheless. "Liam, it didn't occur to me—well, yes, I suppose it did, right at first, but I decided it was the lamp."

"With everything else that's going on," Dan said.

Paige ignored him. "First, there was that damned boat running without lights way too close to shore, and then when I came back inside—"

"When were you outside?"

Paige widened her eyes at Liam in a "you remember" look, but then she realized he probably didn't know at all. He'd been sound asleep until she woke him. "When I let Shadow in, I stepped outside for two seconds. Two, that's all."

"Long enough to see a boat running dark," Dan said. "And you didn't think to say anything about that either to your boy—"

"Liam. His name is Liam. What we are to each other is our business and doesn't need your sarcastic references."

To her astonishment, both men laughed. "Understood," said Dan, with an enigmatic glance at Liam. Liam had the grace to look uncomfortable. Dan shrugged. "How long before you saw the light in the living room did you see the boat?"

"Only a couple of minutes. I watched the boat until it was out of sight and then I came back inside. That's when I went to the window. Liam, you woke up and found me there. I had already dismissed it."

"And then what?" prompted Dan.

"And then nothing," Liam answered for her.

"Got it," said Dan. "Anyway, your boyfr—Liam here believes it's the same guy who went into your place."

"I gathered that from what I overheard. What is your opinion?"

"I agree."

"Why would he break into Liam's house? Because of his association with me?"

Dan looked to Liam, who responded with a brief inclination of his head. "It would appear so. This time, though, we're hoping he left usable prints."

"And if he has," Paige said, "will that really get you any closer to finding him?"

"I hope."

"In the meantime," said Liam, "you need to clear out of here for a while. Not back to Tennessee, but maybe into town? There's a bed and breakfast on Pine that might be able to accommodate you. Isn't that right, Stauffer?"

"Run by an ex-cop and his wife," Dan said. "I think you'd be safe there."

Paige looked from one man to the other, studying expressions nearly identical in determination. The last thing she wanted to do was hinder the police department's investigation, now that they were paying more attention to the case. She didn't want to cause any further trouble for Liam, either. "Okay, that's fine. If you'll give me the number, I'll call. If they're full up, I'll try somewhere else. I understand you need me out of here. Consider me gone."

Dan pulled a card from his pocket and wrote the number across the back. "Thank you, Paige."

His gratitude for her cooperation was genuine, which made Paige suffer more than a pang of guilt for her attitude earlier in their conversation. She took the card from him with acknowledgment of his concern and tucked it into her pocket.

Liam stepped close, lowering his voice. "I'll come by in a few minutes to see how you're making out with those arrangements and to help you carry everything to your car."

"I can manage. I'm not that broken."

"Oh, come on, Paige, let a man be a man," Dan said before walking away in response to one of the other officers calling his name.

Paige bit her lip, raising her gaze to Liam's. "He's right. Thank you. I appreciate the help."

"I think you've been used to being on your own for a long time. We'll have to work on that."

Why? By the end of the summer she'd be back home, needing her resilience.

The same thought appeared to occur to him. His lips twisted into a closed, crooked smile. "A little change won't hurt you. Won't hurt me, either. No matter where we are."

Grabbing a fistful of shirt, Paige pulled him down and planted a kiss on his mouth, not caring who witnessed the action.

Chapter 23

The room at the bed and breakfast—owned by friends of Dan Stauffer's, as it turned out—was the type of space designed for a romantic getaway from the world. Paige sat on a white, eyelet coverlet on the bed by herself, thumbing through a glossy monthly publication from the nightstand. When Liam departed, he told her to use his number frequently. She'd wanted to dial it within two minutes of him walking out the door.

Instead, she'd called Billy Woodward's mother, Felicia, and left her a message, hoping to meet up with her in a day or so. After noting the sky had taken on the look of an impending storm, she plugged her phone in to charge the low battery. God forbid the electricity went out and left her with a dead cell.

The B&B was very quiet. The crisp flick of pages sounded loud in the room. Flip. Flip. An ad showing a lovely couple eating dinner at the charming, nearby Hideaway Restaurant. Flip, flip. A story about the stone circle at the nature preserve. Flip. Another attractive couple standing at the prow of a sailing ship, hair tossed by the wind, teeth white as snow, champagne glasses in hand. She didn't bother reading the copy beneath. Flip.

Across the room, her suitcase sat open on a low chest, the box of photos Liam had insisted she take beside it.

Flip. An article about the benefits of an appointment with a local spa, accompanied by an image of river stones and water lilies. Flip. A double-page collage spread showing shop fronts, advertising the upcoming Fourth of July sales. Paige closed the periodical to glance at the date on the lower left-hand side. She didn't bother to open the magazine again, but folded her hands over the cover and sat contemplating the box beside her case.

Why had all these photos been in her father's possession? There were many more than those she'd examined, possibly able to provide her with further revelations about her family's life when she'd been a young girl.

This was the reason she'd come to Alcina Cove, to address and understand the nuances of her parents' relationship, her own with them, and yet she couldn't bring herself to look in that box again.

She cringed in self-reproach over her inability to be the brave woman her mother always exhorted her to be. Cowardice was an unbecoming trait. She hadn't viewed herself as particularly spineless in the past, but she'd never quite been put to the test.

Paige rose and stretched, tossing the magazine back where she'd found it. She thought of Liam's break-in. If she'd left when he'd asked, that night in the hospital, it wouldn't have happened. Liam had told Dan nothing was missing, but she'd thought the same thing. What might this psycho have stolen from Liam's home that he would only find later? Had she left something behind? Not that it would matter. An outsider wouldn't know. Which meant yes, he'd been singled out because of his association with her.

Parting the curtains, Paige peered out at the street beyond. Located down a picturesque side street, the bed and breakfast had an English-style garden out front complete with a white picket fence, stepping stones, and a quaint wooden bench. The Dieters knew what they were about when they'd created the Timeless Inn from a rundown home. She'd seen transformation photos downstairs in the lobby.

There was a lot to admire about Alcina Cove, most of which had been lost to her as a teenager. Directly across the road stood a stately Victorian, a huge house built by a wealthy captain at the turn of the last century. The lawn was impeccably tended, shaded by several old growth trees, gnarled and twisted by nature and weather. A man in a battered hat, likely the gardener, started to step out from behind the nearest tree, but paused. His head lifted, showing graying hair beneath the brim of his hat and what appeared to be redness, perhaps a birthmark on his face. Behind a pair of glasses, the man's eyes found her with unerring accuracy in the window where she stood. Paige lifted her hand and waved. He did not return the gesture. Instead, he backed away, losing himself behind the huge trunk. A moment later, he disappeared through the rhododendron, vanishing completely in the flowering bushes.

Paige frowned. In all likelihood, he hadn't been able to see her at all behind the reflective glass. The man had looked familiar, though, in a way she couldn't quite place. Perhaps the fellow was an old neighbor she'd known years ago. After all, she was bound to run into someone she could place other than Dan Stauffer. She hadn't existed in a vacuum, although it certainly felt as if she had.

Turning from the window, her gaze alighted on the box as if drawn there. Steeling herself, she crossed the room and plucked the container off the chest, dumping half the contents onto the bedspread. She set the box on the floor, then climbed up onto the mattress and sat, cross-legged, to contemplate the images.

After a couple of minutes spent picking up photograph after photograph, a sense of hopelessness returned. Searching through old photos for glimpses from the past wouldn't work. Sure, she'd get caught up in the excitement that prodded memories could bring about, but she'd already realized half the images meant nothing to her. Many photos showed other people, strangers, and some revealed faces she vaguely remembered, but whose names eluded her. The rest filled her with a burning need to know why and how her father had come to possess them. With no one to provide that answer, her curiosity would remain unsatisfied. She began to scoop the photos up again when one in particular caught her eye. She flipped it quickly for a name and found none, but she didn't really require identification.

"Dad."

The utterance sounded to her ears like a child's plea. Her heart felt the echo of tone, hearkening back to a time when she'd known nothing but love for her father—a time she'd forgotten, pushed down, and left behind. It hurt her to recognize the emotion now. Hurt her to the point of physical pain. Her respiration became ragged in the battle against tears.

"Daddy."

Damn you, damn you, damn you, she raged silently, gripping the photo between her fingers with the intent of ripping the print in half. Instead, she set it down again on her leg. Her jaw ached from the strain of holding back the noise that thundered in her head, demanding escape.

She understood now why the gardener looked familiar. Though slight, there was a resemblance between that man and her father, the similarity one found in distant relatives where genetics managed to survive despite dilution. She'd been operating under the assumption she had no family except her mother's sister in California. But did she know that to be true? It was information that had been fed to her by a parent who wanted nothing to do with the life she'd left behind.

Swiping dampness from her cheeks, Paige stood and tucked the photo into her pocket. She grabbed her phone and the keys to the room. She pulled a hair from her brush on the way past and took a moment outside to wrap the curly strand around the lock's plunger before pulling the door shut. A short length of the hair stuck out past the doorframe. With any luck, only she would know it was there. She'd seen this trick in a movie once. The only way the hair would disappear from that spot was if someone entered the room while she was gone.

Clinging to a sense of security she recognized as altogether false, Paige left the Timeless Inn and hobbled across the street, intending to continue up to the huge double doors with a request to speak with the gardener or groundskeeper in order to show him the photo of her father. With any luck, the man wouldn't be as clueless as she in terms of family ties and could tell her straightaway if any kinship existed. Even if he knew nothing about her parents, he would be family. Maybe that alone would be enough to make her feel a little less dispirited.

As she reached the property, she saw that the landscape wasn't quite as well maintained as it had appeared from her room at the bed and breakfast. Despite the vivid shining of the sun, a huge portion of the grounds remained shadowed and overgrown. Paige hesitated on the sidewalk, pacing back and forth in front of the long walkway leading up to the home. The perfect spot for an ambush. Less than a week ago, such a frightening thought would never have occurred to her.

After a moment, she pulled out her phone and sent Liam a text, telling him she'd possibly found someone related to her father, and if he had the chance at some point, she'd appreciate the bolstering adjunct of a little company in tracking the man down. A few seconds later, she received a reply.

I know you. You've left the B&B. Get back there until you hear differently.

His written tone left something to be desired, but she appreciated the sentiment. Turning her back on the overgrown estate, she stepped off the curb to return to the Timeless. Movement in her peripheral vision jerked her back around.

Nothing but a squirrel in a tree, attracted, no doubt, by the huge nut standing in the road. As she took another step, she again caught sight of movement. This time, however, she spotted someone in furtive retreat. "Hello?"

Through the swaying of rhododendron blossoms from forced passage through the bushes, she finally glimpsed a battered green hat. "Look, I only wanted to talk to you." The man stopped, nearly invisible in the greenery, but didn't speak. Paige shifted her weight from foot to foot in indecision. After a moment, she backed away.

No. She wasn't some ingénue in a cheap horror movie making bad decisions left and right. Whoever this guy was, she had no desire to go in after him. She'd wait for Liam and they'd tackle him together. Frankly, she was getting a little tired of the eccentric behavior of the people she'd met in this town. They all couldn't have been so peculiar when she lived here. Of course, she'd only interacted with a few residents since her return. The fates had not favored making this easy for her.

Paige returned to the inn and climbed the stairs slowly to her room. At the door, she examined the knob to make certain the single hair remained in place before turning the key and going inside. On a hunch, she walked straight to the window and peeled back the curtains a couple of inches in order to see the yard across the street once more.

Nothing.

She let the curtain fall back into place. Returning to the bed, she gathered the photos she'd left spread across the coverlet and put them back in the box. Her phone rang. She answered without looking.

"Liam, I'm back in the room safe and sound—"

"I'm sorry, not anyone named Liam. Hope you're not too disappointed. This is Felicia Woodward. Paige?"

"Yes! God, I'm an idiot." Paige sat on the floor beside the carton of photos, leaning her spine against the mattress. "Thank you for calling me back."

"Not a problem. You've got a hoot of an accent. Billy warned me about that. I love it."

Paige closed her eyes. The woman's voice—no longer the stilted message on her voicemail, but her actual voice, filled with nuance and energy—came rushing at her through the years. Somewhere back in the days of early childhood, she had known this woman and liked her very much.

* * * *

"I've got tonic—'pop' I guess you'd call it down South?"

Paige smiled. "I still call it soda."

A head taller than Paige with short salt-and-pepper hair, Felicia Woodward bent for another look in the refrigerator. "Wine? Too early, I guess. Water. Milk." The woman wrinkled her nose, sticking her tongue out between her teeth. "That belongs to Billy. He likes it. It's probably out of date." She opened the container and sniffed. Her face contorted. She hurried with a comical leap to the sink and dumped the white liquid down the drain, then filled the plastic bottle with water to soak. "Or I could make us some coffee. How's that sound?"

"Perfect. I'd love one. Do you need any help?"

Felicia shook her head. "You just stay right there." She pulled a can of coffee out of the closet.

Paige stood instead and crossed the floor to look out the window of the country-style kitchen. The stone circle was visible through the trees, silicate particulates winking in the afternoon sunshine. "They look quite beautiful from here."

Felicia glanced through the glass and returned to the preparation of the coffee maker. "Quite a marvel, they are. Some people don't like them. Believe they're evil or a sign of devil worship or some such nonsense. I don't think anyone's really figured out how they came to be there. One might suppose the native peoples set them into place, though I don't know if that would have been something they'd do. But the stones aren't evil. They're magic."

Paige shivered involuntarily. "Magic? How so?"

Felicia favored her with a long, speculative look. "Sometimes you can feel something when you're standing within the circle that you can't feel anywhere else, as if your connection to the earth is stronger. Of course, that might just be my former Wiccan phase cropping back up. You had the chance to visit them yet?"

"I have. I don't know about feeling anything special, but I did see something there."

"You've seen the shadow, then."

Paige turned her back on the window, folding her arms across her chest. "You and Liam, you speak so matter-of-factly about ghosts, as if they're nothing out of the ordinary."

Felicia pushed the button to start the coffee brewing. "I don't know that the shadow is a ghost. I'm not really sure what it is. But ghosts are ordinary. They're everywhere. Just not everyone can see or sense them."

"I never saw them before, but now I've come home, I'm getting quite the education on what exists among us." Including psychos, she almost added, but maintained silence on that matter. At least for now. Depending on her comfort level, Paige decided she might bring the subject up later, if only to bounce the situation off someone who wasn't directly affected.

"Who's Liam?"

Paige smiled at the change of subject. "Liam Gray. He…he lives in the house I grew up in. Bought it off my dad."

Eyes flickering with an emotion Paige couldn't decipher, Felicia reached into the cabinet to grab two mugs. "Grab the sugar bowl, will you? It's on the other side of the stove."

Paige retrieved and delivered the lidded bowl to Felicia.

"I'm sorry about your dad. And your mom. Deb wrote to me when she first got sick, did you know that?"

"No," said Paige, "I didn't."

"We hadn't communicated in quite a few years, but we started writing regularly after that, and calling. Old-fashioned things, letters are, but holding a letter in your grasp, putting it away somewhere to pull out again later and re-read beats an e-mail hands down. It's like having a piece of the person with you."

Paige plucked at a stray hair lying on her sleeve. "You kept them? My mother's letters?"

"I certainly did. In a shoebox. Like when we were kids."

Paige drew an agonized breath. She hadn't found any box of letters from Felicia when she'd gone through her mother's possessions and wondered what had happened to them. As if reading her mind or her expression, Felicia smiled at her with a nod.

"I've got the ones I wrote to your mother in the same box. She sent them all back to me just before she died."

A constricted exhalation shuddered out of her lungs. Oh, God, she was going to break down right here in front of her mother's oldest friend. Paige turned away so Felicia wouldn't see the tears coming faster than she could blink them away.

"Cream and sugar?" Felicia asked in a way that indicated to Paige she'd seen her tears but wouldn't fuss about it. They were going to have coffee, and that would be that. Even so, Paige's breath throbbed in her chest, as if she couldn't quite draw in enough oxygen.

"Here. Come sit down. I'd offer cookies but that son of mine ate every last one before I left. Potato chips might be a good substitute."

"Where are they?" Paige volunteered in haste. "I'll get them." Following the jerk of Felicia's chin toward the pantry, Paige whipped out the bag and removed the clip from the top, then set the open bag between them on the table as she sat.

"You all right now?"

"I'm all right."

"Good."

For a full five minutes, they sipped their coffee and munched on rippled chips without speaking. The kitchen became silent enough to hear the wall clock's battery-driven motor in between chewing and the rustle of the coated bag.

"So," said Felicia at length, "this Liam, is he someone your mother would approve of?"

Paige's cheeks heated. She'd hoped she hadn't given herself away. "I think Mom would approve of anyone who wasn't Dad."

Felicia lowered her mug to the table. "I wouldn't be so sure of that."

"Okay, not anyone," Paige backtracked, "but you know what I mean."

"Your mom only ever wanted the best for you, to keep you safe."

Paige stopped with her hand mid-way to the open potato chip bag. "Keep me safe? She was the one who needed protection. Dad never went after me the way he did her."

Felicia lifted the mug again, taking a long, noisy slurp of tea. "It might be time to unlearn what you've collected in that head of yours over the years."

Sitting up, Paige pulled her hand back to her lap. "What do you mean? This is why I'm here, you know, to see what you might be able to tell me."

"I figured as much. But let's talk about Liam first. You like him, do you?"

Paige nodded mutely.

"How long have you known him?"

"We met...we met the night I got here." Goodness, how ridiculous. How could a person develop an attachment to another that quickly? Lightning fast connections didn't have a good track record. Not for her anyway. But then again, she hadn't known any other kind but the swift physical interactions, which she'd experienced in plenty. It was the affection, the emotion, unnerving her.

"Don't worry," Felicia said with a smile, "I'm not judging. Love works in mysterious ways, or so the saying goes."

"I didn't say anything about love."

"Right. You didn't. And your face?" Felicia indicated the bruises with a nod.

Paige darted her gaze to the mug, to the cartoon on the side depicting a man in a hospital gown and the words *get well soon*. "Not Liam." She yanked the mug off the tabletop, the tea sloshing around inside, and drank.

Felicia tipped her head to the floor near Paige's feet. "What's in the box?"

"Photos. I haven't looked at them all yet, but they're mostly of me. Some have other people in them, with or without my face, and I don't know all of them. I thought if you wouldn't mind going through some...?"

"Of course I wouldn't mind going through them. I'm honored."

"Not all the photos are old. Some are relatively recent. Liam found the box in the attic, which makes me think Dad had them. I just can't figure out how he got them. They don't look like the fodder of a private investigator."

Felicia's expression remained a study in neutrality. After a moment, she got out of her chair, lifted the box from the floor, and set the container on the table between them. She flipped the lid back. "I know how he got them, Paige. I gave them to him."

Chapter 24

They had moved into the living room, box and all. Paige couldn't remember how they got there. They hadn't said anything, but had gotten up as one accord and gone to a place where they could settle in. This conversation wouldn't be a short one once it began. Paige sat on the sofa's far end, staring out the window, not quite ready or willing to start the exchange. The sky had gotten darker. She supposed the rain was finally coming.

"Paige, it was your mother who asked that I give the photographs to your father."

Paige believed Felicia when the woman spoke those words. She couldn't imagine, however, why they might be true.

"At first, it was one or two here or there, but then she started sending them on a regular basis, passing them through me because…because it was safe to do so. Before she died, she sent a huge envelope. The newer ones she didn't mark with any caption in order not to reveal your location."

Paige lifted her hands and rubbed her eyelids with the curve of each palm. "What was she trying to do? Make him feel guilty?"

Felicia's prolonged silence drew Paige's gaze. She dropped her hands back down to her lap. Felicia's brow had furrowed and her mouth was turned down. She looked exasperated and perhaps a little angry. Paige clasped her fingers into a knot to keep them still.

Despite her expression, when Felicia spoke again she sounded calm. "How much do you remember about those months before you left?"

"I remember Mom's eye blackened. I remember the blood running from her mouth," Paige said.

"Not the night you left. Your daily life leading up to that moment."

"What do you know about that night?" Paige demanded.

"Think, Paige. It's important."

"I remember it wasn't the only time. I remember seeing Mom apply makeup to her face to cover marks. I was told recently the police had been called to the house, but Mom wouldn't follow through and told them everything was fine."

Felicia reached for the mug she'd carried in with her and lifted it, taking a mouthful, swallowing carefully. "Those incidents stand out because they were traumatic. What else do you recall?"

Paige leaned forward, elbows grinding into her legs a couple of inches above her knees. "What are you digging for? What is it you want me to say? That was all a long time ago. Why would I want to remember anything about that?"

Clutching the mug against her stomach, Felicia leaned back into the cushioned chair. "Do you remember your parents arguing? Do you remember seeing your father hit her?"

"I—" Paige stopped, recalling her thought processes on the beach a few nights past, and often since. She shook her head. "I never did. I guess he hesitated to do it in front of me. That would have made me a witness. As for the arguing, well, yeah, of course they did, but I can't call to mind anything more than the normal type of quarrel except in the days immediately before. I'm not sure. How can I be? It was sixteen years ago. I do know that I didn't want other kids coming around. That had to mean something."

"I'm sure it did."

Paige narrowed her eyes. "What are you trying to tell me, Felicia? I spent more than half of my lifetime far away from here because my mother was in fear of my father."

"No, Deb stayed away to keep you safe."

"My father would never have hurt me!" Paige's hand flew to her mouth, shocked at her own vehemence. She'd never said those words aloud before. On and off she'd believed them, coveted them like a talisman against her feelings of abandonment, but to admit them out loud seemed to betray her mother. "Debra Waters lived in fear of her husband," Paige stated quietly.

"Did she?"

Paige's vision glimmered with angry tears. "Of course she did."

"Did she say as much to you?"

"Of course she did." Paige considered, remembering past doubts. "She didn't like to talk about it! When I asked questions, it upset her, and she would…she would tell me everything was all right. To not ask. To let it go…"

Shoulders slumping, Paige dropped her head into her hands, shoved her fingers into her hair, and pulled it from the clip binding the locks at her nape. Across from her, Felicia stood and walked to a cabinet against the living room wall. She opened the door and removed a bottle that she carried back to the coffee table. She poured a bit into Paige's tea. The strong smell of alcohol reached her nostrils.

"Whiskey," said Felicia. "It won't kill you."

Paige peered up at her. "It's not even three yet, is it?"

"Who gives a crap? Drink it. You're going to need it. Me, too." She poured a healthy dose into her own mug, then screwed the cap back on and set the bottle on the table before she sat back down.

Paige pulled the tea nearer and leaned over it, breathing in liquor's hard, sweet scent. She'd wanted answers and was very much afraid she was going to get them. With determination, she brought the mug up to her lips and downed the contents. An immediate coughing fit followed, but warmth spread from her belly to her limbs within a few seconds.

"Better?"

Paige wiped her hand across her lips. "Better."

"You might want another one."

"I'll wait."

Felicia reached into the box and drew a photograph out. "Nice dress. Who's the lucky guy?"

"Ashford," said Paige with a snort of suppressed laughter.

"Ash-what?"

"Don't ask. I think his parents had pretensions."

Felicia dropped the photo back into the box. "Your father wanted to know about your life. Deb couldn't contact him directly so I was the go-between."

"He wanted to know about…me?" Paige frowned down into her empty mug. She reached for the bottle and poured an inch of liquid into the bottom.

"Want a little soda with that?"

"Nope."

"It's your funeral. Water and aspirin for dinner, got that?"

"Got it. And pancakes. Don't people eat pancakes when they've been drinking?"

"Yeah, I suppose they do."

Paige leaned back into the sofa, wincing at the discomfort in her bruised hip. She clutched the mug to her breast, planning to nurse the whiskey inside. She didn't relish a possible hangover. "Go on."

"They probably would have divorced, your mom and dad, if things hadn't happened the way they did. But they remained married for all those years apart."

Paige waited. She didn't think she could ask a sensible question with the information she'd been given because none of the dots appeared to connect. It wasn't the alcohol confusing her since she wasn't drunk, but she decided she would be before too much longer. If she'd been less cowardly, she might have chosen sobriety for a conversation she sensed was about to change her life.

Be brave, Paige.

Mom, I'm afraid.

Pushing the mental conversation with her deceased mother from her brain, Paige focused on Felicia in her chair. "What did happen?"

"Deb—your mom—had an affair."

"What?" Paige gulped a mouthful of liquid from her cup, squinting as it burned its way down her throat.

"I don't condone it. I didn't then. But that's what happened."

Paige frowned. "That's it? That's your explanation for everything? For why Dad beat her? Or was the abuse the reason she went outside the marriage? I really, really don't understand where you're going with this."

Felicia leaned forward, dumped a shot of liquor in her cup, another in Paige's, and sat back. "This story's only just beginning, and your father never touched your mother. He wouldn't have laid a finger on her. It was her lover who did that."

* * * *

Liam's cell vibrated in his pocket. He yanked the phone out and checked the caller ID. Paige. With a glance toward the activity below, Liam texted that he would call soon. After a second, he forwarded another advising her to dial 911 if it was an emergency and then call him again. Otherwise, they would talk later. He'd almost stowed the phone away when her reply pulsed in his hand.

K. Lts to tell. Ned to tlk. xo

He frowned at the errors in the text. Or were they meant to be abbreviations? He knew she'd gone to spend the afternoon with an old friend of her mother. Even if Paige hadn't told him, the undercover cop tailing her had relayed where she'd gone and that she remained there safely. That had been hours ago. The day had come and gone with night settling down like a stifling blanket.

Liam shoved the phone into his pocket, wiping his brow with his forearm afterward. The men below moved in near silence, speech truncated and barely discernible over the thundering waves. They worked without benefit of illumination with the exception of the flashlights utilized once inside the entrance of the cave, a cave that wouldn't be visible come high tide. Even the flashlights were held in such a way as to center the beams inward, with no more than a flash to be glimpsed by anyone out on the water. Had they been more sophisticated, they would have used night vision goggles, but they worked in much the same manner men had since the first pirates and privateers had moved illicit goods from ships to the caves all along the shoreline around Alcina Cove.

Tonight, the crates being moved into temporary hiding below held weapons. The usual operation was taking place. Store the cache away from prying eyes, wait until the appointed day, and restore the crates to the ship for an exchange out on the water. It wasn't safe to keep the goods in a warehouse and certainly not on the ship while it was still being used for other jobs. Liam had been involved in these exchanges for nearly six months, waiting for the right one.

A stone shifted with a sharp clatter, striking another. Liam turned his head. He saw a familiar silhouette against the sky behind and waited until it had neared.

"Why aren't you down there?" A harsh whisper.

Liam shrugged. "You posted me as lookout. Make up your mind." Liam played a dangerous game with his disrespect but it also kept the bastard on his toes. Raleigh never knew quite what to make of Liam, how far Liam would go. But with Edwin gone, Raleigh needed Liam in order to continue operations in the cave on his property. Liam remembered again the day Raleigh had approached him with suspiciously blasé questions about the natural features of the area, not as if they were new to him, but as if he were feeling Liam out. The moment couldn't have been more opportune. Liam had followed through with arrangements for the cave's use, including making every effort to keep people off the beach. With Raleigh's mercurial personality, though, Liam wasn't sure how long he could count on remaining in the man's tentative good graces. He hoped he wouldn't have to find out.

"Some lookout. I crept right up on you."

"No," said Liam, keeping his voice low. "You didn't. If you had, you'd be lying on the rocks right now with a broken neck."

"Bullshit."

Liam said nothing, continuing to observe the work transpiring on the narrow stretch of beach by the cave. He heard the snick of something metal and tensed, but after a moment Raleigh chuckled. "You've got balls, Gray, I'll give you that. Being a ladies' man, though, I don't have much use for anybody's balls but my own."

The muscles in Liam's abdomen tightened. "So I've heard."

"Yeah, and I know a bit more about you than you'd probably like, but we'll talk about that another time."

"Confessions before you try to kill me?"

For a full half minute, Raleigh didn't speak. Liam's entire body tensed in preparation for attack. He wondered if he'd gone too far, but he didn't care. He'd recently found himself grown impatient with waiting for the final strike.

"Wouldn't be the first time, but I usually don't bother with pretty speeches beforehand."

Liam's shoulders didn't relax, not even a little. "I've heard that, too."

"Anything you heard," said Raleigh, before beginning a descent to the beach, "is only half the story."

And therein existed the problem. In order to make good on six months' careful planning, waiting for all the pieces to come together in order to grab every player, what he needed—what *they* needed—was more than half the story. They needed it all.

Chapter 25

Nearby, a tray dropped. Paige flinched behind sunglasses at the ungodly clatter. Letting her breath out, she speared the cut, stacked pancake triangles laden with syrup and forced them into her mouth. Dan and Liam had arrived at the diner two minutes ago, one right after the other, and were exchanging heated words in an undertone by the entrance. The heck with them and whatever man business made them act like a pair of idiots. She shoveled in another mouthful of her breakfast.

When their legs paused beside the table, Paige set her fork down. "Gentlemen."

"Slide over, would you?"

Paige made room for Liam. Dan took the seat opposite. He placed his elbows on the table, vibrating the utensils. Paige winced.

"Hungover?" asked Dan.

"Yeah," she said, "a bit."

"Why, did you have more than half a beer?" Liam said beside her.

She mopped pancake through syrup puddles, then set the fork down on her plate. "Split half a fifth of scotch whiskey with Felicia."

Dan whistled. Paige squeezed her eyes shut. "My freaking hair hurts." She lifted her right eyelid in time to catch one of those damned inscrutable looks between Liam and Dan. She didn't possess the energy to question it. Liam's arm came up across the back of the booth, his fingers settling on her left shoulder. Even that hurt, but she kept quiet.

Both men waited to place orders for coffee with the waitress before interrogating her again. She went back to eating, slowly and steadily, keeping her head down.

"So," said Dan, dumping a huge amount of sugar into his coffee cup. "What have you found out?"

Paige pushed her plate away, fighting nausea. "I would have called last night, but I passed out on Felicia's couch. And stop looking at each other like that. What is it with you two?"

Liam stroked her shoulder through her blouse. She bit her lip. "Was she able to tell you much?" he asked.

"She was able to tell me...everything." Emotion clogged her throat. She picked up the ice water and drank—all of it—and asked for more. "Dad never hit my mom."

"But the report—"

"Screw the report." Paige recoiled at the noise her own voice made inside her head. "It wasn't him. It was...it was her boyfriend. Her lover. The man she was having an affair with. And don't you look at each other. Look at me. I'm the one talking."

Liam leaned over, pressing his lips to her temple. "You're cranky when you drink."

Paige started to cry. Neither man spoke, but both started shooting glances around the diner, probably to see who was noticing. Paige gulped on a sob and straightened, angry. She blew her nose in her napkin. "I'm fine. I was lied to my whole life. I was allowed to believe my father had abused my mother. And you know what? Part of me knew it wasn't all true. I pretended I was wrong, though, and took the created version of my parents' relationship as gospel. So many things I didn't quite understand as a child, and I let them fade into the background. That much is my fault, without a doubt, but because of what my mother had done, I had no relationship with my dad for sixteen years. For my safety, Felicia said. And now he's gone, and it's too late."

Dan and Liam exchanged another glance. She let it go. "Apparently, I witnessed something I'm not able to remember. Now that I'm back here, glimpses keep popping up, but I can't make sense of them. My mom took another beating from the bastard she was sleeping with as a warning. The next time we'd both be dead, he said. My father, however, was A-okay as long as he continued to cooperate. It was the deal he struck with the man his wife was screwing while she was married to him. What the fuck."

Crossing her arms, Paige stared out the tinted window to the parking lot. She almost wished the whiskey had been enough to make her sleep for days on end so she wouldn't have to think about any of this. But sticking her head in the sand had been one of the strongest reasons Paige had accepted the falsehood fed to her by her mother. "Those photos in the attic? Mom had been sending them to Dad through Felicia for years. I don't understand how my parents could let their lives get so out of control."

With a deep sigh, she unfolded her arms and reached into her purse. "And this man who delighted in violence? It appears when he vanished from the area, my father was questioned about his disappearance, but someone at this table didn't see fit to mention that to me." She glared at Dan from behind the dark lenses. "My father was only cleared completely when Raleigh was arrested somewhere else on a warrant. Guess that prick did his time and got out, just in time to hassle me."

"I'll check into it," Dan said, deadpan. Not a flicker of interest, confusion, or concern. Either he'd known, or he was trying hard to cover the fact he'd missed something that monumental. "I've been meaning to get into the archives."

"Aren't there computer records?"

"Records more than ten years old are incomplete."

Paige frowned at him, not caring for his glib responses. "I can only assume since my mother and I didn't come running back to Alcina Cove that Dad knew Raleigh wasn't really gone." She slid a photograph to the center of the table, refusing to look at her mother's smiling face and the brutal, remarkably handsome younger man beside her. Despite the damage of time and whatever had altered his appearance, she had recognized Regan Raleigh as the same man who'd been stalking her as soon as she saw the eyes.

"Since I didn't know the truth, I walked right back into danger. What's his point in toying with me? Is he testing, in his own twisted way, if I remember him? I know who he is now though. I know what he did to my mother, to my family. I only wish I could remember what I had seen that caused him to threaten our lives. Because it had to have been bad, and I'd love to make him pay for all of it."

Paige sucked in a breath, jerking upright. Liam lowered his arm across her back, pulling her close. She clung to his shirt with her fingers, inhaling the dulcifying scent of his laundry detergent.

"Regan Raleigh," said Dan softly, lifting the photo between thumb and forefinger.

"Yes," Paige said from beneath Liam's sturdy arm, "Regan Raleigh. That's what Felicia called him. He and my dad were involved in something together. That's how Mom met him. I guess she fell for his pretty face." Liam gave her a short squeeze, presumably to keep her from flying off on a tirade.

"What else did Felicia tell you?" Dan asked. "I'm probably going to want to speak with her, by the way."

"You already spoke with her son. Billy Woodward? Or you were going to. There's no association with this Raleigh guy. You can't think there is. She was my mom's best friend, which is why she knows all of this."

"I'm not accusing her of anything. She may have knowledge that could be helpful, though. Knowledge she doesn't realize is important." Dan looked at Liam at that point. Not one of those fleeting looks, but eye to eye in a prolonged fashion. "That's the connection," he said.

Paige lifted her head to study Liam's expression. "What's he talking about?"

Liam's gaze remained steady on Dan's. "I'm not sure."

Dan rubbed his eye, smoothing the arch of his brow with a brush of his fingertips. He returned his attention to Paige. "The connection to you. Why you come back to town after sixteen years and immediately become a stalking victim. That's all I meant. But this is good. This is something to go on, and we have a photo now. Can I keep this? We can age the image."

"Yes, keep it. I don't want to ever see that photo again."

Dan tucked the photo into his shirt pocket behind his badge. "Paige, it'll be all right."

"Really?" She pulled away from Liam's protective embrace and gathered her purse from the seat. "I don't think all the whiskey in the world would make me believe that."

* * * *

Tiny bubbles popping in the water sounded like the whispers of fairies. Paige hadn't taken a bubble bath in years, but it felt like the thing to do right now. The fragrance of lavender soothed her aching head, and the warmth relaxed her muscles. In the bedroom, Liam held a running conversation with someone on the phone regarding dinner reservations. He was going to take her to a restaurant he wanted to try somewhere near Bar Harbor. Odd moving on, "business as usual," but perhaps he only wished to allay her fears in this fashion. She wouldn't fight him on it. She figured he needed normalcy as much as she.

Liam knocked on the door, cracked it open. "You okay in there? You didn't fall asleep, did you?"

Paige stirred, almost as if she had been dreaming. "I'm awake. I think I have about another ten minutes before the water gets too cold."

He stuck his head inside. "May I come in?"

"Sure."

Liam crossed the cramped space and sat on the mat beside the tub. He stretched his long legs out over the floor, crossing his ankles. His shoelaces tapped the tile. "How do you feel? Besides the hangover, I mean."

"Betrayed," she said without needing to think, and then added, "Angry, too, for a variety of reasons."

"Not scared in all of that?"

"Odd thing about me, I don't stay scared. I probably should, but dwelling on fear has never been part of my makeup. That's probably not such a good way to be, considering the present situation."

Be brave, Paige.

I am, Mom. You know I am.

Paige bowed her head until her chin touched a mound of bubbles. Tendrils that had escaped the clips trailed along her jaw and into the water. Liam pulled one away, tucking it behind her ear. Tepid bathwater dripped along her neck as he traced her cheekbone with a finger.

"Living in fear isn't necessary as long as you remain cognizant of the danger and take necessary precautions."

"You see how well I've done with that, Liam."

He laughed and leaned over the tub's curved edge. Cupping her head in his hand, he kissed her. "We'll keep you safe from here on in, Stauffer and I."

Her faith in Dan had been shaken, and Liam allying himself with the man, especially considering their antagonistic relationship, didn't provide her the comfort Liam obviously thought it should.

"For two people who didn't know one another before a few days ago, you're awfully edgy in each other's company." Paige tipped her head back, hoping he would kiss her again. He did, taking a tad longer in the process.

"Look at the two of us after only a handful of days. Relationships can progress rather quickly." He lowered his chin onto the arm he folded across the side of the tub. He dropped the other into the foam, curling his fingers around her wrist. Opening his mouth, he blew gently across the bubbles, causing them to skitter away from her breasts. Hard and glistening and very pink, her nipples rose above the surface of the water. Releasing her hand, he ran the pad of one finger across the tip of the nearest. Heat rushed through her body. "It's not just sex between us, Paige, but sex can be a very powerful motivator. People will make the most asinine decisions based on its lure."

Fluffing the bubbles back into place, he shook the clinging soap from his hand and stood. "You need to forgive her, Paige, somehow. You came back here seeking answers, and now you have them. Or some of them. I never got the impression you hated your father. I think you had forced yourself to a kind of ambivalence because it was the only way you could reconcile the father you had always known with the father you thought you had discovered."

"And now I find my mother wasn't at all what I thought, either."

"She was human, like the rest of us. We all make mistakes. We all have our shortcomings. We all keep our secrets."

He removed the fluffy bath sheet from the rack and opened it, holding it up. When he saw she had no plans to get out of the water, he sat on the closed toilet seat, the towel draped across his knees.

"Felicia said I shouldn't blame my mother, that people make foolish choices. But it's not like buying a pair of three hundred dollar shoes when you don't have the money for groceries. This choice caused long-term consequences and a loss that can't be rectified."

Liam remained mute, watching her.

"I had every right to know my father."

He picked up the empty packet of bubble bath with the Timeless Inn label on it and lobbed the object at her. She didn't bother to try to catch the packet, and it landed with a plop to float atop the creamy foam.

"Paige, even if you had known him, there's no guarantee you would have had a relationship with him. Families aren't always tight-knit little microcosms of community. Sometimes they just don't get along."

Paige wondered if he spoke from experience. He hadn't said much about his family, if anything at all. "I would have liked the opportunity to find out what our relationship might have been." Paige flicked a bubble, and then another, trying to stem the anger that kept rising to the surface, the strongest emotion in a barrage of them.

Liam reached up to scratch the stubble along his jaw. The sun through the bathroom window illuminated the scar like a silver trail. "You want that chance now, in retrospect, but did you before? Maybe your mother hoped that one day you would. Maybe—and don't get angry at me for saying this—maybe, as you suggested, that choice was yours to make, and you didn't. I know your mother let you believe the worst, but you didn't have to take it at face value."

Paige moved her knee, causing the soapy water to rush toward her face in a small wave. Liam was a good man, and a smart one, but she really didn't think she was ready to hear anything quite so sensible from him. She wanted to lash out, to condemn, indulge in a dose of self-pity along with the recognition of her responsibility.

He held the towel up again. Giving in, she climbed out and let him wrap the soft terry around her. He kissed the top of her head. "I know it's hard, but you'll get through it. You're stronger than you realize."

He left then, pulling the door shut behind him. Paige yanked the towel closer, hugging herself beneath its folds.

"And I think I love you, Liam Gray," she whispered. "Will I still be strong then?"

Chapter 26

Paige spent the day semi-somnolent, waking on occasion to see the same story playing over and over again on low volume on the Weather Channel. A fierce storm was moving swiftly up the coast, already in the Carolinas, threatening fierce weather in New England sometime in the next twelve hours or so. For now, though, the sun continued to shine brightly, forcing Paige to place the pillow across her head to block the light from her eyes. When Liam returned late in the afternoon, Paige was still lounging in bed. She answered the door with an apology.

"It'll take me two minutes to get dressed. Or maybe it'll take a couple minutes longer. You look nice. I guess this isn't a totally casual dinner."

She eyed him in his shirt and tie, the former a deep blue that brought out the shade of his eyes, the latter a variation of the same blue in a simple pattern with a turquoise pop. His dark hair had been trimmed but it was still long enough to curl over his collar. Paige stepped back to let him in. "Do you realize how good you look?"

"I did my best," he said.

"I hope I have something suitable with me. I hadn't planned on fine dining." She went to the closet and yanked open the door to reveal the garments hanging in meager assortment inside. "Well, I brought one dress." She whipped it out, holding the garment by the hanger across her body. In sea foam green, at least it wouldn't clash with his attire.

Liam gave her a slow onceover, grinning. "Perfect."

She had the feeling he would have said the same thing even if the dress were a pumpkin-orange sack. Hurrying to the bathroom to change and apply makeup, she called over her shoulder, "There's a storm coming. Did you see that?"

"I did. Time to batten down the hatches. Or soon, anyway."

Leaving the door ajar, Paige stood behind it to shed her clothes and slip into the dress. She put on some mascara, frowning at the bruises on her face. Any attempt at covering them would only make them look worse. If Liam didn't care, neither would she. She slipped a pair of earrings into her ears for good measure before subduing her hair. When she returned to the bedroom, she paused in her hunt for proper going-out shoes to frown at Liam, who was staring out the window and wearing the oddest expression.

"What are you looking at out there?"

He turned quickly. "I—"

She peered through the glass beside him at an empty street. She'd half expected to see the man she'd spotted yesterday.

"What man?" he asked when she told him.

"Don't worry, it wasn't Raleigh. It was the groundskeeper, I think, for the property across the street. At least, he was dressed like he did that kind of labor. I thought he might be a relative of my father, as he resembled him a tiny bit. Not much, mind you, but enough. Felicia said she wasn't aware my father had any family in this area, but she would see if she could find out. After everything I've learned since yesterday, I have mixed feelings about speaking with a member of my father's family, if it actually turns out there are any of them around. I don't know how much more disturbing information I can take." She laughed so he'd know she wasn't being morose and slipped her sweatshirt jacket from the chair back. "In case it's chilly in the restaurant. I don't have anything else."

He studied her a moment, a frown deepening in his brow. Then he shrugged. "Good idea. We need to get going, though. Reservations are for six-thirty."

Before they left, he took the time to yank the shades down on the windows and switch on the bedside lamp. "If anyone's watching the place, let them wonder if they've missed your return. Plus, I don't like the idea of coming back to a dark room. Not now."

Paige nodded, the light tread of phantom feet skipping along her spine.

"You okay?"

"Yes…no. We're going out to dinner like everything is right with the world, and it isn't. Not even the teensiest bit."

He took her hand. "I know. And I'm not going to utter some stupid platitude to try to make you feel better. You're too smart for that. It's a bad situation and it could get worse. But in the meantime, we need to eat and we need to talk, and this restaurant is one I've wanted to go to for a while. I want to spend that kind of time with you. So, I think that's a good enough reason for going, even if the world has spun off its axis."

"I trust you," Paige answered quietly.

His lovely blue shirt lifted and fell with a nearly silent sigh. He jiggled the keys to the Jeep in his right hand. "'Trust thyself only, and another shall not betray thee.'"

"Excuse me?"

"Sorry. It's an old quote that popped into my mind."

"Not a very reassuring one."

"Ignore me. And make sure you leave room for dessert."

His mood had turned strange. She knew she shouldn't be surprised. The good face he was putting on for her benefit had to be difficult to maintain. She squeezed his fingers and released them in order to secure the door, then preceded him down the stairs. She bid Dan's friends a goodnight in passing.

"Will you be late?"

Paige glanced at Liam for a clue. He answered for her. "Not very. No later than eleven, I should think."

"We'll keep the lights on," said the wife, whose first name Paige thought might be Constance. She uttered this statement with deliberate emphasis. Outside, Paige turned to Liam as he held the Jeep door for her.

"Do they know? I mean, they're friends of Dan's, and he's an ex-cop…"

"Oh, I'm sure they do." Liam left it at that, assisting her into the seat.

More than an hour later—having traversed twisting, narrow roads in what Liam referred to as "the scenic route," but which she suspected was a way to ensure they weren't followed—Liam pulled the Jeep into a parking lot outside what had once been a rambling white mansion with huge windows, white colonnades, and a wonderful view of the ocean. The building now housed a thriving restaurant. Despite the hour, the lot was more than three-quarters full.

"Smart move, Gray, getting reservations."

He smiled without answering. She realized for most of the trip he'd been quiet, leaving her to carry the conversation. She'd been too enthralled with the scenery to notice, but it both moved and troubled her to think her situation weighed so heavily on his mind. She touched his arm in assurance. He blinked and snapped his head in her direction as if she'd roused him from sleep.

"Are you sure this is what you want to do?" she asked.

"Yup." He climbed out of the vehicle. "Waste of gas if we don't at least go inside and breathe the aroma."

Walking beside him, her hand tucked into his elbow, she wondered if Liam's odd behavior might be caused by the changes occurring in their relationship. They'd come far in the short time they'd known each other.

The speed of it certainly unsettled her, and he had even more reason to be unprepared for the forward momentum. She'd had no one in her life. A year ago, he'd had a wife and the hopes of a family.

Releasing his elbow, she moved her fingers along his arm to his hand and clasped it. Not hard but with a gentle restraint. *Don't be afraid, Liam*, she thought at him. *Please don't be afraid.*

Odd, that plea coming from her. She might jump on a stalker's back and wallop him with an ill-aimed punch, but God forbid she should trust a man enough to love him. The things she feared in life had been misaligned by the reality of living.

* * * *

With the phone pressed to the side of his face, Liam raised a finger in Paige's direction to stop her from getting up from the table. "One minute," he mouthed at her. Dan's voice continued in his ear.

"Things are coming to a head. You need to get her out of here."

"I know," Liam whispered, overly cautious. Paige couldn't hear him. He knew she couldn't, and yet the scope of what was taking place without her knowledge filled him with guilt and anxiety.

"No one asked you to involve yourself in this. You volunteered."

He didn't care for Dan's reminder of the obvious. It was too late to back out, even if he wanted to. Yes, the choice had been his, but where would any of them be right now if he hadn't agreed to Raleigh's coercive offer? "I have my own reasons for that. They haven't changed."

"I understand. Doesn't make me any happier about the situation. And Paige—"

"Paige is my problem," Liam stated.

"Paige is everybody's problem. She needs to go."

Liam hung up without the courtesy of a goodbye. "Fuck," he whispered, and headed back to the table.

* * * *

Paige studied Liam's eyes as he observed the seascape beyond the large panes of glass. She wasn't sure he even saw it. She placed her hand on the table next to his, hooking her pointer finger over his pinkie.

"Thank you," she said.

He started. "For what?"

"Bringing me here."

"Of course. I thought you would enjoy it."

"What's wrong, Liam?"

"Nothing." He spoke too quickly. She had already begun learning his "tells," the little mannerisms and actions that gave him away when he was being less than truthful. Was this how it began, in this small way, the things that tore a couple apart after years of knowing one another?

Stop it, she commanded silently. She'd spent too long entwined in a falsehood. Like Felicia had said, she needed to unlearn what she'd believed. Time for faith, Paige supposed, but it wasn't going to be easy. There were going to be hiccups and relapses in abundance.

Liam removed his hand from hers to take the menus offered by the waitress, listening with rapt attention to the recitation of specials for the evening. Once the server left, Paige tapped Liam's shin beneath the table with her sandaled toe.

"What gives? Seriously, I feel like the sky is going to fall on us any second. What are you holding onto that you need to let out? You can tell me."

"Paige…"

"Go on. I'm all ears." She put her fingers behind the appendages in question and pushed them away from her head. He barely cracked a smile. Dropping her hands back to her lap, she folded them in the linen of her napkin.

Liam cleared his throat, turning his gaze to the window. "I haven't been entirely honest with you."

"I think we've had this conversation before. I don't need to know every little thing about you. I like mystery in a man." He didn't laugh. She tightened her fingers in the hopelessly creased napkin. "Unless it's something really horrible, like you killed somebody, I really don't care." At his look, she straightened her spine, eyes widening. "You didn't, did you?"

"Not yet."

"Liam?"

"I'm kidding. And I guess I shouldn't be. Because with the mood I'm in, you can't tell. With the mood I'm in, neither can I."

She waited, blindly pleating the napkin into a fan. When the waitress returned with their drinks, Liam asked her to give them a while longer before they ordered dinner.

"As much as I'd like to," he said, "I *can't* do anything about recent events and the danger you're in."

Paige reached for his hand again. He withdrew before contact occurred, pulling his water glass closer and whisking the condensation from the side with an angled finger. He wiped the moisture on the tablecloth.

"It's all right—"

"It's not all right, Paige."

"The police—"

"The police aren't doing enough."

Paige smiled gently. "I thought you said you and Dan would keep me safe."

"I did, and I'm not faulting him or his department. It's... it's complicated."

"I know that, Liam." She glanced around for their server. "Let's enjoy dinner and forget about that for now. We're far away from Alcina Cove—"

"Not far enough. I want you to go home, Paige. To Tennessee." Across the table, Liam, handsome, competent, confident man, looked both determined and a little frightened. "In the morning."

Paige didn't hesitate. "No."

"No? It's not up for discussion."

"Ouch. That smacks a little of...I don't know, dominance, maybe?" Placing her forearms on the tablecloth, she began to tick off points on her fingers. "First, I told you before, I don't take orders. Second, I'm an adult and the risk is mine. Third, you're not responsible for me, for my safety or my well-being. Fourth—"

"But I am, Paige. Responsible for you. In ways you could never imagine and I hope you'll never know."

His tone chilled her. She coiled her fingers into a tight knot. "What's that supposed to mean?"

Expression guarded, he shook his head. "Do you think I want you to leave me? Just the thought of it creates a gaping hole in my chest. But how much worse would I feel if something happened to you?"

Comprehension filled her with relief. "It wouldn't be your fault, Liam. Not your fault. Understand?"

"It would. This time it would be."

"Nothing's going to happen to me. Dan and his department know who they're looking for now, and you're with me. You're with me, Liam, okay?"

He reached across the table and draped his hands over hers. "Stauffer would prefer you far away, too. You know that, don't you?"

"Liam..."

Releasing her, he opened her menu and pressed it into her grasp. "Let's figure out what we're going to eat. We can continue this conversation on the long ride home."

By the time dessert and coffee arrived at the table, Liam had lightened up to the point he'd begun regaling her with stories of his childhood. He did have a family, most notably a younger sister who he made out to be the bane of his existence, but Paige could read between the lines.

She observed the emotion playing across his face with an overwhelming recognition of her own affection for him.

"Paige, what's up?"

"Nothing's up. Why?"

"You're a piss-poor liar."

"No worse than you."

He flinched. "You look happy, though."

Paige jabbed the last bite of her chocolate cake with the tines of her fork. "I am. That's what's up."

His smile faded. "Paige, you really need to go home. You could come back after."

"After what? This lunatic is locked up for giving me back my belongings? Nothing proves he took them. Think about it. It's not like he was caught pawning a gold watch with my initials on it. What could he even be charged with? There's no proof he'd broken into the cottage. No proof he'd been stalking me. Nothing that would hold up in a court of law. Heck, he could claim I had dropped those items and he picked them up. That's what he told me had happened the first time."

Liam's nostrils flared. He shook his head. "The comments about hurting you? About your mother?"

"My word against his. And I jumped on him, not the other way around."

He closed his eyes. "Fuck."

Paige glanced around at the other diners, seated too far away to have heard. "Liam, school's starting in just a few weeks. If I go home, I won't be back." She paused, her words like a punch to the middle of the chest. "I don't mean never, but not...not soon."

"It's all right," he whispered. "I know you have a career, a life."

She did. She had both those things, yet suddenly they weren't enough anymore. Like a car on a roller coaster, her elation of a moment ago plummeted. "I'm not going home. I want the time we have left."

"So do I. But I want your safety, too."

Paige popped the cake into her mouth, chewing slowly and speaking around the remnants. "Besides my going home, is there something else you might suggest?"

"Remembering."

She lowered the fork to her plate with a distinct click of stainless on china. "Remembering?"

"Whatever precipitated Raleigh's threat. Whatever drove you and your mother away from your home. Felicia Woodward said you had witnessed something."

Paige rubbed her eyes, staring at Liam through her splayed fingers. "She said Raleigh *thought* I had witnessed something. I don't remember anything concrete, just bits and pieces that won't gel. Besides, aren't there statutes of limitation for criminal activity?"

"Not all criminal activity," said Liam, spinning the coffee spoon on the tablecloth. "Murder has no home-free."

"Murder? You can't—no." Paige crossed her arms, shoving closed fists against her body to keep them from shaking. "Why would you say that?"

Liam's hand opened flat over the spoon, ceasing movement. He placed the utensil back on the saucer. "Because it's a distinct possibility."

Paige shook her head. "How would you know? Has Dan been speaking about this with you?"

"Dan talks. A lot. I've been listening."

The man who'd broken into the cottage, a murderer? That put everything in an entirely different perspective. She understood now why Liam was so insistent about her returning to Nashville. "But I don't know anything."

Liam didn't speak. All around, the clamor of flatware on plates, the conversation of diners continued in an almost surreal din. Paige's head began to spin. She put both hands out, clutching the table's edge, the cloth smooth and cold beneath her sweaty palms.

Mom, what is that?

Sweetheart, don't. It's nothing.

Mom, no, I can see—

Come away. We shouldn't be here.

Paige pushed away from the table and hurried to the bathroom, throwing open the door without ceremony. Standing over the toilet, she gasped and clutched her stomach in an attempt to keep her meal where it belonged. Knuckles rapped hesitantly on the door.

"There's someone in here," she called.

"Paige, it's me."

"I'll…I'll be out in a minute."

"And I'll be right here, waiting. Yes, sorry, there's someone in there." The last uttered, she supposed, to a patron seeking the facilities. Paige went to the sink. She splashed water on her face and patted her skin dry with a paper towel as she stared at her pale, bruised reflection. More than ever, she looked like her mother. It surprised her no one had stared at her when she and Liam came in. She'd almost forgotten the condition of her face.

Leaning closer, she gazed into her eyes, trying to dredge up the elusive memory. She *had* seen something. Disturbing and only half-recalled, a terrifying nightmare as a child, dismissed as an adult, and always blocked from conscious recall. She couldn't drag the memory out of the darkness to which she'd consigned it even now. If what Liam said was true, she needed desperately to remember.

Paige opened the door. Liam was in the process of slipping his cell phone into his pocket. "I'm okay," she said.

Liam touched her bare shoulder. "I'll get the check and we'll go home."

Nodding, she headed back toward the table. Several yards away, she stopped. Liam halted beside her. Despite her distress, she smiled. "Oh, Liam, that's so sweet. Where were you hiding it?"

She continued forward and bent to breathe in the heady scent of a single, blood-red rose in a narrow vase. A tiny card in a white envelope had been rolled to fit against the inside curve of the container's upper edge. Paige lifted her hand to pull it out, but Liam reached past her and yanked the card free with enough force the vase wobbled, splashing water on the tablecloth. He stopped the waitress on her way by.

"Where did this come from? Did you see who placed it on the table?"

Paige straightened. The server indicated she hadn't seen. Paige lifted her eyes to Liam's, whose gaze shifted away as he tore the small envelope open. He swore. A woman at a nearby table gave a timid gasp while her husband placed his napkin on his lap and turned, trying to decide whether he should speak. Liam tossed the card down on the white tablecloth.

"Is that—?"

"Blood?" said Liam. "I think so."

Crimson had soaked into the card like porous litmus paper. Nothing was written on the surface. Paige's stomach roiled again as she frowned at it. "Maybe you should ask the waitress for a box."

"For what? There's nothing—"

"For all of that. We'll give it to Dan."

Liam stepped away to see to the task. Paige sat slowly in her vacated chair. How had he known where they were? She'd been watching in the Jeep's side view mirror the whole way. There had been only one or two cars behind them, and none had been with them from start to finish.

Paige pulled her purse and sweatshirt jacket from the back of the chair and set them in her lap. She reached into the front flap of her bag for a mint to calm her stomach, fingers encountering a slip of paper. She drew it out. Cold washed like an arctic wind through her soul.

WHOSE BLOOD IS IT?

Chapter 27

"I can't get her on the phone."

Liam glanced from the road to Paige's panic-stricken features. She clutched the silent phone in her hand, her gaze glued to the windshield where the last of the evening sun made long shadows across the surface of the road in front of them. Instead of going for a box, he'd headed straight outside and had a look around the parking lot. When he'd returned, he'd found Paige pale and shaking, holding the note out to him. He'd recognized the bold printing right away. Fortunately, she didn't.

After, he'd spent a few minutes questioning the patrons at the nearest tables. He'd received vague descriptions of the height and build of the man who'd delivered the vase—none of which could be said to exactly match Raleigh at all—all of the witnesses being more intrigued by the delivery itself. No one had seen the man approach Paige's purse. Liam left them to speak further with the local police when they arrived, wanting only to get Paige out of there.

"Stauffer or one of the other officers is on his way to Felicia's house," Liam said. "Someone will call you soon and let you know she's fine."

Paige had been insistent the note referred to her mother's old friend, and her reasoning was sound. Who else was Paige connected to in Alcina Cove? What other person did she care about? Besides him, of course. Coming home had been her first mistake. Caring about him had been her second.

"All those people who didn't want to talk about my parents? Maybe it wasn't Mom or Dad they were hesitant to talk about. Maybe it was Raleigh."

"I don't know, sweetheart." Given what he knew, what he had done, and what he was prepared to carry out, the endearment rang false in his ears. It had never been his intent to care for Edwin Waters' only child.

Even less to hurt her. He'd made promises in a wicked hour. They'd become very hard to keep.

"Felicia opened up to me. And now she's targeted. How the hell does this guy know?"

Liam's jaw tensed. He let her ramble uninterrupted, his concentration on navigating the tight curves in the road in excess of the posted speed limit. So far, Paige hadn't noticed, her hand coming up to clutch the dashboard or the door handle at intervals in unconscious response to twists and turns.

This had to come to an end. He'd known for a while the final outcome of his dealings with Raleigh might not be exactly as anticipated. Too many variables had always existed, even before the unexpected event of Paige's return. If he'd maintained an emotional distance, only kept his eye on her as he'd been asked, they might have survived the tightrope walk between his daily existence and his nocturnal affairs. Everything would still have begun its inevitable unraveling, but now the stakes were higher than he'd ever imagined.

"Paige?"

She looked at him, eyes wide, the phone still gripped in her hand.

Liam sighed. "You need to start listening to me. You need to do whatever I say without question."

She thought about what he said. He witnessed the process in her mobile expression. He didn't want her to think. He wanted her compliance. His fingers tightened on the steering wheel.

"I'll try," she said, "but I'm not going home."

When the road opened temporarily into two lanes, Liam took the left, passing a line of four slower vehicles in the right. For the first time, Paige asked him how fast he was traveling. He glanced at the speedometer. "Right now? Eighty-two."

She made no further comment, dialing Felicia's number again. His own phone rang. Liam checked the ID and snatched the cell close to his ear.

"Gray here."

"Yeah, I know who it is. You're going to be a dead man, Gray, if you do anything but what you're told."

* * * *

Dan found Felicia Woodward. He stood a moment, waiting for his heart rate to slow, remembering, oddly, a trip to the hospital a couple of years past. This didn't feel the same. Not at all. But it made him remember. He didn't like fear. Tried to avoid it when he could. He didn't like uncertainty, didn't like the anticipation of bad things, didn't like finding them. And yet his job made all of those things inescapable.

"You okay, Stauffer?"

He nodded. "Yeah."

Because this time he was.

Striding across the parking lot, he left Higgens waiting by the car. The woman standing in the open garage bay with her son turned at his approach. "Ms. Woodward, where's your cell phone?"

Felicia patted her pockets. "Goodness, I don't know. Did I leave it at home again? What's wrong, officer? Oh, God...Paige?"

Dan planted his feet apart on the concrete floor of the garage. He nodded at young Billy, wondering if he'd mentioned his visit to the station to his mother. "Paige is fine. Something spooked her and she thought you might have been hurt. She's been calling you, as has the switchboard. Glad to see you upright and animate."

"What happened?"

"I'm not at liberty to say, but I believe she discussed something of what she's experienced lately with you?" He shot another look at Billy, who remained stone-faced. Nope, hadn't mentioned it to his mom. Probably because the incident had also involved being underage and drunk. Dan had warned him about the behavior. He hadn't cited Billy despite his admission, mostly because Woodward was sober when they talked, but also because Dan had been that age and up on that hill once or twice. Billy hadn't been much help with a description, either, since he'd been inebriated when the man approached him in the dark. Didn't matter now, though. They knew for sure it was Raleigh.

"Yes," Felicia said. "Paige and I talked about it."

"Good. I'm going to have an officer escort you home when you go." The woman's eyes widened, deer in the headlights. "Just as a precaution," he added. "Is there anyone who could stay with you or, as a better choice, somewhere else you might stay for a little while?"

Felicia's expression changed, hardened. She lifted her chin. "It's my home. That Raleigh's not going to scare me out of it. Because that's who we're talking about, right? He's back."

"He's back," Dan said. Billy's hand lifted and dropped gently onto his mother's shoulder. She patted his fingers. Dan recognized stubbornness in the set of both jaws, both pairs of eyes. It was no wonder Paige liked the woman.

"I'll stay with my mom," Billy said. "I have a late job to finish and then I'll pack a few things and we can go."

"We'll stop for groceries on the way," Felicia informed her son in an aside. "You finished off the cookies last time you were there. I had nothing to offer Paige."

Yes, thought Dan, nothing to absorb all that whiskey. Cookies, though, would not have been his first choice. With a nod at the two of them, Dan started back across the lot. He spoke into the radio on his shoulder loop to inform dispatch the search was over. He called Gray next, wanting a little more information out of him.

"Hey, tell Paige Felicia's fine. She'd forgotten her cell phone at home. Her son's going to stay with her for a while." Dan listened while Liam relayed the news to Paige. Although he couldn't hear her response clearly, the relief in her voice was plain. Dan went on. "I'm damned glad the blood wasn't Felicia's, but if not hers, then whose? We don't even know for sure it is blood. That hasn't been determined."

"I know that," Liam stated in a flat tone.

Dan frowned. "What's up?"

"We need to talk."

"The two of us?"

"Yeah. We're ten minutes outside of town."

"I'll meet you at the station."

* * * *

Paige paced the interview room, skirting behind the chairs. Dan had taken Liam somewhere else, somewhere they hadn't wanted her to join them. Did they think she wasn't frightened enough already without them discussing in secrecy some dire conclusions they'd both drawn?

A policeman came in, offering her a cup of coffee. She took it out of politeness.

"I put in two creams, two sugars. That okay?"

Paige nodded. "Perfect. Thank you."

She waited until the officer had gone before setting the cup down on the tabletop. Her third time past, she picked it up again, warming her nerve-chilled hands on the thick paper surface. A few minutes later, she heard a commotion outside the partially open door. Carrying the coffee with her, she went and peered into the hall.

"Chief, thanks for coming back in. Sorry to disturb you. This office."

Dan touched the arm of a man in a police chief's uniform at the same moment he found Paige watching. He reached for the door and pulled it shut, leaving Paige standing on the other side with the coffee cup clutched to her chest. She decided to drink it. The night might be another long one.

Half an hour later, the door opened again. She rose from the seat she'd taken, expecting to find Liam there. Instead, the officer who'd brought her coffee stood in the hall. "I'm Officer Jonathan Green and I'm…I'm supposed to take you home."

"To Nashville?" Based on her earlier conversation with Liam, her southern home was the first thing to pop into her mind. The officer appeared temporarily thrown. He recovered with a small laugh, as if he thought she'd made a joke.

"No, to the Timeless in town. Once I see you safely inside, I'll station myself outside for the night. Overtime, miss. Glad of it."

"All-righty then," Paige muttered to herself as she dropped the empty cup into the trash can. "May I speak to Liam before I leave? Liam Gray," she appended, in case this man had no idea.

Green inhaled, expanding the vest under his shirt. "I don't believe he's available right now. I'm sure you'll see him soon."

And that was that. The officer had positioned himself in the hallway in such a way as to block her from turning in the direction Dan and the Chief had been heading earlier. She strode toward the front door. Officer Green came behind. Outside, she climbed into the back seat of a patrol unit. Like a criminal. She supposed insurance didn't allow passengers up front. Even so, as soon as the door shut and she found herself separated by a presumably bullet-proof, or perhaps fluid-proof, panel from the officer sliding behind the wheel, she began to envision not ever getting out. She'd heard the rear doors of police cars didn't open from the inside, like a family vehicle with childproof locks. Willing herself calm, she slumped against the seat, holding her purse on her lap.

A few minutes later, the unit pulled up in front of the bed and breakfast. The inn's owners were waiting out front to hasten her inside. Green preceded them to the room and entered to check the space before allowing Paige to cross the threshold. After ascertaining she was safely locked inside, the officer announced from the other side of the door that he would be stationed on the street. Resolved to imprisonment and lack of answers, Paige changed into comfortable clothes and turned off the lamp. She dragged the chair up to the window to watch the road outside, her phone on the sill beside her elbow.

She couldn't imagine what was taking Liam so long with Dan. She hoped Dan didn't still suspect him of something—what, she really couldn't imagine. He hadn't broken into the cottage, he had no connection with Raleigh, he certainly hadn't soaked his own blood onto the paper in the few minutes she'd been in the bathroom. However, he had been found in the cottage, she had no clue who he knew or didn't know, and whatever was on that paper—blood or food coloring—the card had been dry so had been prepared in advance.

Appalled at the split-second shift from confidence to suspicion, she left the chair and strode across the room, where she retrieved the box of photos from the dresser. Resuming her seat, she held the box on her lap in the dark. For sixteen years her father had thought about her, wondered, perhaps even continued to love her. What hold did Raleigh have over him that he maintained silence for all that time? Was it only fear for his daughter and his wife, despite what she'd done? Somewhere inside, Paige held the key to Raleigh's downfall, or so that man believed. There had to be a way to play that card, draw him out.

Closing her eyes, she tried to bring the elusive scene of childhood to the forefront of her consciousness. When she'd been young, her mother had always soothed away her nightmares, told her to forget them, focus on the wonders new to each day. Had this been one of those horrors prone to rear their heads during slumber, relegated to the subconscious by the mind's self-protective functioning, and then urged to remain there by her mother's nurturing ways?

She thought of her father then, and wished with an ache in her chest for the time back. True, she might not have liked the man he'd become, but at least she would have been able to make up her mind for herself.

Paige observed the activity in the street dwindle to nearly nothing and realized with a start that almost two hours had passed. A car door opened and slammed shut, out of sight around the front of the bed and breakfast. Paige got up to turn the television on, pausing when she sighted a shadow moving across the thin strip of light that showed beneath the door. With a gasp, she hopped toward the handle to test the lock. Finding it secure, she leaned her ear against the wood to listen.

Muffled footsteps fell on the runner as someone strode to the end of the hall and returned, pausing outside her door. She lifted the phone in her hand, preparing to dial the police. Abruptly, the wood beneath her ear vibrated. She jerked her head back as the knock repeated.

"Who is it?"

"It's Dan, Paige. Let me in."

Paige switched on the nearby lamp and unlocked the knob. Before she could turn it, Dan had done so and stepped inside. Paige glanced into the hallway, looking for Liam.

"Where is he?"

"He's not with me, Paige. Liam Gray has been arrested."

Chapter 28

"No." Even though the room was empty now, she kept saying the word into the quiet, over and over. Liam hadn't done those things. He hadn't been involved. Her ability to judge a man's character was not so fucking impaired by the upheaval of her childhood that she couldn't recognize the fundamental qualities of a criminal.

Paige punched the pillow with her damaged hand and gave a little cry. Then she proceeded to swear profusely.

Liam had been charged and brought for arraignment before the district magistrate. Dan had made sure to tell her the conditions of his bail. No contact with her at all.

"You'll have to stay here for now," he'd said. "You can't return to the cottage with him right next door, at least not before the hearing. To be honest, I'd like you to head back home tomorrow bright and early. There probably will be no need for you to testify. He confessed to everything. It was Liam in your cottage, like I thought. Not Raleigh."

"But Raleigh—"

"They were working together, Paige. Whether to frighten you off or to find out what you remembered, I don't know."

"Raleigh broke into Liam's place. What about that?"

"A ruse? Retaliation of some sort? I don't know. Raleigh's always been a loose cannon. When he went away years ago, the town thought they were well rid of him. Apparently not."

"And you've known more all along than you've ever told me."

"I'm sorry, Paige. I'm…I'm sorry."

Hours later, sleep eluding her, Paige threw herself face first onto the bed, still too angry, too shocked and disbelieving, for tears. "Fuck," she said for the hundredth time. Poor Liam, his hair would stand on end at the words coming out of her mouth. But he wouldn't hear them. Not ever again. In a sane world, she should be relieved by that knowledge, but all she discovered was an extraordinary, deep sorrow. After only a handful of days of knowing Liam, the thought she'd never speak with or see him—a man who'd been charged with having a hand in terrorizing her—left her empty and hollow. The world wasn't sane. No, it was not. But the idea of Liam doing this thing ventured into a realm she couldn't recognize.

"Or maybe it's just a case of 'like mother, like daughter,'" she said, tossing the pillow to the foot of the bed. But though Debra Waters hadn't been a good wife, she'd been a loving mother. Paige belittled her mother's memory with her lack of understanding. As Liam had said, she needed to forgive. Did that sound like the words of someone intent on harm?

Paige rolled over and sat up, reaching for her vibrating phone. She stared at the text from Liam with her heart sinking into her stomach, and then it split in two.

* * * *

Liam threw items of clothing from his dresser into a duffel bag on the bed. He'd opened the windows and lifted the shades to let the cool, moisture-laden air circulate through the house. Anyone in the dark outside could see him, but he didn't care. In fact, that was the point.

Every few minutes, he paused to listen. The house was quiet tonight. He used to believe the spirit inhabiting the house was Alice, but recently he'd begun to realize guilt fostered that belief. Alice wouldn't follow him here, to a place she'd never known, and she certainly wouldn't be separated from their daughter. Whoever it was had gone silent, as if waiting. It shouldn't be long. If spirits could be disturbed by changes in a home, like renovation, how much more disruptive would the reckoning of a sudden, heartbreaking truth be?

Leaving the bedroom, Liam went to his office and dumped his paperwork and discs into a second duffel bag before slipping the laptop into its carrier. He had to make this look good. Like he meant it. Straightening from the task, he listened again. The stairs creaked, first one, then the next. Several after were silent until the top two, which made the slightest noise as if pressure had been carefully applied. Pretending he hadn't heard, Liam slid the handle of the computer bag over his shoulder and called Shadow's name as he approached the door. The start he felt at finding someone standing right beyond the threshold wasn't feigned, despite knowing he was coming.

"Going somewhere, Gray?"

Shadow scooted out from behind the desk and ran past Regan Raleigh's legs, heading full tilt for the landing. *Good boy*, Liam thought. *Get as far from this house as you can tonight, buddy.*

"Yeah, Raleigh, I am. I believe the term is 'jumping bail.'"

"I heard you got popped. Good man."

"Paige had already figured out there'd be no charges short of a confession, so I provided it. The ploy worked. You got what you wanted." Liam yanked the duffel from the floor and pushed past Raleigh, returning to the bedroom.

Coming into the room behind him, Raleigh laughed. Liam continued to pack.

"I'm surprised you didn't figure out it was me sooner," Raleigh said.

"What makes you think I didn't?" Liam didn't look back. He listened, though, closely, for any sign the man had moved nearer.

"You surprise me. Never figured you for a loyal soldier."

"Threatening me didn't matter. The fact you threatened Paige did."

"Now, Gray, did I actually use her name?" Raleigh drawled.

"You didn't have to. I'm no fool."

"I can see that. And your next step?"

"What do you mean?"

"Think you can kill me?"

"Why would I bother?" Liam zipped the bag shut and straightened, looking around the room as if to make certain he hadn't missed anything.

"Because you've been fucking the bitch."

Liam didn't miss a beat. "Not anymore. You know that information you were looking for? I got it. It'll protect me, and it'll protect her, long after I'm gone. What Paige saw that night is written down and notarized, waiting in a sealed envelope for delivery to the police if anything happens to either one of us."

Raleigh came into the room, walking in a wide circle, eyeing Liam's belongings with mild curiosity. Liam could see the man's mind wasn't on anything in front of his eyes. Except Liam. The bastard was sizing him up. "Then why haven't you given the envelope to the cops yet? Something like that would have been good leverage, rather than confessing to this other business. Why didn't you point the finger in my direction?"

Liam shrugged. "Because no one knows you're here. It would be like pointing fingers at a ghost. And I just want to be done."

Regan turned his head aside, coughing into his shoulder. He smelled, Liam realized, like alcohol. Not a good sign.

"So, you'll leave her," Regan said, "just like that."

"That's the plan. After the job."

"After the—" Regan laughed again, so hard he staggered sideways against the doorjamb.

"Yeah, the job. I'm going to need the money. You said you wanted the load out before dawn with the storm coming up the coast. You haven't time to waste, and I just want to put all of this behind me."

Regan straightened, his pale eyes glittering in the lamplight. "You want in, you're still in. I'm short a man. And then what? You're really gone? Leaving her behind without a backward glance?"

"What do you think? She's not going to want me back, thanks to my confession."

"Maybe I'll take her on myself then."

Liam bent to adjust the zipper on the duffel bag, hiding his face. He couldn't be sure Regan wouldn't read his expression. "Doubt it. She knows now what you did to her mother."

"She doesn't have to be willing, Gray. You know that."

Liam kept himself from taking a deep breath, giving his emotions away. He tossed the second duffel beside the first in the middle of his unmade bed and turned. "Was that really blood on the card with the rose?"

"Yeah, stroke of genius, that." Raleigh held up his hand, wagging his middle finger. "Paper cut on these rough old hands. Couldn't resist."

"Your intent was only to scare her away? If you'd only ignored her, you would have been better off."

"Needed her away from here, though, didn't we? Besides, it was fun."

Fun. Liam's gut clenched. "I tried to get her to go back home. She wouldn't listen."

"Not surprising. She thinks she's in love." The man started chortling again. "And the end game? Well, you've changed that now, haven't you?"

Liam's eyes narrowed. He knew better than to believe the bastard was giving in this easily. Liam needed a little more time, that was all, and he hoped he'd bought it. He couldn't count on any more than that.

"Fuck you, Raleigh. Let's get this over with."

He took a few steps into the hallway and turned in front of the bathroom door, waiting for Raleigh to exit the room. After a moment, the man sauntered out with a jerk of his thumb over his shoulder. "Had her in there once, I did. Edwin's wife. Right here in his bed. She was too scared to say no."

Liam stayed quiet, his teeth grinding together. From the corner of his eye, he glimpsed the attic door swing open several inches. He looked away. "Last job, and I'm gone."

Raleigh nodded. "Yeah. Last job."

Liam didn't much care for the way Raleigh uttered those three words, but he couldn't change them.

* * * *

Paige crossed the porch, careful where she placed her feet. Storm clouds had begun to amass sometime overnight and, with the hour barely past four, the night remained dark as ink. A cool, damp breeze tugged at her hair, whipping loose tendrils into her eyes, while light rain clung like mist. Something bounded at her from the corner.

"Shadow!" Bending, Paige scooped the black cat up with one hand and tried the knob on the screen door with the other. Unlocked. So was the interior door. Paige walked into the unlit kitchen and lowered Shadow to the floor. Light filtered down from a room upstairs, lining the steps in the living room with a soft glow. Otherwise, the house was dark.

Had he already gone? Idiot. Such an action would only solidify a guilt that wasn't his. Paige crossed the floor and climbed the stairs. Standing on the threshold to Liam's bedroom, she studied the empty, rumpled bed, the drawers in the dresser hanging open, clothing obviously removed from them. In the office, she found the same conditions, drawers not fully closed, papers and laptop missing.

Paige's shoulders dropped. "Liam, no."

She was too late to stop him. Defeated and empty inside, Paige turned and headed back down the hallway. Two strides away from the door leading to the attic, she heard the feeble squeal of hinges and glanced back to see the door swinging open to reveal the darkened stairwell inside. She stopped. "Liam?"

Her question was followed by a sound in the bathroom that made her think of a struck match. She spun in time to witness the flare of white-gold light at the end of a cigarette and the face revealed behind it. The man puffed to get the cigarette going. Paige darted toward the stair head, but a stocky, balding man with a fierce tattoo the length of his arm already blocked her descent from the landing below.

"Hey, babe," Raleigh said, coming out into the hallway behind her. "I see you got my message."

She looked back. Regan Raleigh lifted his hand to reveal a cell phone cupped in his palm, her reply to Liam glowing on the screen.

Don't leave me, Liam. Just don't leave me. We'll work this out together.
"Where is he?"

The man blew a perfect smoke ring into the air between them. "Gone. Just like he said." He tipped the phone from side to side. "And you, of course, opted to go with him. After all, you looooove him. Stupid emotion, love. Fucking waste of energy."

Paige glanced again into the ransacked bedroom. "Did you hurt him? Is he here in the house?"

Raleigh took a few steps closer and stopped at a point where she had to look up to meet his eye. Not far, though. He was nowhere near as tall as Liam. She could only hope the man was lying through his teeth. Unless Liam had been pounced on by more than one attacker, she felt confident Raleigh couldn't have overpowered him. Not alone. Yes, now that she stood closer, she could see a definite swelling in Raleigh's jaw and the beginnings of a black eye.

"He's not in the house. He's waiting for you…sweetie. I couldn't very well leave him somewhere he could be found. Had to follow through with his bid for freedom, didn't he? And you disappear with him. Simple." He bent close. "We'll have a little fun beforehand, though, won't we?"

Paige drew a clenched fist. She kept it at her side, remembering the end result of the last time she'd taken a swing at him. Besides, the other man waited behind her. If she cooperated, she might find a way to help Liam. Patience had never been one of her virtues. It was time to establish that practice, if only for Liam's sake. Wherever this man had taken him, she wanted to be there, too. Together they would—they would what? Probably both die.

"I'm not my mother. She was afraid of you."

"You will be, too, before I finish." He nodded to the man on the steps. Paige ducked away, up against the wall.

"What about—"

"The envelope containing the statement of what you saw on the beach sixteen years ago? Believe me, you'll sign another saying it was all a lie to try and frame me because of this whole harassment thing they've charged lover boy with. If you don't, you'll just prolong the agony I'm going to subject him to before he dies."

She had no idea what he was talking about, but she latched onto the fact that Liam lived. "Why do you want to kill him?"

He appeared affronted that she'd even ask. With a smirk, he took another drag on the cigarette. "Do I need a reason? He irks me."

"I don't believe you."

"That he irks me? Why would I lie about that? He's been working for me for six months now and has never shown an ounce of respect. I never quite trusted him. And I've dumped men in the ocean for less. As soon as he hooked up with you, though, I knew it was only a matter of time before he learned the truth about that night. That truth makes him a danger to me. Just like you."

Paige risked a look to her right, where the second man stood less than six feet away now. "I don't—"

A knife flashed out, sparking light from the single burning lamp in the bedroom. She raised an arm to ward off the blow and felt the blade slash across her forearm. Not deep. Please God, not deep.

"That's just a taste of what's coming," Raleigh said with a smile.

Blood dripped onto the floor, a few crimson spatters on the hardwood. More ran warmly over her skin. She lifted her hand to her shoulder to elevate the wound, clamping her right over the cut, and turned toward the stairs. "Where are we going?"

"Just shut up. I'll let you know when you get there."

He marched her outside and down the stairs to the dark beach, the knife inches from her ribs and his tattooed companion on her other side. She had no doubt she'd break down when this was over, but for now she felt preternaturally calm. Like the atmosphere. Eerily still before the pending storm. Even the wind had died. Not a star could be seen over the ocean, and the mist had ceased its fine spray. Waiting. Everything waiting.

"The old broad? Bea something? I was in the house that day you came back to talk to her. I was there to make her shut up. Her grandson told me she'd been blabbing to you. Couldn't have her saying too much. She might have let something slip without even knowing what the fuck she said. You passed the place I was hiding twice. I could have reached out and touched you."

Paige's stomach rolled. "Did you hurt her?"

He chuckled. "Nah. Scared her good, though. Couldn't hurt her. She reminds me of my granny."

Sick freaking bastard. Paige stumbled on a dimple in the sand and was jerked upright with a rough wrench to her arm. Biting her tongue to keep from crying out, she scanned the beach from side to side for any sign Liam had preceded her. For all she knew, Raleigh was lying about that.

Before they'd gone far, he appeared—the seaman's ghost. Lantern swinging. Looking back at her. Paige gasped. Did ghosts do that, look at people? The man to her right sucked a breath in through his teeth, his eyes bulging.

"Shit fuck, what is that?"

"You see him, too?" Paige asked, ever so calmly.

"I told you to shut up," Raleigh hissed.

Oblivious. No chance to frighten him with it, then. But his buddy was faltering. Hell, Bea Hunt had been right. Sailors were a superstitious lot.

This guy probably viewed what he was seeing as a premonition of death. One could only hope.

"Cap'n, you don't see that?"

Raleigh stopped. "Who is it? Where?"

The man raised a hand, pointing. "Right the hell in front of us. It's a haunt."

Snorting impatience, Raleigh shoved her at the man, who grabbed her arm. Raleigh then marched forward, straight up and through the specter, pausing on the other side. Even at this distance, Paige witnessed his shoulders jerk in a quick shiver. He spun on his heel to stare back at her and then down to the beach at his feet. The apparition vanished. Where it had been, Paige spotted again the long, low rock, free of seaweed. This time, instead of the black stone, she saw an actual body and the remembered stance of Regan Raleigh sixteen years ago standing over it, bloody knife still clutched in his hand. The man's plea for his life and the whispered suck of his dying breath reverberated in her head with all the force of the present, rather than memory. The victim of Raleigh's savagery had been a stranger to her then and remained a stranger now, but it didn't matter. Raleigh had killed a man in front of her. She had witnessed his horrendous crime and spent a lifetime blocking it from her mind. Well, it was back now, the memory, and it both sickened and enraged her. Her jaw tightening, she raised her gaze to Raleigh's bone-white countenance and knew he had seen the vision of the body on the sand, too.

He rushed back in her direction. "Lights out," he said.

And they were.

Chapter 29

Paige awoke to the vile stench of her own vomit. She struggled up onto her knees but couldn't stay there as the surface beneath her rolled and dipped, tumbling her onto her side. Duct tape bound her hands behind her back as well as her ankles. Using her heels, she shoved herself backwards until she hit something solid and worked her way into a sitting position against what appeared to be a metal wall. The world plunged again. A voluminous spray of seawater crashed down over her and flooded across the deck. She was on a ship.

Without warning, another stream of vomit churned from her stomach.

"Seasick, little butterfly?"

"She's probably got a concussion, Raleigh."

Paige jerked away from the visage of Regan Raleigh bending over her to Liam's voice, locating him similarly trussed about ten feet away. He'd been tied about the chest, too, secured to what appeared to be a barrel affixed to the deck. The sun had not yet lipped the horizon and black clouds roiling overhead limited her vision. Raleigh straightened, unaffected by the tossing ship.

"You're a fool if you think you can ride out the storm in this vessel," Liam shouted.

"You're a fool if you think it should matter. Not to you, Gray. Not to your lady, either. I've faced worse. You, however, have about another ten minutes for concern. After that…" He made a theatrical slashing motion across his throat.

"What's another ten minutes going to do?"

Liam, Paige thought. *Shut up. Don't taunt him.*

Raleigh crouched again. A flash of metal preceded the downward motion of his hand. Paige flinched and turned her face away, feeling a tug at her ankles. Two seconds passed before she realized he hadn't stabbed her but only severed the binding on her legs.

"Turn around."

She complied. He cut the tape on her wrists before yanking her to her feet. Good. Having her hands free evened the odds a bit.

"What are you doing?" This from Liam. Paige tried to reassure him with a look, but the deck's plunge and roll across huge waves prevented her from focusing.

"I said ten minutes, didn't I? Think about what's happening to her while we're gone. I don't like them bound. I like them to fight."

A wordless growl gurgled up from Liam's throat as he struggled to free himself. Raleigh grinned. She wanted to knock his teeth out. As he dug his fingers into her arm, Paige envisioned the photo of her mother and Raleigh, both of them smiling. It had to have been taken before Deb Waters understood what a monster this man was. Another wave of nausea took her and she lurched over. Beside her, Raleigh jumped back, avoiding the spray.

"Fuck. This isn't going to work." Striding angrily across the reeling deck as if on dry land, he threw his hands up, the knife still in his left hand reflecting what little light existed. None of it came from the ship. They were running dark. Overhead, lightning seared the sky, followed by a blast of wind that threw her sideways. She caught herself on a coil of rope. A shrill keen filled the air. The storm was upon them.

"Too late, asshole," she said, and charged Raleigh with her head down. She hit him square in the bony, concave structure of his lower back, sending him sprawling. The impact rolled her hard across the deck. The other men onboard stared, as if unsure what to do. An instant later, she realized they weren't looking at them at all, their attention fixed starboard where an ominous black shadow, whether cloud or water, loomed toward them. If the latter, she understood the ship could flounder at any moment.

Raleigh was slow getting up. When he did, she spotted blood streaming from his head. She also saw the knife lying in a rippling puddle of seawater half a dozen feet away. She lunged for it. Chilled and wet, her fingers slipped off the handle and caught the blade. Blood clouded the standing water. Grabbing the carved grip with her left hand she rolled onto her back as Raleigh rushed her. The ship rose and dropped into a huge trough, throwing the man off balance. Paige lashed out, slicing into the tendon at the back of his ankle. A crippling blow, Raleigh went down.

On her knees, Paige scrambled over to Liam. Behind her, she heard Raleigh screaming for someone to stop her. She doubted anyone could hear it over the freight-train noise of the wind. Breathless, shaking, she cut through the duct tape on Liam's limbs, struggling with the wet rope.

A hand reached to take the blade. Liam, who had been ripping the tape from his wrists, looked up. So did Paige. "Oh, God, you."

Not a gardener after all, but Raleigh's crewmember. No wonder he'd been watching her. She wrestled him for the knife. Rain lashed across her face with the sting of sleet.

"Let him have it," Liam shouted in strangled tones. Paige turned and followed his wide gaze to the ocean rising toward them. She released her grip on the handle.

The stranger snatched the knife before it fell and sawed through the rope. "No man should be forced to die when he has even the smallest chance to live."

Paige's attention snapped back to the man beside her, to his red, burn-scarred face, familiar features and recognizable voice. *Oh, God, oh, God.* "Dad?"

The monster wave hit, flinging them all into the sea.

* * * *

She couldn't move. Every bone in her body had been broken and badly glued back together. Water flowed through her head and pounded each nerve into screaming confusion. The black, black sea was going to claim her, suck her down into a place where she'd never be found. And that was okay. She wanted to go. If only someone would release the chain around her wrist.

"I've got you, Paige. I've got you. Stop fighting me."

She relaxed her body, gave in to this new pressure, allowed herself to be pulled up and out and onto something cold and unyielding. Hands rolled her onto her side. She puked out salt water like bile.

"Paige, honey. We can't stay here. With the storm surge, high tide will fill this cave to the ceiling in minutes."

Thrashing, she managed to get into a sitting position. Her bones still hurt but at least now she understood why. Raising her head, she looked into her father's eyes.

"Dad, Dad, you're alive."

He nodded, his scarred face creasing into a smile. "Later. We'll talk later. We're not out of danger yet." He tugged her hand. Her muscles shivered in protest.

"Wait. Where's Liam? Where's Liam, Dad? Where is he?"

"Not here. That's all I know. And we can't be, either."

Paige gaped at the crashing waves. No beach remained. Soon, the cave floor would disappear beneath the surging tide. She cupped her hands around her mouth. "Liam!"

"There's no time. He wouldn't want you to die here, waiting for him. We were lucky. I don't think anyone else on that ship survived."

"No, Dad. No. Liam!"

Wind rushed into the cave, carrying with it salt spray and a cacophony of sound. Water followed. Paige pulled herself away from the retreating surge. Next wave would drive even deeper. Their exit was blocked. "We can't get out."

"Not that way. Can you follow me?"

Paige gave one last cry for Liam, her voice drowned by the storm. Sobbing, she clung to her father's hand as he led the way back into the cave into utter darkness. Soon, though, they left the echoing vastness behind, climbing up manmade handholds through a narrow stone corridor. Still crying, she paused when her father did. He placed her hand on the rung of a ladder. "Climb," he said. "It will take you to a small trapdoor at the top. Open that, and you'll be in the crawlspace underneath the cottage where you were staying. I snuck in that first night. Just that first night only. I wanted to know…to know you were there."

"Dad."

He let go of her. "I'm going back for one more look."

"Wait, Dad, no. You'll be—"

"I have to, Paige. He saved my life when Raleigh blew up my ship. We both lost a lot that day, but him most of all. I need to do this."

Paige reached for his shoulder, but missed it in the darkness. She listened until she couldn't hear his progression anymore and then she climbed up rung by rung. She pushed open the trapdoor at the top, shimmying onto the crawlspace floor where she sat with her knees pulled up and her arms wrapped around them. She wasn't going anywhere until one or both men appeared at the top of that ladder.

What seemed like hours later, but was likely, in the time-warping dark, no more than fifteen or twenty minutes, she heard the old ladder creaking beneath the weight of an ascent. In sudden fear it might not be either man she wished to see, she didn't call out, but waited in mute anticipation.

"Paige?"

"Dad! Is Liam with you?"

He hesitated. "No. I'm sorry."

Paige bit back a cry of anguish. Crawling toward the opening, she assisted her father into the blackness beside her. "We'll find him," she said. "I swear we will. But for now, we have a more immediate problem."

"What's that?"

"I nailed the trapdoor in the cottage shut. With about fifty nails."

Locating a piece of a cement block lying on the dirt floor, Paige banged it against the floorboards above. "I don't get it, Dad," she said, punctuating each word with a slam. "Where have you been? Why did you let me believe you were dead? What the hell were you doing on Raleigh's ship?"

She heard her father scrabbling around in the darkness, soon joining her efforts, wedging an implement of some sort between the boards. "I'm not proud of the choices I've made in my life, Paige. I never meant for Liam to get involved in this investigation. When I saw the two of you being loaded into the dinghy with the last of Raleigh's cargo, I slipped onboard. In the commotion, no one questioned me. Once the dinghy was winched up onto the ship, I hid inside. I couldn't let either one of you pay the price for my past mistakes. Not again."

"Why didn't he tell me?" Paige wiped the sweat from her face on her forearm. "Why didn't you?"

Her father pulled down on the piece of metal, splintering wood. "It was an impossible situation. We were trying to make things right."Another board gave. Paige bit back any further questions as she worked beside her father to tear an opening to the cottage above. A half an hour later, they emerged from the cottage into gale force winds. Paige's cell phone had disappeared in the ocean, but she knew Liam had a landline. She only hoped it would still be working in the storm.

When they entered through the back door, Paige found water on the floor from the open windows. She quickly closed them as she made her way across the kitchen to the phone hanging on the wall. Shadow darted from his hiding place and she reached for him. He ran past her into her father's arms.

"Hey, Spooky," he said, scratching the cat behind the ears. "How are you, old man?"

"Spooky? What happened to the white spot on his chest?"

Her dad nodded. "It's him. Still going strong, your old kitten. The markings on his chest spread apart as he aged."

Paige shook her head. "Would you close the windows? I think Liam left them all open." Speaking his name, Paige's throat closed. She blinked back tears. Lifting the receiver from the cradle, she listened for a dial tone. None.

"Paige!"

Pivoting on her wet sole, Paige looked toward the sound of the voice. Dan Stauffer stood in the living room with several other officers. Over the storm's racket she hadn't even heard them.

"Why didn't you shut these windows?" The complaint was the first thing that came to mind. She couldn't help thinking the floors Liam had worked so hard to refinish would be ruined, which was senseless and stupid. He could be beyond caring about anything at this point.

No. No! She mustn't think like that. Liam had to be all right.

"It's a potential crime scene," Dan told her. "We didn't touch anything. Came through the front door. Afraid we damaged it. Waters?"

Her father went forward and shook Dan's hand. "Stauffer. What the hell happened? I thought you were supposed to be there before the dinghy returned to the ship with the goods?"

Paige sat abruptly on the high stool beneath the phone, still cupping the dead receiver in her hand. They *knew* each other? Why wasn't Dan surprised to see her father? And what the hell were they talking about? Looking at the other men, she noticed the officers were all dressed in black.

"We set up the perimeter, but didn't move in until the appointed time. Raleigh shipped off early. I thought maybe he learned we were coming. Gray said—where the hell is Gray?"

For a moment, neither Paige nor her father answered, and then Paige cleared her throat. "The boat capsized. We don't know what happened to him." Moisture slid down her cheeks. She didn't bother to wipe it away.

Dan frowned, turning to hold a quick conversation with one of his men, who promptly fired up his radio, heading back toward the front of the house. "I'm sorry. I don't know what kind of rescue can be mounted with the severity of this weather, but we'll do our damndest. I promise, Paige, the Maine patrol will find him."

Paige compressed her lips, shaking her head. There could be no guarantees. She understood that with a knowledge that chilled her soul. "Why did Liam confess? It was Raleigh all along, wasn't it? Not Liam. And you arrested him."

Dan stepped into the kitchen and removed the phone from Paige's hand, returning it to the cradle. "No, I didn't. That was a ruse. Raleigh demanded Liam confess as a sign of his loyalty and to lead us off Raleigh's trail, and we needed Liam back in his good graces. I wasn't sure Raleigh would actually believe it. In fact, I wanted Liam out at this point, but he refused. I always felt the scheme was too dangerous, but Raleigh approached him half a year ago, and he became our 'in.' I've never been a fan of civilians in this type of situation."

"Damn it, Dan, what 'type of situation' are you talking about? Why did you two lie to me? You knew my dad was alive. You did, didn't you?"

Dan let out a long breath. "Yes." He glanced at her father, who said nothing. "Edwin's been in hiding since Raleigh tried to kill him by planting explosives on his ship. Gray saved him, but Edwin spent a long time in the hospital. The ship went down with two crew members. Raleigh thought he'd been successful. Even before we convinced your father the time had come to help put the prick behind bars, we made sure the story got out that the ship went down with no survivors. In order for us to pull this off, Edwin had to stay dead to Raleigh. Believe me, Liam wanted to tell you. It was too risky letting you know, especially once we suspected Raleigh might be the one harassing you."

"You suspected? You mean, even before I gave you that photograph? God, Dan, how could you leave me in the dark? Didn't I deserve the truth?"

"Paige," her father said quietly.

She ignored him. "You have a lot of explaining to do."

"What happened to Raleigh out there?" Dan asked, disregarding her statement. He looked to her father for an answer to that question, but Paige responded.

"After I sliced his Achilles tendon with his knife, I'd say he became shark bait in the water."

Dan stared. "You? You were on the ship?"

"I was gullible enough to fall for a text he sent with Liam's phone and showed up here. He was waiting for me. On our way across the beach he or the guy with him knocked me out cold and I woke up on the ship. I should probably see a doctor to make sure I don't have a concussion."

Dan's gaze didn't leave her face. "And you managed to stab the guy. With his own knife."

"Yep."

"You scare me, Paige Waters."

"I scare myself sometimes."

Dan studied her a moment before getting on his radio again to make arrangements for transport of the two of them to the hospital. As she was heading out the door to a waiting patrol unit on the front lawn, Paige paused beside Dan. Her father continued on, leaving them alone.

"Raleigh was planning to kill both Liam and me. Liam had apparently told him a story about me remembering something I had witnessed before my mother and I left Alcina Cove. I had only flashes of memory of it. I remember it now. It came back to me in our walk across the beach before I was knocked out. Raleigh…Raleigh is a murderer." With that statement, the danger of the situation, both past and present, struck her hard.

"That's something we've always suspected," Dan said. "The only reason this current investigation has gone on so long was because we hoped to get enough on him that he wouldn't walk away with a slap on the wrist. Between the guns he was moving tonight and other information your dad supplied..." Dan shrugged. "Probably moot now. I would have liked proof he planted the explosive on Edwin's sailboat. Without physical evidence, though, it would have come down to his word against your dad's. Paige, if Raleigh has survived, perhaps with your help we can piece together what took place all those years ago. There's no statute of limitations on murder."

Liam had said the same thing. When was that? Last night. It seemed like years. Paige looked toward the police car. Exhausted and defeated, Edwin Waters limped across the scraggly lawn. Paige turned back to Dan. "My dad's been watching me, you know. I spotted him outside the bed and breakfast."

"I'm not surprised he took that risk. You're his daughter."

"Yeah. I am. I just can't figure out what either of my parents was doing with the likes of Regan Raleigh."

"That's something you'll have to ask him."

Paige nodded and began walking toward the waiting vehicle again. She paused once more, looking over her shoulder at Dan framed by the open, battered doorway. "I want him back."

He didn't ask who she meant. There was no need. "I know."

On the way to the hospital, Edwin spoke quietly of the day Liam saved him. Paige listened with tears still running down her face. She dashed them away.

"While Raleigh was in prison, I made an honest life for myself. Your mother knew he'd gone, but his release was imminent. By that time, she had a life of her own down there in Tennessee, and there was no guarantee Raleigh wouldn't make good on his promise if she showed her face around here. When he got out, he kept coming around, trying to talk me into taking small jobs here and there until I threatened to turn him in. Big mistake. I should have gone to the police first instead of after. My crew would still be alive."

"I don't understand why Mom never went to the police in the first place, years ago," Paige whispered, leaning her head back against the seat.

"It was a twisted, nasty affair. I kept working with him, though, more to keep an eye on him than anything else. When he left town, I was relieved. I suppose I could have given him up when the cops questioned me about his disappearance, but I just wanted it all to be over. I hadn't meant to get caught up in Raleigh's trade. At first I liked the easy money, and then I was in too deep to get out."

Paige closed her eyes. From the things her mom had said at the end, she'd suspected her father had been involved in something illicit. That both of them had. How casually he spoke of it now. Yet she could hear the shame, the torment underlying his words.

"After I was released from the hospital following the explosion," her father continued, "I went to the police. Word was given out my ship had gone down. I went into hiding. Plans had been underway to infiltrate Raleigh's group as soon as the cops realized he'd come back. He approached Liam about six or seven months ago, though, because of the cave on the property. I think Raleigh considered himself invincible, smarter than most men. And Liam…well, he felt Raleigh was responsible for the fact he hadn't been with his wife when she died. And he's right. If he hadn't been saving me from my burning ship, he would have been. I lost my men that day. He lost everything."

Paige sighed. "Raleigh didn't recognize you tonight."

"No. He didn't even notice the extra man when I slipped onto the dinghy. As you can see, I don't look the same." He fingered the burns marring half his face.

"What about all these years, Dad? What were you doing? Did you ever think of me?"

Edwin Waters was silent a moment. His lips twisted. Moisture glistened on his lashes. "Of course I thought about you, Paige. Can we talk about this later?"

Paige narrowed her eyes, her stomach twisting. "All right, Dad."

He nodded. "And I'm sorry about the fact Dan and Liam had to keep you in the dark, couldn't let you know I was alive. Or any of what was going on. I don't think they knew for certain at first that Raleigh was after you."

"But they suspected," Paige whispered.

"They were protecting you. You need to know that."

An angry growl escaped her lips. "You know what? I don't want anyone ever fucking protecting me again."

"Language, Paige."

"Oh, now you sound like Liam." At the utterance of his name, she felt as though her heart had ripped from her chest to land on her lap.

"I'm sorry about your mother, too. At the end, we reached an understanding. I'm guessing you never knew that."

Paige said nothing. She thought of what she'd viewed as her mother's ramblings in those final days. She hadn't been rambling at all. She'd been trying to let Paige know the truth. All of it. Those jumbled, confusing words were what had driven Paige to return to Alcina Cove after all the years away.

Chapter 30

"Why are you staying in the cottage, Dad? You could be here in the house."

Edwin shook his head. She'd gotten used to his scars in the past twenty-four hours, almost didn't see them, only the man she was starting to remember. "I'd rather not. I was here, on and off, in hiding, which made it difficult for Liam these last few days when you were around. I saw Raleigh take you out of the house."

"You were in the attic?"

Edwin nodded. "I think Raleigh suspected Liam had something of value secreted away and came looking for it the night he broke in. I wasn't in the house at the time, fortunately. I don't think Raleigh ever expected the thing Liam was hiding was me."

Paige nodded, her arms on the porch railing, hands folded as she observed the darkness lowering over the sea. "So it was you and not a ghost I saw."

"Oh, I don't think I'd say that. Except for the time you saw me outside The Timeless, I was very careful to avoid coming out into the open. And the night you jumped on Raleigh. I almost blew it then. I had been following him around a bit, keeping my distance, but I nearly revealed myself when I came running. Fortunately, he just took off."

"God, you mean you were right there? You'd think I would have sensed it or something," Paige muttered.

"Why?" He sounded bitter. "What kind of dad had I been that you would expect something like that?"

She touched his arm, but said nothing. He was right, yet what kind of daughter had she been? If remembered love hadn't been enough to make her reach out to him despite what she'd believed about the man, a need for answers should have. But she'd let it go until she thought him dead.

"There is something in this house," Edwin said, returning to the prior topic. "Not when you and Deb were here, but after, much later, I encountered some things I couldn't explain. I sometimes thought it was your mother's grandfather."

"Why would you think that?"

"This house used to be his. You don't remember that? Your mom always thought her grandfather died of a broken heart when his wife drowned. I thought if that were true, maybe he was even more devastated when Deb left, and he started to haunt the place then. She was his favorite of the two sisters. Don't ever tell your aunt I said that, though."

With a crooked smile, Paige promised to keep his secret. "I've seen a ghost on the beach, too. This place really is 'Haunted Alcina Cove.'"

Her father laughed.

"I think he might have been the man Raleigh killed in front of me and Mom, but I don't know. I guess I never really will."

He patted her hand where it lay on his arm. "Don't question. Just accept. There's so much in this world that defies explanation."

Paige grunted. "You remember Bea Hunt? She said something about your improper renaming of your sailboat being bad luck. She never said what you'd called it, though."

"Debra's Hope. That's what I renamed it after I learned she had cancer. Not supposed to christen a ship with a name ending in an 'a.' Hogwash, if you ask me. That was a sound ship and would have continued on the seas if it wasn't for Raleigh sending it to the bottom of the ocean."

Paige bowed her head. "Do you think he's dead, Dad?"

"You're not talking about Raleigh."

"No."

"I don't know, honey. They've been out all day looking for survivors. But don't give up hope. Don't ever give up hope."

He patted her hand once more and left the porch to stroll slowly in the direction of the cottage. Spooky-Shadow trotted at his side, two men growing old by the seaside. Paige released a breath she hadn't realized she'd been holding.

"Please, please don't let him be dead." Paige prayed in earnest, her eyes closed. She'd prayed for her mother, too, but those prayers hadn't been answered. Or maybe they had in a way she hadn't understood then. More than anything, Paige had wanted her mother's suffering to end.

Shoving her hands in her pants pockets, Paige walked down the steps to the beach. She strode in the opposite direction of the jetty and the cave beyond, picking up the occasional shell and sticking it in her pocket. Love hurt. It hurt deeply. Maybe she would have been better off without it, but it was too late now. Though she told herself over and over again he would be found, Liam's absence left her bereft and hollow and aching.

Night fell with remarkable softness due to the change in the atmosphere from the storm. Paige took the shells from her pocket and dumped them into the waves before turning on her heel to head back to her old home. She had no reason to stay there except lying in Liam's bed the night before made her feel closer to him.

A light flared on the beach ahead of her. Paige narrowed her eyes and increased her pace until she got close enough to see the hair, the beard, the outline of the coat—the absence of legs.

Heart pounding, she continued her pursuit. The figure turned, looked back. Paige felt her knees turn to jelly. He lifted the lantern and swung it, as if urging her on. What did he want from her? She'd thought the ghost's purpose had been to make her remember the murder on the beach. But he was still here, still beckoning.

When Paige got within a handful of yards, the phantom dissipated, shredding like fog on a breeze. Something dark and tall moved where it once had been. Her heart leapt, first in fear and then in joy. "Oh, my God." She ran, all physical discomfort forgotten, skidding to a halt a few steps away. "Liam, you're not…you're not dead, are you?"

She heard his deep, rumbling voice over the waves. "Put your arms around me, sweetheart, and let me know."

She did that very thing, afraid she'd discover him an insubstantial being like the ghost who had vanished at his approach. She found him quite alive, solid and shaking and soaked to the skin. As soon as her limbs slipped around him, he collapsed against her and they dropped together to the sand.

"Liam!"

Paige pressed her fingertips to his throat, seeking his pulse. Locating a strong, steady beat, she shifted her position and tightened her grip around him. She kissed his forehead, his eyes, his mouth, tasting salt water on her lips.

"Where the hell have you been?" she demanded. Everywhere her body touched his, warmth returned to his flesh, but those places exposed to the air remained icy cold. She rubbed her hands up and down his arms in an attempt to dispel the chill. He leaned his head against hers.

"I was trapped in that blasted cave. The storm surge threw me up into a crevice and knocked me out cold. Paige, I'm sorry about all of this."

"Stop. It doesn't matter."

"It does. Because I lied to you. All I ever wanted to do was make Raleigh pay. For the loss of my crew members. For the fact I wasn't with Alice when she died. I had a plan…*we* had a plan—me, your father, the police, the Maine patrol. Even the frigging FBI. But none of us ever counted on you showing up."

"I bet you didn't." Paige chafed his hands between her own, uttering a silent prayer of thankfulness that he had survived. She released his fingers and pulled on his arm. "Must have been quite a shock when I appeared on the beach that first night. You probably crapped your pants. Now get up. We need to get you to a doctor. Now."

"I'm all right," he said. "Just give me a minute."

She struggled onto her knees, trying to drag him up with her. "A minute? I'll give you the rest of my fucking life if you'll have me."

He laughed, the low, thunderous chortle she'd come to adore. "Your mouth, Paige…"

She grinned at him. "You love my mouth."

"Yes, I do, because it's attached to the rest of you."

She tugged him, hard, by the shirt and elbow, knowing she at least had to get him some place warmer and out of his wet clothes. "So my admittedly foul mouth's not a deal breaker?"

He managed to gain his feet again and wrapped an arm around her shoulder, leaning his weight precariously in her direction. "I love you, Paige Waters. I think I did from the first expletive you uttered in the dark. I'll take the rest of your life, sweetheart, if you'll take mine."

She pulled him close and kissed him soundly, his temperature flaring beneath her fingertips. After the doctor declared him sound, she'd make sure the rest of his body received the same treatment.

"Deal," she whispered against his lips. Together, they climbed up the slope toward the house. The lights shining through the windows beckoned her back to the home where she'd always belonged.

Meet the Author

Celia Ashley lives in rural Lehigh County, Pennsylvania, an area rich in history and beauty and from which she has drawn inspiration for many of her tales. She is the mother of three grown sons and their significant others, as well as the companion of five cats. When not writing, she is a garden enthusiast (not an expert, by any means, but growing things makes her smile) and spends time painting in a variety of mediums. Published in historical romance under the pen names Alyssa Deane and Robin Maderich, she has most recently taken to writing spicy contemporary paranormal romance as Celia Ashley, for which she has received enthusiastic reviews. Ms. Ashley is a member of the Penn Jersey Women's Writers Guild and credits many of her fellow authors in that group for inspiration.

Be sure to read the first book in the series, Dark Tides. Each gripping tale is set in the fictional coastal town of Alcina Cove and is a standalone novel.

Dark Tides

The depths of the ocean hide more secrets than one...

When a man without a memory washes up outside her lonely seaside cottage, Meg can't explain the connection she feels to him. She should be afraid, suspicious, even angry that he would disturb her hard-won peace. But something about Caleb Hunter calls to her. On instinct, Meg asks this stranger into her home, her life—into the place left vacant by her dead husband, who drowned at sea a year to the day before Caleb appeared.

But something isn't right. Half-buried memories begin to haunt Meg's dreams, Caleb seems to know things he can't possibly know, and there are signs that someone else is watching them, someone with a heart as cold as the sea...

Chapter 1

Swiping a handful of sodden hair from his eyes, Caleb Hunter scrambled upright, stepping away from the water purling around his bare feet. An expanse of sand stretched as far as he could see into a soaking fog, although beyond the crest of dune in front of him, a slate-roofed, decrepit white Victorian rose out of the shimmering haze. The house didn't look at all familiar. Neither did the beach. Nothing did, no matter what direction he turned.

With a deep, painful breath, Caleb considered what he did know. His name, for one. Good. He thought he might be thirty-five or thirty-six years old. Somehow, he knew he stood six-foot-one, he had brown eyes, and his nearly black hair badly needed trimming. At this point, it needed a great deal more than that, plastered with salt and sand and a bit of debris hanging in front of his eyes. Yanking a piece of seaweed from above his brow, he tossed the vegetation down, tracking its descent past the length of his naked body. He pivoted in a slow, searching circle. Not a stitch of clothing lay in the sand.

After a moment, he lifted his hands, turning them palm up and finding them well-formed, calloused across the pad of flesh below his fingers. The skin of his fingertips had wrinkled from long immersion, and fine sand had embedded in the bend of each joint. Salt and sand encrusted the hair on his chafed arms. A black, ugly bruise throbbed on his right forearm. When he flexed his hand, the injury burned deep into the muscle. More sand coated his torso and his groin, clumped in the hair on his legs, and grated in places more private. He planted his feet apart and bent to brush the sand away, discovering this only made the situation worse.

Dismayed by his lack of recollection, as well as his lack of garments, Caleb closed his eyes and pushed both hands through his hair. Clasping his fingers behind his neck, he frowned when he located a hard knot of tender flesh at the base of his skull. Something had struck him there. He remembered that.

No, not something. Someone. Someone had tried to kill him.

Shit.

That fragment of recall brought no further revelation, but his skin crawled in reaction to a danger he couldn't fathom, and he checked again to make certain no one else occupied the stretch of beach. Shredding fog revealed a woman approaching him from a short distance. Walking with her head down, she bent every now and then to collect small items from the water's edge. Not knowing what else to do, Caleb sat in the sand once more, pulling his knees up close to his chin and wrapping his arms around his legs. After ascertaining he'd tucked everything neatly out of view, he waited.

She stopped little more than a dozen feet from him, bending to pluck at a polished stone to deposit with the array of minuscule treasures on her palm. The wind fluttered the length of a dark blue shawl from her shoulders, dragging the fringed edge in the sand. Tan trousers, rolled to the knee, exposed the curve of her calf and slender feet washed by the surge of the tide as she crouched. Caleb lifted his gaze again to her face. Even at that distance, he could see her eyes were quite green and staring straight into his.

Clutching her treasure trove against her breast, the woman straightened. Her lips moved in speech, words drowned by the low growl of the tide. Caleb cleared his parched throat, uncertain what to say as the woman continued to stare at him with an unreadable expression. After a moment, she dropped the items from her fingers into a heap on the sand and backed away, placing one bare foot behind the other, gaze never leaving his face until she turned on her heel and started an awkward run across the shifting sand. The blue shawl flew from her shoulders.

Leaping to his feet, Caleb darted forward and snatched up the garment, draping the soft wool around his waist. He tugged the folds to cover as much of his hip area as he could. Scooping the woman's discarded treasure into his hand, he went after her, following her toward the white house. Already a good distance ahead of him, she leaped up the long flight of wooden steps from the beach two at a time, crossing a seaside garden to a porch, where she yanked open the door and disappeared inside. Caleb paused in uncertainty. He hadn't meant to alarm her, and she appeared frightened, not merely startled. Nevertheless, if he didn't speak to her, he had no hope of receiving any answers to his many questions.

Girding his determination, as well as his grip on her shawl, he set his own bare feet to the first step and climbed to a brick pathway that led through the garden. At the porch, he paused again, studying the length of the covered area, the blank face of each window for any sign she peered out at him. He found only the milky reflection on glass of the fogged-in sea.

He walked across the porch and halted in front of the door. "Hello?" he called, listening hard.

She responded in a muffled demand through the solid wood. "Who are you?"

"I'm sorry if I startled you."

Silence.

"My name is Caleb Hunter," he said with a crazy expectation she would throw open the door and announce him welcome, perhaps apologize for not recognizing him in his present state. Instead, he heard nothing. The door remained closed.

"I need help." He waited. "I thought I would return your shawl to you, but…but I have a specific need of it at the moment."

"Keep it," he heard her say. The fact she had spoken again gave him a glimmer of hope.

"I don't know where I am," he persisted. "I don't know who I am," he added, frowning down at the worn boards of the porch floor. Aloud, the statement sounded ludicrous. The brief flare of fear surging through him at his own words held no humor at all.

"What do you mean, you don't know who you are?"

The door creaked open. A security chain stretched taut in the space between frame and door. Her leaf-green eyes regarded him intently from behind a fringe of honey-colored bangs.

"I don't remember much of anything specific," he said. "I believe I was hit on the head and…and maybe I washed up onto the beach from the ocean. I'm not sure. My name is about all I do remember with any certainty. Is the name Caleb Hunter familiar to you?"

"No," she said. "I don't know anyone by that name."

The door shut again. Scoured by the salt winds, the light blue paint had peeled away in places to show the bare, weathered wood beneath. A moment later, the door opened again, enough for her to toss something out at him. He bent and picked up a crumpled pair of pants. Light blue fabric, heavy and faded with wear. Jeans, they were called. He remembered that. They looked like they would fit him.

Turning his back, Caleb dropped the shells, stones, and bits of sea glass onto the lacquered surface of a nearby wicker chair. He set the shawl beside them and hastened into the jeans, grimacing as sand abraded his flesh. If the woman still stood in the doorway watching him struggle with the pants, she gave no indication. He glanced over his shoulder. Through the narrow opening, he saw nothing.

"What was that in your hand?"

At her question, he slowly pivoted to face the door, feeling more naked now than he had in her shawl. Talking to her half-dressed, wearing nothing but a pair of borrowed blue jeans, he contemplated picking up the shawl and draping it across his shoulders. Instead, he seized it from the floor where it had fallen and placed it beside her rescued treasure. The door opened a little more and her face appeared.

"Your things," he said by way of explanation. "I never meant to frighten you, to make you drop what you'd been gathering."

She frowned at the shells and oddments he had placed on the chair before turning her gaze to meet his. Slow to speak, she studied him a moment. "Thank you."

The door closed again.

Caleb moved to another chair and sat down. He leaned forward, elbows on thighs, hands folded together between his knees. The shifting of his body renewed pain in every muscle and tendon. Reaching up, he fingered the back of his head to trace again the contours of the vicious lump. He remembered a flurry of fists, grunting blows, and male voices raised in harsh invective, but he didn't recall the words. Was one of those voices his? Could have been. Yes, it could have been his voice. He remembered…nothing. Nothing else.

Damn it.

Once more, the door opened. The woman stepped onto the porch holding out a T-shirt. Gratefully, he took it, then slipped the garment over his head. It smelled as if it had been left sitting in a drawer. Not that it mattered.

"Your husband's?" he asked, not certain from what part of his brain such a question came.

She nodded.

"Is he here?"

"He's dead," she said.

"Oh." Caleb ran his hand through his salt-encrusted hair. "I'm sorry."

"So am I."

She moved to the chair where her shawl lay and bent to pick up the items he had deposited there. Brushing the sand and crushed shell from the seat into her hand as well, she walked to the porch railing and sprinkled them into the garden below, permitting them to flow through a loose fist. Her eyes closed as she did this, as if something ritualistic existed in the execution of her action. He wondered what had happened to her husband, if maybe she did this in his memory.

"His ship went down in a storm."

He started, meeting her eyes. Her direct gaze made him shiver.

"That's what you were thinking, wasn't it?" she said, brushing her hands clean. "You were wondering how he died."

Caleb shivered again within the confines of a dead man's shirt. "Yes," he admitted, "I was."

She nodded, her longs bangs swinging forward. "A year ago today," she told him quietly.

Today. Caleb said nothing.

She moved back across the porch, stopping before the chair opposite him where she gathered up the shawl and sat, holding the garment balled against her stomach. With her feet tucked around the outside of the legs of the chair, knees angled together, she appeared innocent and vulnerable. Caleb's stomach churned. He shoved a fist against his abdomen in an effort to control the response.

"I dream about him most nights," she confided in a voice barely above a whisper, her eyes intent on his own. "But not always. This morning, though, on the anniversary of his death, I dreamed about someone else. I didn't realize it until I saw you on the beach. I'm fairly certain I dreamed of you."

Stunned by her speech, Caleb sat back hard against the chair frame. His breath exploded as the knot at the base of his skull met wood, causing him to jerk forward again, bright pinpoints of light dancing before his eyes.

He couldn't remember the fundamental particulars about himself and his life, but he knew what dreams were without requiring an explanation. What she said made no sense to him. None at all. Unless—

"What do you mean? Do you know me?" he asked again. Perhaps she didn't know his name, but she might recall having seen him somewhere. Something. Anything.

She raised her eyes from a fierce contemplation of the air between them. After a moment of consideration, she shook her head. He licked his dry, salty lips as he shifted on the seat, frowning at the pain wracking his body. Observing his movements, she reached into her pocket and drew out a narrow black object, holding it on her palm. From somewhere in the recesses of murky recognition, he recognized a cell phone. "What are you doing?"

"Calling the police," she said.

Don't let her. Don't let her. Don't let her.

The force of the voice in his head caused him to gasp, recognizing without understanding that an instinct for preservation spoke to him. "Don't," he said and added "please" more sedately at the widening of her eyes.

She displayed no further consternation at his command, just cocked her head to the side, her gaze turning contemplative as if studying him. Even so, he could see the pulse beating beneath her jaw, the momentary suspension of her respiration.

"Why not?" she asked after a moment, still holding the phone at the ready in her hand.

He tried to dredge up a reply she would find suitable. He couldn't imagine where to begin. "God, I don't know," he answered, lowering his head into his hand, shoving fingers deep into his tangled hair. "I don't. I don't know. I…I don't know."

He heard a short, decisive inhalation and looked up in time to witness her returning the phone to her pocket. Fingers curled loosely, she lowered her right hand into her left across her stomach. "Don't you want to go to the hospital?"

"Why?"

"Aren't you hurt?"

She waited for his reply. Caleb didn't believe he'd ever seen eyes so green, though he couldn't recall for certain. He straightened in the chair, folding his hands in his lap. "What makes you think I'm hurt?"

Blowing out a breath, she stood, tucking the sand-spattered shawl against her abdomen. "You can hardly move," she said. "And the wound to your head—"

"How do you know I have a head wound?"

Her mouth twisted in wry amusement. "I could say I dreamed it, but I didn't. You told me you thought you'd been hit on the head. Even if you hadn't, you wince every time you touch the back of your skull. That and the fact you can't remember who you are are fairly good indicators of some sort of head trauma. Which," she added, "is why you should have a doctor check you out. Even if you don't want the police involved, I could call an ambulance or, well, I suppose I could drive you to the hospital myself."

Possessing a certain amount of defiance in her expression, she did not look away from him. Her stance shifted, and her hand lifted to assist him in rising. He wondered at her trust in a stranger, standing so close to him with her hand extended, as if she had no idea how easily he could overpower her if he had the inclination. He could remember nothing about his past life. For all he knew, he could be a nasty sort of person, a dangerous man. After all, someone had tried to kill him, hadn't they? Somebody must have had good reason for that.

"Not yet," he whispered. His aversion to the possibility of questions, of a need for answers he could not provide, worried him. Was he taking a foolish risk, not getting medical help? Still, he didn't think his injuries were life threatening. He felt no weakness, no disorientation beyond his inability to recall.

"You could be bleeding internally. You could have a skull fracture."

He rubbed his eyes, sand grating across his lids. "Are you suggesting I might die?"

"I don't know," she said. "I'm not a doctor."

Through the slats of the porch railing, he saw the sea, the fog lifting above the waves. Possibly, he'd walked to the beach from somewhere else and collapsed here, but that didn't seem likely. In fact, he knew better. The sensation of plunging into the ocean, tumbling through the cold, salty tides, though not quite memory, had the resonation of truth.

"I know a doctor who will come to the house. I've had him here before. He is…well, discreet. At least he can check you out, and if he feels you need to go to a hospital, you will. If not, well, that's up to you then."

Up to him. What would he do if this doctor pronounced him well enough to avoid treatment? How would he even begin to know what steps to take next? Avoiding thought of all the unimaginable possibilities, he nodded at her. "Fine," he said. "Let him come."

She walked to the far side of the porch, talking into the instrument she'd pulled back out of her pocket, glancing at him over her shoulder as she spoke. After a few minutes, she returned. "He'll be here shortly. You may as well wait inside."

He eyed her with bewilderment. "You're not afraid to have me in your house?"

"Should I be?"

"I don't know."

"I do." She held out her hand again. Swallowing, he slipped his fingers into hers and allowed her to pull him up from his seat with surprising strength. Standing before her, he smelled the sea in her hair, the fresh air, and a faint suffusion of citrus. The top of her head barely came up to his collarbone. A feeling of protectiveness stole over him, making him frown.

"Are you sure you don't know me?" *Because it sure as hell feels like I know you.*

"Positive," she said. "And by the way, my name is Meg. Meg Donovan." Clutching the shawl in her fist, she headed inside, leaving the door standing wide. Confounded, Caleb followed her into the house, the inside of his borrowed pants chafing like sandpaper over thighs and calves and along the tender flesh of his testicles. He trailed her from the back door into the kitchen, where she indicated he should sit in a chair she slid from the table. She pulled back the curtains to allow more light into the room and walked behind him across worn linoleum to take a glass down from a cabinet. Outside the window, he saw the sun had broken through the fog, golden light reflecting in a shimmer on the pale blue ceiling of the porch. She opened the refrigerator and rummaged around inside before returning to stand beside him.

"Here," Meg said, handing him a glass of something orange. Orange juice. Yes, he remembered that. "Drink it slowly. Are you warm enough? I can get you a blanket if you need one. Sometimes shock—"

"I'm fine," he said.

"Hardly."

Circling around the table, she pulled out a chair on the opposite side and sat, folding her hands on the scarred painted surface. "So you know your name."

He nodded.

"Amnesia is a fascinating condition," she went on. "Not to you, I'm sure, but it's odd what the brain might pick and choose in terms of recollection. I'm thinking in the most severe cases, you wouldn't be able to walk or communicate or even pick up that glass, but I could be wrong."

Mulling over her words as he took several sips from the glass, he welcomed the slightly acidic burn in his throat. He set the glass down. "So you're saying I'm not too bad off, even though I can't remember a single goddamn thing except my name?"

"But that's not exactly true, is it?" Her gaze held his until she rose and stepped away from the table, leaving to answer a distant knock on another door. He clutched the glass of juice in both hands on the tabletop, staring past to a series of lines scratched into the table's wooden surface. Not random, but seeming to spell out a word, a word he couldn't focus on as he thought about what she had said. How did she know? How did she know about the jumble of thoughts he held inside this fragile bubble in his mind?

"Caleb Hunter?" a deep voice said. "I'm Dr. Redecker, and I hear you may need my help."

Caleb spun on the chair to face the man standing between him and the interior kitchen door with a vague hope the man's face would be familiar. The gray hair, heavy countenance, and steady blue gaze meant nothing to him. This total lack of recollection made him understand something else, something he hadn't understood earlier. When looking into the eyes of the woman in whose kitchen he sat, he didn't see a stranger.